Grand Illusion

LESSON OF A BALINESE LOTUS

NINA PURTEE

Copyright © 2025 NINA PURTEE
All Rights Reserved
First Edition

PORTO BANUS PUBLISHING 2025
St Pete Beach, FL

This novel is a work of fiction. Any references to historical events, real people, or real places are used fictitiously. Other names, characters, places and events are products of the author's imagination, and any resemblance to actual events, places or persons, living or dead, is entirely coincidental.

ISBN 979-8-9911007-5-5 (Paperback)
ISBN 979-8-9911007-4-8 (Digital)
ISBN 979-8-9911007-6-2 (Hardcover)

Acknowledgements

Mara, the Balinese designer born Ni Made Sudra, is the last of the original cast of characters from the first book in the series, *Beyond the Sea: Annie's Journey into the Extraordinary*, to get their own book. Throughout the series, Mara has been a constant, with her uncanny ability to sketch a scene on the move, to mastering the art of painting on silk, to the heartwarming Balinese wedding blessing she performed.

The months of research required in the books that I write hopefully bring an authenticity to the stories. Ironically, that is one of the key subjects of this book. Learning rice production throughout its growing process, the Balinese caste system, and the Balinese purification and healing rituals, was an enlightening experience for me as the author. The rituals offered a unique way to bring closure to the other key characters of the series, as well as offer Mara direction as to how to balance her two worlds.

On a personal note, having been the owner of a fashion catalog in the 1990's, I did go to Bali to visit one of our suppliers who produced batik fashions, so Allison Ford's character rang true to me and gave a reason, previously unexplored, how Mara managed a scholarship to Kenneth Patrick's art program.

Lastly, I would very much like to thank my new editor, Laurie Chittenden, whose encouraging critique and edits had me dig deeper into the essence of the story, and a fitting end to the series.

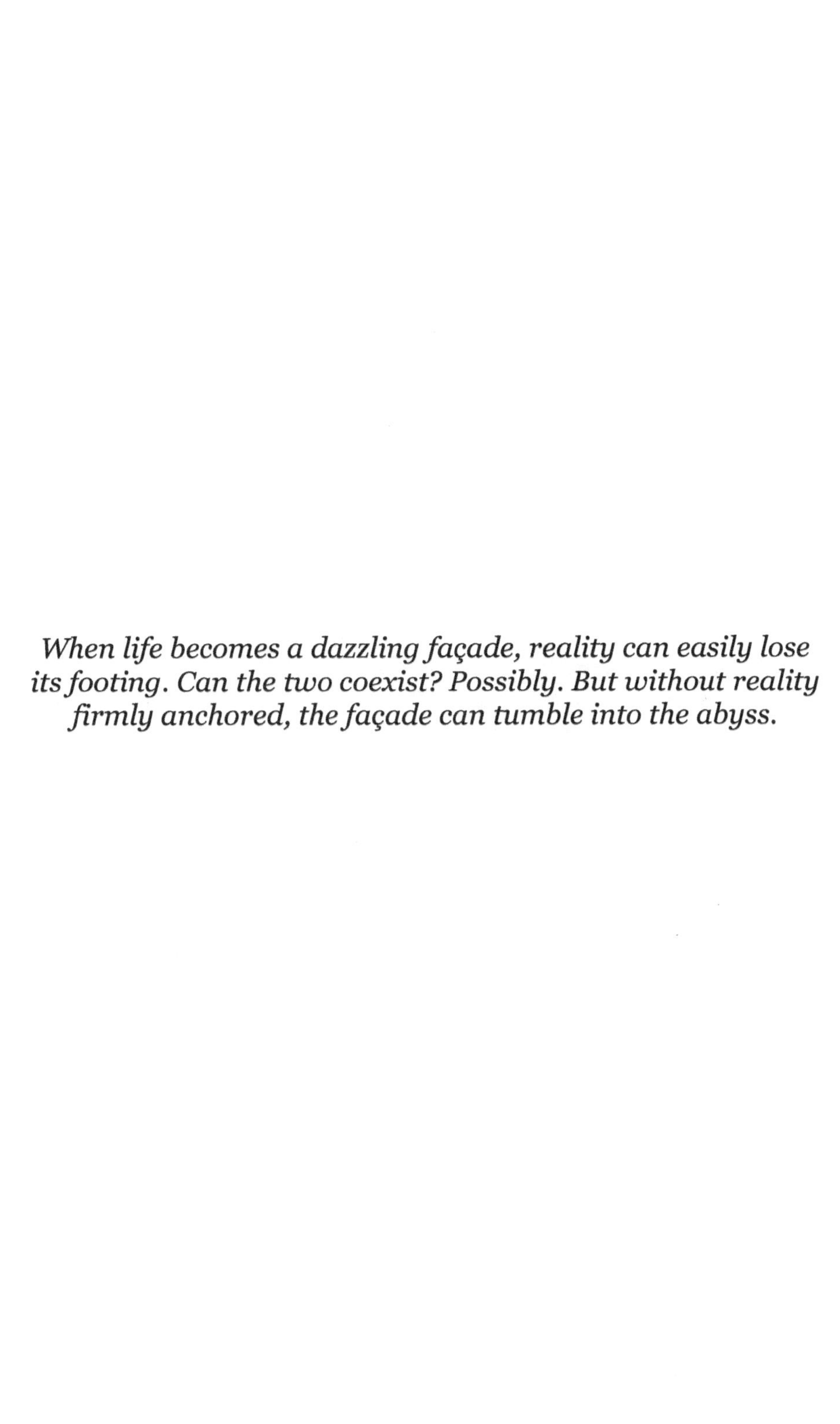

When life becomes a dazzling façade, reality can easily lose its footing. Can the two coexist? Possibly. But without reality firmly anchored, the façade can tumble into the abyss.

CHAPTER 1

For centuries, Italy has been the center of fashion and the fabric that goes into making the garments that dazzle fans around the globe. Even today, the talented designers who create their unique fabric patterns and set global trends remain the driving force behind the vibrant and fast-paced scene in this trend-setting city.

As the countdown to Milan's famous Fashion Week ticks by, the great fabric houses are immersed in a whirlwind of creativity and collaboration with the iconic fashion designers who would soon showcase their innovative bolts of cloth on the catwalk in their latest fashions, ready to push the boundaries to make each season surpass the last.

Mara, a Balinese artist known for her skill in creating hand-painted masterpieces on silk, was among those working around the clock as Fashion Week approached. She drew her inspiration from a myriad of sources, ranging from art and architecture to the rich tapestry of colors and traditions that characterize the artistry of her ancestors. Her keen eye for intricate detail and passion for quality positioned her to play a crucial role in enhancing the high-fashion designer collections to be presented on the runway.

Mara's studio was buzzing with interns bringing in armfuls of bolts of textiles sourced from local suppliers and exotic locations from around the globe, including her homeland of Bali. Others were checking dimensions against the specs on the large cork storyboard. Mara stood at her massive workstation, tirelessly translating her creative concepts developed on silk into wearable masterpieces. From sketching the original designs, to creating a textile geometry that repeats within a length of fabric, to sourcing materials and overseeing the production process, the activity was nonstop, particularly before Fashion Week. She glanced at the clock that seemed to be racing ahead, willing her hands to move faster.

Two meetings were planned with independent designers and one with a renowned fashion house that afternoon. She poured her heart and soul into her designs and personally collaborated closely with each designer, translating their ideas and concepts into exquisite fabrics that would set the tone for their creations.

The energy in the studio was palpable, as sketches turned into swatches, and swatches into full-fledged masterful creations ready to steal the runway. One of the fashion designers meeting with Mara was Lucca Accardi, known for his avant-garde approach to fashion. He drew from Mara's fabrics to push the normal limitations through his bold and innovative designs that challenged conventional ready-to-wear.

On the other hand, Sophia Romano favored timeless elegance and sophistication, drawing inspiration from Mara's rich heritage of art and culture in her work that combined modern techniques with age-old craftsmanship.

No one knew better than Mara how critical the collaboration between fabric and fashion designers was during this hectic period, as they worked in harmony to ensure the fabrics selected perfectly complemented the designs envisioned. This afternoon's meetings would strive to perfect each final detail. The models should arrive any moment.

Mara had to admit, having only been in her studio in Milan for less than two years, that she thrived on the energy that took place twice a year. It was a time of intense creativity where ideas were brought to life, dreams realized, and the magic of fashion was woven into every stitch and seam. Anticipation and exhilaration were mounting as the culmination of weeks of hard work and dedication would finally be revealed on the grand stage of Fashion Week in Milan.

* * *

However, beneath the glamorous veneer of Mara's professional life lay a complex web of contrast and contradiction. It wasn't always like this. The Hindu stone prayer necklace hanging from the hook next to Mara's jacket on the studio wall held the story of her humble beginnings. Despite being surrounded by opulent wealth, couture fashion, and pomp, the necklace served as a reminder to Mara to hold on to the simple values of her childhood. Born and raised in a small village among the remote rice paddies of eastern Bali, Mara lived with her extended farming family that included her parents and many cousins. Her family was part of the primary Balinese caste population who were in the lower class of *Sudra*.

Within the caste system, and particularly in Sudra, a child was given a name that labeled them as to their caste and what number child they happened to be. Mara was named *Ni Made Sudra*, or second child of the Sudra caste. Even within their own compound, there were both boys and girls from the various families named Made. At an early age, the cousins nicknamed her Mara, and the name without a surname stayed with her. Her youth was filled with hard work and discipline as each morning she was up well before dawn to help the adults in the rice fields before boarding an old pickup truck with the rest of the children to go to school. Much of her early childhood, when she wasn't working or in school, was spent chasing dragonflies and drawing patterns in the sand with a stick.

One day, Mara's teacher gave her a sketch pad, and every day at recess, instead of playing with the others, Mara opted to sit to the side and draw. Her teacher watched and marveled as Mara filled up pad after pad, showing a natural talent for bringing her vision to life. Farm animals, buildings, the other children, flowers...she would sketch anything in front of her, quietly drawing inspiration from the beauty of the vibrant Balinese culture surrounding her. Mara's parents could not afford to send Mara to art classes. It was her uncle who gave her a paint set when she turned twelve years old who changed the course of her life and recognized Mara's innate talent for original designs. With the support and encouragement of her family and teachers, Mara was determined even at a young age to pursue her passion for art in spite of their limited resources.

Mara's grandmother was an expert weaver and would use the petals of vibrant tropical flowers to teach her granddaughter about colors and shades, while her father carved intricate designs on wooden trinkets for her to paint. But it was her mother, most of all, who dreamed of a better future for Mara and persistently encouraged her artistic pursuits, telling her to expand her horizons and share her passion with the world.

At the age of sixteen, with her parents' approval, Mara left the family compound and moved with several of her cousins to Ubud. A distant relative gave them shelter, and it was there Mara, working relentlessly to hone her craft, caught the attention of a local company working on block prints and batik fabrics. Mara began sketching designs that the block makers would copy and carve into soft wood to make a stamp. She learned the meticulous technique of what would or wouldn't work on a block stamp when it was reproduced on fabric. The company grew and so did Mara's reputation.

The turning point for Mara came when a retail catalog company from the United States discovered the line and began to feature the designs worn by beautiful models on the pages of the catalog. The owner, Allison Ford, flew to Bali to meet with the owners of the company and view the operation. What she learned was the value of the designs Mara did for the fashions that sold so well off her catalog pages. At first, Allison thought how lucky she was to have discovered Mara and that she should choose her to do custom batik styles exclusive to the catalog.

But, back in her hotel room that night, Allison came up with a better plan. Checking the time on her watch, she placed a call to her old friend, well-known commercial artist Kenneth Patrick in Australia. He was in the process of assembling a group of fifteen young aspiring artists who stood out from all the rest to come work under his tutelage for nine months. Allison described Mara's extraordinary talent by calling it a rare blend of raw skill and untapped potential. When Kenneth heard how highly Allison spoke of Mara's ability to capture the essence of Balinese culture in her art and her need for proper training, he immediately dispatched his staff to interview her and bring back samples of her work.

Much to Allison's delight, Mara was among the fifteen chosen for the Kenneth Patrick program. It wasn't until several years later that Mara found out it was Allison who initiated such an opportunity, and she made a pledge to herself to always ensure Allison got some of her best fabric designs.

The winds of fate shifted the day Mara packed her bag and left for the picturesque coastal town of Byron Bay, Australia, not knowing a soul. Armed with nothing but her talent and determination, she joined Kenneth Patrick's unconventional program that would lead her to painting on silk fabric and launching her career.

CHAPTER 2

Mara was eighteen when she boarded the plane that would stop in the city of Ballina, on her journey to Byron Bay, Australia. Allison Ford had provided the batik company the funds to use for Mara's ticket, asking that it remain an anonymous *gift*. It would then be a short bus ride from Ballina to Byron Bay. The curriculum under Kenneth Patrick would be taught in English. Mara spoke no English, but she had learned a limited amount of French. There was also a boy from Germany who did not speak English. His name was Hans Schuman. Since Hans spoke French, the program director arranged for one of the other students who spoke both fluent English and French to come early to work with Mara and Hans to help them with their English. Sarah Wilkinson was an artist from England who had been training in Paris so French was second nature to her.

The student housing arrangement was vastly different for Mara who was used to sharing a single room with her cousins. When she realized she had a private room to herself, she was almost giddy with delight. During the month in Byron Bay prior to the start of the program, when she wasn't working on her English, Mara fell into her old habit of sketching for hours.

Sarah often expressed her amazement that Mara could so quickly sketch a scene unfolding before her. Mara smiled, reluctant to share that she hadn't had access to anything but a pad of paper and a piece of charcoal until her uncle gave her a paint set. Part of the requirement to get a scholarship to this program was that the artist had to have sold three pieces. Kenneth had worked around that with Mara, accepting that she made the primary designs for at least three separate clothing patterns that had sold in Europe and in the United States.

Mara found it hard not to be intimidated by Sarah's impressive Paris art school training, along with the master-pieces she had painted and sold for a substantial sum of money. Mara could tell Hans felt that way too since his entry to the program was through his precision-oriented nautical designs, not painting. Ironically, it was Mara and Hans who had found their unique interests, or what others called artistic vision, long before Sarah did.

Kenneth Patrick, a legendary figure in the world of com-mercial design, had a reputation that preceded him, yet during that first month, Mara was just learning about him. From humble beginnings himself, starting with painting surfboards in California before finding his way to Byron Bay, Kenneth's unorthodox path to success inspired Mara. This opportunity marked a significant milestone in Mara's life, and her living arrangement was a simple luxury that sparked a newfound sense of independence and freedom within her. Here she had been given the opportunity to find a direction for her craft while exploring her own identity.

That first month established a strong bond of friendship between Mara and Sarah and Hans as they immersed them-selves in the local art scene and embraced the chance to learn from Kenneth and their fellow artists. They quickly discovered the state-of-the-art facilities and supportive group of creatives he had at his disposal. When Sarah and Hans fell into a romantic relationship, Mara never felt excluded and actually enjoyed the extra time alone to focus on her art and learning English.

Kenneth Patrick sought her out just as the curriculum was about to begin to personally welcome her and offer his mentorship. "Mara, I understand you have had limited resources in Bali. I intend to change that. My process is to allow you and the rest of the artists in this program to try a variety of mediums until you find one that lights a passion in you to not only pursue it but to be the best you can possibly be. If you make a commitment to hard work, determination, and an unwavering belief in your own abilities, it would not surprise me to see you transform from a humble village girl to a formidable artist in your own right."

Mara could hardly believe the faith Kenneth expressed in her and she found it hard to hide her insecurities. "Sir, I feel so blessed to be here, but to be honest, I am far behind these artists like Sarah, who have had such extensive training and experience."

"Mara, no one here, especially not me, will hand you a map that precisely directs you to the exact path for your talent. I sincerely believe much of the joy of discovering your passion comes from finding your own way there. My role is to give you various options for you to decide which to pursue. What I think you will discover is that your gift is unique. It is not the same as Sarah's or any of the other artists. Let the process unfold. Believe in it. You will see."

* * *

The classes began in earnest and the students were told that professional instructors would teach the group a new artistic medium every two to three weeks. The students were to give each creative method a focused effort to determine if that was an area they wanted to pursue.

Three months had gone by before Mara stretched her first piece of silk fabric taut on a square wooden frame, creating a smooth and even surface. Once she applied her first brushstroke of specialized silk paint, she was mesmerized by the way the colors bled and blended on the delicate fabric. The meticulous process required a steady hand, a keen eye for detail, and a deep understanding of color theory and composition. Mara learned how to carefully apply layers of color to the fabric, building up the design gradually with precision and patience. When Sarah and the other students were giving up in frustration, Mara was delighted to discover how each calculated stroke of color could move to the desired texture and vibrancy of the overall result.

She spent hours observing how a certain brushstroke on her part would affect the way the fabric interacted with the paint and how the paint would be absorbed by the silk fibers, creating a beautiful translucency that added depth and dimension to her designs. Every step of the process intrigued her, pushing her to immerse herself in mastering this delicate technique. When she told Kenneth Patrick she had found her passion, he nodded his approval and it was under his guidance that her nimble fingers learned to dance across the delicate fabric, weaving together intricate designs and vibrant colors that left Sarah and the other artists in awe.

Throughout the rest of the year, Mara's skills flourished under Kenneth's watchful eye and she infused her work with a unique blend of Balinese artistry and contemporary flair. By the spring, Kenneth brought in a clothing stylist to work with Mara and another designer to create a small, specialized line of hand-painted clothing that Sarah referred to as *wearable art.*

Mara put her full effort into each piece, critically building up the design to the right depth and richness. Kenneth showed her the dazzling results that could be created with a sprinkle of salt on the wet paint, or dry brush stippling...each creating a unique texture and effect. Kenneth could see the dedication on Mara's face and in her finished works of art. By the end of the program, he sent her to Sydney to display her fashions during market week alongside a designer he knew. The designer included them in his fashion show and they were an instant hit, creating a buzz about this new Balinese up-and-coming fabric designer, earning Mara recognition as a rising star and generating her first orders. Mara was elated!

Kenneth Patrick had laid the foundation. Now it was up to Mara to unleash her creativity and delve into making a business out of her love for silk painting. By the time she left Australia, Mara's artistic journey was just beginning.

CHAPTER 3

At the end of the program, Mara knocked on Kenneth Patrick's door one last time to say farewell. She could not refrain from the tears that glistened with her emotions. "Kenneth, it is impossible to express the gratitude I feel that you allowed me into the program under your guidance. This experience has been life changing. I will never forget you or Byron Bay."

Kenneth held out his arms to take her into his embrace. "You did the work, Mara. We are all going to be buying Mara fabrics someday. My advice to you...focus on the fabrics. Let the clothing designers come to you. They will. Be true to yourself. Keep your imagination fluid, open to experimenting, and never settle for the mundane. You will go far and I will be watching. Call on me anytime. I am a phone call away."

If saying goodbye to Kenneth Patrick was hard, the good-byes with Sarah and Hans were even harder. The three of them had done everything together for ten months. Hans had discovered glass-blowing and had made a collection of pieces that were to be featured in an art gallery back in his hometown of Hamburg. Sarah was about to embark on a month-long sojourn in East Africa to paint wildlife in their environment, and Kenneth Patrick had shown her how to create the semblance of motion in her paintings to further explore during her time there. The masterpiece Sarah had created there in Australia of a phoenix rising from the flames was surely museum-worthy.

Mara was the first to leave and both Sarah and Hans were there to see her off. It was Sarah who said, "It feels like we have shared such a life-altering time together and now are separating to opposite ends of the earth." There were no dry eyes between them.

Hans answered, "The three of us are so close that distance won't change that." He took Sarah's and Mara's hands and held them to his heart. "You will both always have a place right here."

Mara reached into her bag and handed them each a small, framed silk painting of a lotus blossom with a long stem. "In my country, a lotus blossom represents beauty, strength, and grace. But look closely at the long, winding stem. Its strong connection to the blossom symbolizes an eternal, unbreakable bond. That is how I see us...the stem may be long but the connection is strong. It shall forever be there between us."

* * *

Life swept the three of them in different far-reaching directions. Mara took the proceeds from the money she earned fulfilling orders from the show in Sydney and attempted to move her parents to Ubud to live with her. Her father declined, however, calling her by her given name, "Ni Made, we are simple people of the land. The city is not for us. You have made us proud, daughter. You deserve to be happy. Dare to follow your dreams."

So instead, she secured a small studio with a tiny apartment attached to live and work in. Mara reached out to the textile fabricator for the batik company she had worked for to show him her swatches and discuss the possibility of a process to turn raw materials such as yarn and fibers through dyeing at various stages that could replicate her silk designs onto other fabrics. It could be a tedious, time-consuming procedure so they agreed to try different techniques to get to an end result she could hope to market.

Her talent as an artist grew, with an unmatched ability to translate traditional techniques into modern and commercially accepted designs. She spent hours painting complex patterns and designs on her silk fabrics, honing her skills and developing her own unique style. Mara was so immersed in her work that she lost all track of time.

The soulful phone call from Sarah came as a shock. She had returned from a month-long stay in Africa painting animals and decided to surprise Hans with a visit to Hamburg. Sadly, Sarah was the one who was surprised when Hans's wife answered the door! Mara and Sarah had talked for a long time about Sarah's possible options but, in the end, she decided to go back to Africa. That move of Sarah's indirectly had a huge impact on the next direction in Mara's career.

It was sometime later when Mara received a cryptic note from Sarah that she had met an adventurous young blonde woman who was on a journey to discover new cultures and meet interesting people. Her name was Annie, and Sarah had encouraged her to travel to Bali. Sarah seemed to think Mara and Annie would get along and asked Mara to be on the lookout for her. Back in her apartment above the studio, Mara studied the note thinking there was no way she had time to play tourist guide. Now she just needed to find a way to get out of this meeting.

News traveled fast in Ubud and the news of the arrival of a beautiful young Western woman traveling solo had caught the attention of the rumor mongers. Knowing Annie was alone, seemingly absorbed with the spiritual Balinese culture Mara herself loved so much, distracted Mara's thoughts to the point where she couldn't focus. Unbeknownst to her, Annie was about to do something on impulse that would have a lasting impact on Mara and ingratiate Annie into her heart.

Mara's favorite cousin, Kadek, had married earlier in the day in a ceremonial Balinese wedding. The reception was taking place in a small courtyard next to the village inn where Annie happened to be staying. The party had already gone on for a while and Mara was anxious to get back to her studio. She gave the bride and groom an embrace and left just before Annie was returning to the inn.

It was her cousin who told Mara all about Annie. Kadek explained that although they did not have a common language to communicate, Annie smiled and left to go get something from her room. When she returned, she had given Mara's cousin a hand-carved stone prayer necklace with such a genuine gesture of affection that the entire wedding party had invited her to stay and she seemed to effortlessly fit right in.

Once Mara heard her relatives' story, her curiosity about this Western friend of Sarah's was piqued and she became anxious to meet her. They finally met during a serendipitous meeting on the hillside after an outdoor performance of the traditional musical drama of the Kecak Monkey Dance.

Meeting Annie was like meeting a force of nature. She embraced life with passion, not wanting to miss any detail. She never hesitated for an instant to sweep Mara into her inner circle, and before Mara knew it, she was invited to travel by yacht to the barrier reef of Australia where she had never had the chance to go when she was studying there. Annie was smart and insightful, and Mara found herself looking at her surroundings through Annie's inquisitive eyes, giving her a unique addition to her perspective.

Would she be where she was today without meeting Annie? Possibly. But, when Annie invited her to Mallorca to offer a Balinese blessing, she was able to give Annie the spiritual wedding she so wanted when she married Ramone on that beautiful island. Then, later, she wouldn't have visited Marbella for the birth of Annie's twins. Her being in Spain was momentous. Sarah had reconnected with Hans, now a widower. He was meeting her in Marbella as she was arriving from Morocco with El Amir, her long-time Moroccan art sponsor. During her time in Morocco, Sarah had befriended a young Arab heiress and had been the mastermind behind El Amir and Elena Al Farooq becoming a couple.

Elena's parents were arriving at the port of Marbella in their new designer yacht in order to purchase an exclusive property along the coveted *Golden Mile* Marbella was known for. Through Elena's friendship with Sarah, Mara was introduced to Bajir Al Farooq, Elena's father, along with her older brother Zayn. Sarah was instrumental in landing a design contract for both the yacht, *Arabian Pearl*, and the new estate home that would include Mara working on a design collaboration with Hans and Sarah. Zayn's father could not have been more pleased with the resulting decor of both extravagant properties. What might have happened to her without being introduced to the oil magnate and his son, Zayn?

Zayn was immediately captivated by Mara's stunning beauty and undeniable talent, and the two quickly formed a deep connection. As part of a prominent devout Muslim family with immense oil wealth, Zayn had the financial security to do as he pleased, and he enjoyed the idea of being a pillar of support in Mara's career without consideration of the vast difference in their upbringings.

CHAPTER 4

Mara's musings were abruptly interrupted, bringing her attention back to the present, by the second urgent call of her name by her spindly assistant, Rochelle. Normally, Mara would stop to appreciate Rochelle's quirkiness with her red glitter tennis shoes, numerous multicolor bracelets on each wrist, and bejeweled eyeglasses. But Mara recognized the tone of Rochelle's voice. "Nicole Manning is here and demanding to see you about the dress Marcus sent over for her to wear to the finale of Fashion Week."

Without a chance to respond, Mara saw Nicole barge through the feeble attempts to stop her as she headed directly toward her. Mara summoned her most patient smile and welcomed the high society debutante who was holding her dress like an unwanted dishtowel. "Nicole, how are you?"

With fire in her eyes, Nicole raised her voice, "Purple flowers! Really, Mara?! I am not wearing purple flowers to one of the most sought-after parties of the season!" Mara absent-mindedly rubbed her temple with a quick glance at her watch knowing she might now be late to pick up Zayn from the train station. It was Rochelle's roll of the eyes at Nicole's audacity that gave Mara the sense of restraint she needed.

Although Nicole was only a few years younger, Mara took on her most maternal voice, "There now, dear, don't worry. Have you spoken with Marcus about the dress?"

Still riled, Nicole retorted, "Of course not! The design is brilliant. It is these purple flowers that wind all over the dress that are the problem." Mara took the dress and studied the intricate lotus blossoms with the long winding stems so reminiscent of her farewell paintings to Sarah and Hans.

"Nicole, would you please try the dress on and let's see what the problem is. The dressing room is over there." She turned to Rochelle who informed her Lucca was waiting in the showroom. "Serve him some refreshments and explain I am finishing up a last minute fitting. Have the models ready and I will be there as quickly as I can."

The dress fit Nicole perfectly, and it was as though the flowers came to life as the fabric stretched across her body. "Lift your chin slightly, Nicole. There, now, look in the mirror. Did you even try the dress on? It is stunning on you!"

Nicole looked in awe at her reflection in the beautiful chemise with a sarong-like wrap skirt. Immediately contrite, she answered, "Well, no, to be honest. I pulled it out of the box and just saw flowers everywhere."

Although Mara understood Lucca was waiting, she took the time to explain, "My homeland of Bali is known for its wide variety of magnificent plants and flowers where each holds a cultural significance and is admired for its beauty. Rooted deeply in Balinese culture, their profound meanings have been passed down through many generations. You are a debutante being presented to the world to begin your life as an adult. Your dress features the lotus blossom, which is called *padma* in my country. The lotus comes in different colors, each possessing its own symbolism. Marcus chose well with purple which represents mystery, dignity, and success. Wear it proudly, Nicole. Marcus did a masterful job. Now, unfortunately, I must go. I have an appointment waiting for me." Looking over at Rochelle, she asked, "Would you see Nicole out once she changes?"

Rochelle's nod was accompanied by a slightly subdued "thank you" from Nicole. That small crisis averted, Mara confidently strode into the showroom and began the meticulous process of matching fabrics to designs for Lucca and then Sophia, finishing the afternoon with an innate sense of accomplishment.

* * *

Mara had just enough time to touch up her make-up and get to the elegant Milano Centrale train station in order to pick up Zayn. Their relationship had blossomed after his offer to invest in her Milan studio alongside his father. He and his family were from Fujairah in the Emirates, and Zayn had been her exclusive companion since their time in Marbella.

Zayn's father, an astute businessman with investments across many industries in addition to oil, saw the potential in Mara's work and was quick to agree to invest in her studio. Between both projects, it took the three artists close to a year to finish, but by the end of that time, both Zayn and his father knew Mara had the potential to make a name for herself in the competitive fashion world. The father-son investment had propelled her career to new heights. With their generous backing, they provided her with the resources and connections needed to establish her studio in Milan's fashion center and get her work noticed.

Mara was able to pursue her dreams and eventually found her fabric designs quickly gaining recognition and acclaim. As Mara's success soared, grateful for such an opportunity, she found herself caught up in the glitz and glamour of Zayn's world, attending lavish events and rubbing shoulders with the elite. Zayn, with his love of fast cars and the luxurious lifestyle his family provided, introduced Mara to a world she had never thought possible.

Zayn was captivated by Mara's talent and exotic beauty and could not stop his pursuit of her, drawn to her not only for her artistic talent but also for her generous nature and strong connection to her roots. Even after sweeping Mara into a whirlwind romance, he had been resistant about pushing their intimacy, knowing in his heart that taking her to his bed would mean a commitment to marriage. Zayn was far from ready to settle down like his sister, Elena, now happily married to El Amir who had convinced their father he was a worthy suitor.

Zayn liked his freedom as much as he liked Mara by his side, so to compensate for his lack of intimacy, he remained steadfast and attentive to Mara yet with the freedom to live his life his own way.

Although they spent much of that first year in Marbella enjoying the company of Sarah and Hans, Zayn never lost focus on Mara and the desire to lift her to higher circles. Marriage and children were far from his mind in keeping with the fast pace of his lifestyle, and for that reason, he did not enjoy time with Annie and her ex-matador husband, Ramone, and their demanding twin babies. Whenever they were included, Zayn often made up excuses not to join them. Mara didn't really notice the coincidence, but Sarah and Annie did. To them, however, Mara seemed happy with Zayn so they remained silent.

CHAPTER 5

Mara glanced around the elegant train station noting the gorgeous architecture and natural style of the people that exuded from the locals. Mara smiled as she noted the visitors always arrived seemingly under dressed. She noted the number on the board and quickly found the platform for the train arriving from Geneva.

As the train appeared on the tracks, Mara mentally ticked off the list of what she knew to expect each time Zayn arrived. He would, of course, have booked a suite at Casa Rugiada since his family had been members there for years. Naturally, he would have made reservations for a table in the library section of Savante Bistro with his favorite maître d, Marceau, for a late dinner.

Mara would have to beg off any late night festivities since there was so much work to complete before the beginning of Fashion Week. In some ways, she appreciated not having the further complications of a demanding live-in man who might distract her from her work. But there were other times that Mara felt alone at the end of an evening or when Zayn was away. She lived in her own apartment but they never spent time there together. He always expected her to come to him.

She shook off those negative thoughts and concentrated on how much Zayn had offered her. Was she ready for an intimate relationship? Absolutely YES. She yearned for the loving experiences she knew Sarah and Annie had found with their men. Was she ready for that intimate relationship to be with Zayn? That answer wasn't so clear. Despite the façade of confidence she presented to the world as a successful fabric designer, around Zayn she felt like she was playing a role in a grand production. The stark contrast between her upbringing in Bali and Zayn's privileged background from the Arab Emirates created a silent divide she struggled to bridge.

For now, Mara's heart raced with a mix of excitement and trepidation. Taking a deep breath, she knew the role she was supposed to play as Zayn's train came to a halt in front of her. She adjusted her flowing silk scarf that was her own creation and checked her reflection in the window, her Balinese heritage evident in her graceful demeanor.

Zayn Al Farooq stepped off the train with an aura of confidence, his dark eyes scanning the platform until they landed on Mara. A small smile played on his lips as he approached her, his designer suit tailored to perfection and his cologne enveloping her in its spicy, intoxicating scent. "*Marhaban*, Mara," Zayn greeted her with a warm embrace, his voice deep and resonant.

Mara returned the gesture and greeted him with a warm smile, feeling a flutter in her chest that she quickly dismissed. "*Ahlan*, Zayn, welcome back to Milan." Zayn's eyes lit up at the sight of Mara, his trademark smirk tugging at the corners of his lips. "Mara, darling, you look exquisite as always," he drawled with the Arabic accent she found irresistible.

As they walked towards Mara's waiting car, the conversation flowed smoothly, filled with lighthearted banter and playful teasing. Mara found herself falling into the familiar rhythm of their dynamic, where Zayn's natural charm and charisma seemed to effortlessly draw her in. However, as they settled into the plush leather seats of Mara's sleek sports car that Zayn had presented to her on her last birthday, a lingering tension hung in the air. He made small talk about his recent business deal-ings in Geneva, but Mara sensed something simmering beneath his charming manner. She knew in her heart that despite the lavish gifts, glamour, and luxurious lifestyle he had introduced her to, Zayn wasn't willing to commit to anything more than a superficial relationship. He might like parading her around by his side, but she questioned whether he was ready for anything more. Although their lives had become intertwined, she couldn't help but feel a growing sense of insecurity and doubt about their relationship.

"So, Mara," Zayn began tentatively, his eyes flickering with uncertainty as he glanced at her from the driver's seat. "How have things been at the studio? Are you ready for Fashion Week? Any exciting new designs?" Mara forced a smile, mask-ing her disappointment at the direction of their conversation. He seemed to always avoid conversations of a more personal nature, always falling back to the business side of their relation-ship. She had to remind herself once again that this was all part of the act that she had chosen to play.

Even knowing that, she couldn't help feeling like there were unresolved emotions in the underlying tension between them. She stole a sideways look at Zayn, his profile illuminated by the soft glow of the city lights, wondering if this trip would provide the moment when they would finally address the unspoken desires and fears that danced between them.

It was a short drive to the hotel. Zayn drove up to the valet who immediately recognized him and fussed over them. Zayn dropped an insanely large bill into the palm of his hand, then took Mara's arm possessively. "I need to drop my bag off in the suite. Do you want to come up or meet me in the bar?" A fleeting thought of getting to the suite and not leaving for hours crossed Mara's mind. Not wanting to make things seem awkward, she casually answered, "Sure, I'll come up. How long are you staying in Milan this time? Will you be here through Fashion Week?"

Zayn gave her a playful roll of the eyes. "And be cast aside while you work nonstop? No way! I will just be here for a day or two. My father is on his way to the villa in Marbella and I need to brief him on my meetings in Geneva. Actually, I think Elena and El Amir might be there as well. I haven't seen my sister in a while, so it will be good to catch up. If it weren't so close to Fashion Week, I would ask you along."

"I did hear from Sarah that Elena and El Amir seem really happy and are spending most of their time in Marrakesh on his estate. Do you plan to come back to Milan? I might need someone to calm my nerves."

Zayn grinned and gave her a squeeze. "Of course, although you have nothing to be nervous about! I wouldn't miss the chance to see my girl light up Fashion Week with her outstanding designs. I will insist Elena come with me."

Mara let go of her unwelcome doubts and agreed. "That would be so special. Sarah said she and Annie would be here as well. Ramone and his brother are working on a transportation arrangement between Venice and Slovenia. He took Annie for a visit there, and she says it is breathtaking. Maybe once all this is over, we might go visit?"

Zayn straightened his tie in the hall mirror. "I have never been to Slovenia, and as tempting as a trip with you sounds, I am going from here to enter the qualifier to see if I can race in the Grand Prix in Monaco in a couple of months. It is hard to break into their tight group, but I have been training with a Formula One veteran and he thinks I have a chance."

Shocked, Mara said, "I had no idea you were even racing! Why didn't you tell me?" There it was again...that feeling of being caught between two worlds. The grandiose lifestyle she found herself surrounded by was moving at a pace she could hardly keep up with and was light years away from the simplicity and community of her upbringing in Bali. *Was she losing touch with her real self and her roots?* She questioned Zayn's persistent pursuit, and what his long term intentions might be. Mara felt obligated by her ties to Zayn and the opportunities he and his father had provided her but found herself yearning for a connection that grounded her in reality.

Looking out toward the bustling night sky of Milan, Mara wondered if it was time to follow her heart and choose a path that kept her true to her humble beginnings. With Fashion Week looming and the Monte Carlo Grand Prix on the horizon, she knew she would need to make a choice soon that would not only define her career but also her sense of self and belonging.

* * *

Mara was at her studio the following morning promptly at eight o'clock ready for the tsunami of details waiting for her. After dinner, she had dropped Zayn at a club within walking distance to his hotel. Although he tried to convince her to go in with him, Zayn seemed to easily accept her excuse of an early workday. He pulled her close with his face close to hers. "You are a special woman, Mara. I am so proud of what you have accomplished." He leaned in for a kiss and Mara thought for a moment this might be the turning point for them. But there was no demand behind the kiss, no sense of passion.

Despite his family's generous support, Mara was disillusioned by the lack of intimacy in their relationship, convinced that Zayn was more interested in luxury and fame than building a meaningful connection with her. She knew that his lofty aspiration to participate in the Grand Prix in Monaco was far from realistic. Those drivers had to train for years and be sponsored.

For now, Mara needed to concentrate on her preparation for the spotlight of Fashion Week, but she made a commitment to herself that very soon she would face the stark realities of love, ambition, and identity in her current world filled with dazzling illusions.

* * *

Zayn sat on the balcony of his favorite suite enjoying his cappuccino and *cornetto* filled with custard. He took a bite of the pastry and remembered why the Italian people shared such a passion for food. It was delicious. He scanned the paper for news without serious intention. Instead, his mind was filled with the trainwreck his relationship with Mara was becoming.

Frustrated, Zayn put the newspaper down and began pacing the expansive suite. He clearly understood that as the youngest son in his family's world of wealth and tradition that his future held certain expectations. He wasn't like his older brothers who had so seamlessly embraced the family business. He was more of a free spirit and much closer in age to his sister, Elena, and they had a special bond that made it easy for them to turn to each other for advice and comfort. Together they tackled the complexities of their family's traditions and expectations which eventually led her to her marriage with El Amir. He really needed her advice right now.

Although Zayn knew his duty was to marry within his own culture, he found Mara's ethereal beauty, creativity, and authenticity irresistible regardless of the stark differences between their backgrounds, religion, and cultures. Even after recognizing her talent and potential, and convincing his father to financially support her dreams, what should have been a business relationship turned into more and his feelings for Mara had deepened. Zayn moaned out loud in annoyance, torn between his heart and his responsibilities.

The prospect of breaking tradition and pursuing a more intimate relationship with Mara filled him with apprehension. He knew that his father would not approve of his choice, and the thought of disappointing him weighed heavily on his mind. Caught between desire and duty, he longed to follow his heart and be with Mara, but his fear of the consequences continued to hold him back. There were social divides that did exist, and he was well aware of the challenges and prejudices they would face as a couple. He was certain Mara's patience was wearing thin. He could see it in her eyes. *How could he blame her?* He had to make a choice, one that would define not only his own future but also that of a possible future family with Mara.

Zayn sat at the antique desk and opened the sealed letter from the qualifying board of Monaco. The rejection letter explained that his experience was "insufficient to qualify for Formula One status." He shook his head. *Just one more foolish decision on a long list.*

He picked up the phone and dialed Elena's number hoping somehow his sister had some ideas. When she answered, he couldn't hold back and shared the pain he was feeling. "*Khalas*, sister! I need your help. My life is in chaos and I don't know which way to turn."

Elena had never hesitated to call on Zayn for support when it came to looking for solace from their shared experiences within the strict traditions and cultural norms that their family required. With Zayn's help, she had found a way to find love within a more softened environment which allowed for Western influences included in El Amir's lifestyle. Now it was her turn to help Zayn. "My dear brother, what is it? How can I help you?"

Zayn held nothing back and confided about his feelings for Mara, along with his inner struggle between his own desires and the expectations of their family. Elena listened patiently, fully understanding the complexities of his situation and responded with a mix of understanding and tough love. "There is a vast difference between you and Mara that crosses many areas, including your religions and your very different upbringing. I understand that you are hesitant to fully commit to her due to the pressure you feel from our family. On the other hand, Mara must be equally confused, torn by the allure of your opulent world and what you have provided for her in contrast to the tug of her humble roots in Bali. I have seen the way she looks at you. I agree that she is seeking a deeper connection. If not, she would not have stayed with you this long."

Zayn clenched his fist but said, "What if she is just seeing me out of gratitude. Considering her background, I must seem self-absorbed and entitled."

Elena laughed. "Well, you have indulged in every luxury and whim that money could buy." After a moment to reflect, she asked, "Zayn, have you tried talking to Mara? Maybe the struggle between you is for lack of communication. Have you considered that?"

"Honestly, I've thought about it, but I have no idea where to begin. I am afraid she has already given up on me."

Elena was determined to get through to her brother. "It is time to follow your heart and be true to yourself. Somehow, summon the courage to stand up for what you believe in, even if it means going against Father's wishes. You know he adores Mara. Give him some credit. And remember something Sarah told me once, 'Love knows no boundaries, no borders, and true happiness can only be found by being authentic to yourself.'"

"That is part of the problem. I don't think I can go against my religion, and I know how strongly Mara feels about hers."

Zayn then changed the subject and asked if she and El Amir would be at Fashion Week to support Mara. Elena quickly agreed and added, "Why don't you come here to Marbella so Mara can prepare. There is time to settle things between you after the big event is over."

Zayn hung up the phone with the sage advice of his sister echoing in his mind. He needed to find time to sit down with Mara and see if they could bridge the gap between their cultures. For now, he needed to let her get ready for Fashion Week without any emotional burden. A smile tugged at the corner of his mouth, and he picked up the phone once again.

CHAPTER 6

There was a moment in the rigorous process leading up to the highly anticipated first runway show of Fashion Week when Mara, as a fabric designer, finally had to turn her carefully curated and meticulously crafted fabrics over to the fashion designers with whom she had collaborated. Mara roamed the empty studio feeling a sense of apprehension hanging in the air. It seemed to Mara like being in the eye of a hurricane for a brief moment of calm amidst the whirlwind that surrounds the fashion industry during these electrifying shows. She held her breath, knowing she had poured her creativity and expertise into each design, experimenting with textures, colors, and patterns to capture the essence of each designer's vision.

The final countdown had begun. Now she would work with each individual designer before their show to inspect the fabrics they selected, to ensure that every thread was in place and every embellishment perfectly appointed. It was the last chance to fine tune and make any adjustments that might elevate their designs from mere ready-to-wear to works of art.

The runway show was not just a chance to showcase her talent, but every show could make or break her career in the competitive world of high fashion. Despite her raging case of nerves, she forced them back, searching for a sense of calm to ease the rising pressure. Her first show put her on the map and she was gaining a following. This show would determine if she was a one-hit wonder. In the time since she had arrived in Milan, she had faced language barriers, cultural differences, and intense competition from other talented designers. It was Mara's determination and unwavering belief in her own abilities that kept her going and helped her push through moments of self-doubt.

Mara glanced up to see Rochelle watering the large arrangement of flowers on the stand by her studio table. The extravagant arrangement of her favorite Balinese flowers, including lotus blossoms, frangipane, and marigolds, arrived from Zayn the day after she dropped him off at the club. Shocked he would leave so soon and without seeing her again, she picked up the card to re-read it for the hundredth time, trying to understand its meaning.

Dearest Mara,

I really wanted to see you before I left. However, I know how busy you must be, and I did not want to take away from that for a moment. I spoke with Elena. She is coming back with me and plans to order every fashion that displays your beautiful fabrics! I am so sure of your success that I have planned a quiet celebration for the two of us. Nothing fancy, and we will leave right after the last show. Get all those preparations done and I will see you at the first show featuring Lucca's designs. I'm sure you have accomplished incredible work with him!

All the best, darling,

Zayn

What does this mean? *It sounds like he cares about me, but is it true feelings or just business?* Mara dropped the note back on the stand. Rochelle was fussing over the flowers muttering, "So beautiful, don't you think?"

"Yes, Rochelle. They are lovely. Now let's get this place cleaned up and my location bags packed for Lucca's show. I would like storyboards of each designer using my fabrics and the order of their appearance. I need them backstage with me so I do not miss being there at the right time to help in any way I can."

Rochelle gave her a genuine smile. "And to be backstage when the model struts down the runway with one of your designs and the audience erupts with applause! The designer with the dates and times are on the outside of each bag. You are ready, Mara. Even more than your first show, this one does justice to how you blend Balinese tradition with Italian sophistication. You will see. This group of designers have loved working with you. Look at how once Nicole put that dress on the fabric seemed to slide into place. This is exciting! Now, go home, get some rest, or have a glass of wine. The first show is tomorrow night!"

Mara checked each bag noting Rochelle's usual efficiency. Just as she was about to leave, she reached for the prayer necklace hanging on the hook and fastened it around her neck to ground her. She was locking up when she heard the office phone ring. Afraid it might be some last-minute emergency, Mara rushed inside to answer.

When she answered, what she got in return was her two best friends yelling, "SURPRISE! We are here and on the way to your flat."

Hearing Sarah and Annie's voices at such an emotional time brought tears to Mara's eyes. "I thought you weren't coming until the show tomorrow night?"

Annie spoke up. "I remember right before the first show, there was a lull and it was nerve-racking to feel so helpless! So we decided to come early and help however we can, even if it is just to lend moral support. Are you leaving the studio now?"

"I was just locking up. I should be home in about thirty minutes. If you get there before me, there is a key under the flowerpot."

Sarah added, "Perfect, we will see you there. Let's order in and have a girls' night. The men won't arrive until right before Lucca's show tomorrow."

Overwhelmed, Mara was happy beyond words to know her friends had come to be with her. "Oh my, I am so grateful and can't wait to see you both!"

* * *

Opening the door to Annie and Sarah's smiling faces was a balm to Mara's taut nerves and there were hugs all around. Sarah was wearing her typical jeans, tank top and short bolero jacket with her signature ponytail. Annie was more colorful, as usual, with a multicolor tiered skirt and long sleeve ruffle blouse. To Mara, they both looked beautiful. "Where are your suitcases? You can't come to Fashion Week with only a carry-on bag!"

Annie was quick to answer, "Ramone and Hans are bringing our other bags to the hotel, so we just packed what we needed for tonight and tomorrow."

Sarah smiled in agreement. "Right, we are here to distract you for a few hours, then help you get ready for tomorrow's show!"

Mara opened a local bottle of Franciacorta sparkling wine from the surrounding Lombardy region. Annie lifted her glass. "Let's make a toast. To wherever our paths take us, we are friends for life and will always be there for each other."

Sarah and Mara in unison replied, *"Cin cin!"*

The three girls curled up on the comfortable sofa and chairs ready to share some girl talk. Mara started, grateful for the company of both these dynamic women. "Tell me everything! Annie, what is going on with the twins?"

Annie, never prone to shy away from conversation, and always eager to share news of her two-year-old fraternal twins, answered, "Salvi and Cece just turned two and a half. The issue going on with them right now is the blend of all the languages that they hear. I have always referred to myself as sort of a mutt since my father is British and my mother half Spanish and French. Plus, I spent most of my youth in the States. The twins seem to be making up their own language that is a combination of English, Spanish, and French. They mostly hear French from my cousin, Sabine, though, when she cares for them if I have to go out."

Mara was curious about Sabine. Such a charming girl. "She and Antonio got married, right?"

Annie took a sip. "Ooh, this is good! Yes, she and Antonio got married in Bordeaux at her family winery. We were all there. They have a small apartment close to us and she just found out she is pregnant so the twins will have a cousin soon! Actually, the twins are with them now. Even though Ramone and Antonio are no longer on the circuit, they still participate in the occasional bull fighting exhibition. However, most of their time is spent in developing new shipping routes for their business. That's why we were visiting Sarah in Venice. They seem to think there is an untapped market in a trade arrangement between Venice and the Port of Trieste which is right on the outskirts of Slovenia."

Mara said, "I just mentioned Slovenia to Zayn and that you said how pretty it was."

Sarah nodded. "There's a ferry that goes daily from Venice to the old town of Piran right on the Slovenian coast. Hans and I have been over there a couple of times and love it!"

Mara asked Sarah, "Do you feel settled in with Hans full time in Venice?"

Sarah laughed out loud. "Well, it couldn't be any more different from the plains of East Africa! We actually have to get to our flat by water through the canal. The tourists ride in the gondolas, but Hans and I found a small *vaporetto* that we just attach to the stoop and lock up on the hook beside our door. Stepping inside, you would not believe how charming it is, and it is spacious enough for company. Annie and Ramone have been there for several days now. You and Zayn will have to come visit. Will he be here tomorrow?"

Mara's disposition changed slightly for a moment, but quickly recovering, she answered, "Yes, of course. He will be here in time for Lucca's show, and Elena is coming with him. I am sure Bajir will be here as well. Knowing they are counting on my financial success does add some pressure to the week."

Sarah nodded in agreement. "I totally understand. It was like that with Amir. Having his sponsorship meant everything to me, and I never wanted to let him down. And I wasn't in a relationship with him like you and Zayn. However, if Elena is coming, I'm sure our friend Amir won't be far from her side."

Annie laughed. "That is true, and my amorous and jealous husband seems quite relieved to have Amir happily married!" Looking closer, Annie thought she sensed something off with Mara. "Mara, what about you and Zayn? How are things between you? Are you enjoying the lifestyle of the rich and famous?"

A feeling of resignation came over Mara, not clearly understanding her own feelings. "I know I like this, being here with the two of you. It feels real. With Zayn, often a sense of reality is nowhere to be found. Sure, the glamour can be intoxicating but there is no intimate conversation, no understanding caresses." Mara absentmindedly rubbed on her prayer necklace. "My roots and basic beliefs of my family and my culture are part of me. Sometimes I feel like I am losing that."

Annie noticed the necklace she had given Mara's cousin so long ago and reached over to give her a hug. Sarah was right there as well to form a group embrace to give Mara the support and understanding that she needed. It was a release for all the pent-up emotion, and Mara's tears flowed freely with her two best friends there to buffer her from the world she found herself in.

As usual, it was Sarah who cut to the chase and said, "Sweetheart, have you considered Zayn might not be the match for you? I know that after my breakup with Hans, I was heartbroken. Sam was there in Africa with me, and it made sense at the time that having so much in common we should be together. I believed it for a while too. But after Hans told me about Camille's terminal illness and that he was no longer married, I finally allowed him back into my life. There was no comparison. Hans is my soulmate, and I love him beyond reason. And no, we aren't married but there are no wedding vows that can bind me to him more than the love that I feel in my soul."

Annie solemnly nodded. "Mara, I feel the same way about Ramone. Sure, I was dazzled for a while by Amir, but he never secured my heart like Ramone did."

Mara had a look on her face that was both miserable and hopeful at the same time. "I owe so much to Zayn and his father. I would never have had the chance here in Milan without their support."

Sarah said, "They didn't invest in you out of the goodness of their heart! They invested in you because they believe in your talent! So do we...and all the designers who have chosen your fabrics to display on their runways. This is your time to shine, my friend. Now, let's all get some sleep to be ready for the week ahead!"

CHAPTER 7

Mara pulled the outfits she had selected to wear throughout the week out of her closet and hung them on a rolling rack for final scrutiny. She would not get called out on stage for each show her fabrics were in, but she might be for the designers who were using her fabrics exclusively. There was an image she understood clearly she needed to convey in order to justify her status within the high-fashion realm. *Today it gets real.*

She rolled the rack out to the living room lured by the smell of coffee and freshly baked croissants. Annie and Sarah were seated at the counter sipping their coffee, and Sarah reached for the pot to pour Mara a cup. Annie spotted the outfits first. "Ooh, let me see!" She sifted through the vibrant colors and sheer silk fabrics that were feather-light against her fingertips. "These resemble the outfit you wore to Ramone's and my wedding. But they seem to take the age-old traditional look and add a more current fashionable feel. Which one are you wearing tonight?"

Mara studied them. "These are what I like to call fusion pieces that blend the old with the new. I am going to wear the yellow *Kebayah* blouse with a batik-like sarong and hand-painted silk sash. I think Lucca will like it, and he is one of the designers featuring my fabrics exclusively."

Sarah also looked through the numerous outfits. "How many shows are you featured in?" Looking at Annie, she added, "I want to be sure we have tickets to each one."

Mara explained, "My fabrics are featured in the one tonight, then seven more scattered through the coming week, then the finale next Monday night. There will be three separate shows tonight, and Lucca's will be third at seven-thirty. I think Zayn plans to take us all out for a late dinner afterward."

Annie went to get her bag saying, "Come on, Sarah. Let's go get checked in at the hotel before Ramone and Hans get there. We can give Mara a little peace and quiet to get ready."

Mara never ceased to be amazed at how Annie could read her and somehow knew she needed some quiet time before all the chaos began. "There is no way I can express how much your arriving last night meant to me. Get there early tonight to get good seats. I will see you after the show for dinner!"

Once Annie and Sarah were gone and the house was silent, Mara walked over to her desk where she kept the pictures of her parents, grandmother, and cousins. She picked up the framed pictures and touched each of their faces, understanding they might be poor in monetary wealth but rich beyond words in culture and happiness. It was true, growing up in her small village surrounded by lush tropical forests and cerulean waters, she was immersed in a world of natural beauty that inspired her even in the midst of hardships, and the Balinese people seemed to always maintain an attitude of joy and appreciation. Mara thought about the so-called *glamorous* people she was now surrounded by every day. *Were they real? Were they even happy?*

Suddenly, Mara knew what she needed to restore her sense of balance...a large dose of her family and homeland. She made a decision right there holding those pictures close to her heart that as soon as these shows were over she would take a trip home to Bali. Zayn's plans would have to wait. Decision made, Mara re-focused her attention to the week ahead. She took calls from Lucca and two other designers finalizing a few last-minute details with her promise to be at each of their shows early. Mara liked to take a good look at each model before they walked the runway to make sure each garment was perfectly draped and every detail was in place before the final approval to go onstage from the designer.

Oddly, there had been no call from Zayn, which Mara finally noticed when she answered a call thinking it was another designer. Instead, it was Zayn. He quickly began, "Mara, I don't want to keep you but just wanted to let you know we are all here at the hotel and so excited for tonight! As a reminder, I have reserved a late seating at Mystique. I've requested a table by the window so we can have a spectacular view of the city. I want everything to be special for my girl!"

His girl? Mystique was one of the most sought-after restaurants for reservations on a regular night. She couldn't imagine what it would take to reserve a table during Fashion Week. "That will be lovely, Zayn. Don't forget Annie and Ramone and Sarah and Hans will be joining us. They plan to stay most of the week through the finale."

"Got it! I know you'll do great tonight. This is your time to shine. I will confirm the rest of your schedule when I see you after the show."

"Sounds good, Zayn. See you tonight." *Hummm. More like business.*

* * *

Backstage at the Palazzo Reale, the air was thick with nervous anticipation among the flurry of designers, models, and fashion enthusiasts. Mara quickly found Lucca, dressed for the runway himself in a navy-blue full length Nehru jacket over a matching shirt and vibrant crimson silk pants finished with a thick set of beaded necklaces to the waist and pointed-toe silk slippers. The perfectly coiffed hair and full makeup left no question he was a star. Mara couldn't resist a smile when she saw him.

Her collaboration with Lucca, a renowned clothing designer and one of her favorites, had elevated her work to new heights, and she knew his avant-garde fashions would be the highlight of the evening. Together they had carefully curated each fabric, ensuring that Mara's distinctive style would show through in perfect harmony with Lucca's fashion innovation and keen eye for design. Seeing her fabrics come to life on the models felt like a dream come true. The energy backstage was electric as Mara made final adjustments to the garments, her hands trembling with excitement.

As the lights dimmed and the music swelled, Mara took a deep breath and watched in awe as the first model glided down the runway in Lucca's stunning creation crafted from Mara's fabrics. The audience was captivated. The intricate patterns and vibrant colors brought Mara's fabrics to life, creating a synergy that was nothing short of magical! Once the last model left the runway, the roar of the applause was deafening, and Lucca winked at Mara before walking on stage to take a bow. After several moments, he reached his hand out for Mara to join him onstage.

It was a pivotal moment for Mara to see her designs take center stage in the fashion capital of the world. As she walked toward Lucca, he applauded her and tipped his head. Deeply moved, she applauded him back to the audience giving him the due he deserved. They walked off the stage together knowing this was just the beginning of a successful partnership between them.

CHAPTER 8

Offstage, Mara felt a surge of emotion like nothing she had ever experienced as she was surrounded by flowers and shouts of congratulations. Out of the corner of her eye she saw Annie and Sarah rushing up to the wings of the stage. But before they could get there, Mara was lifted and twirled about. Shocked, she saw it was Zayn! He couldn't stop gushing. "Mara, you did it! They just kept coming...one show-stopping design after the other. Your intricate fabrics with Lucca's daring silhouettes had the audience in awe! If any of your other shows go like this, it is just the beginning for you!" Zayn finally set her down but Mara hardly had time to catch her breath, much less decipher the pounding in her heart before Annie and Sarah arrived with hugs and enthusiastic congratulations.

Annie was bubbling with excitement. "You should have seen the audience! You and Lucca have established a devoted group of new fans."

Sarah said in wonder, "How can you top this? You have another one tomorrow? This is incredible."

Mara laughed as she saw the stage manager trying to clear the area. "Yes, tomorrow is Lôndine, but I am not exclusive with them. Wednesday with Sophia will be another exclusive. Her designs are remarkable."

Bajir picked his moment to approach and shake Mara's hand. "You have made us proud, young lady, and I can see that our faith in you was well founded. Amina and I will not be joining you young people for such a late dinner tonight. However, I would like you to take a moment and come by my suite tomorrow. You can arrange a time with Zayn. There are a few things we should discuss."

Mara barely had time to nod before Elena was at her side with El Amir close behind. She handed Mara an order form. "See, I ordered every single one! I cannot wait to be the envy of Morocco in these gorgeous styles."

El Amir had his arm tightly around his bride's waist and looked more than pleased. "Mara, excellent work! I looked around the audience. Elena was not alone writing orders. I think you and Lucca will be surprised at this line's success!"

Mara glanced over at Zayn, easily taking charge of steering the group toward the exit and to dinner at Mystique. A commanding figure with his jet-black hair and impeccable sense of style, Zayn also exuded charm and confidence easily capturing the attention of anyone around him. Mara had to admit he was hard to resist, but she couldn't shake the feeling that his motives were unclear. *Was their relationship based on genuine affection and mutual respect, or was it merely a transactional arrangement disguised as romance?*

As the group arrived at the exclusive restaurant, the atmosphere was charged with anticipation and speculation. Zayn, ever the generous host, guided them to their table with a confident smile with his hand comfortably at Mara's back. Annie, Sarah, and Elena each had their respective partners at their side to celebrate Mara's success. Mara was torn between her desire to trust Zayn and her fear of being taken advantage of, and as hard as she tried, she could not determine the emotions hidden beneath his charming smile.

Conversation flowed nonstop as the evening unfolded. Annie glanced at Mara several times as if to question the authenticity of her relationship with Zayn in this opulent setting. She tried to pinpoint what was making her uneasy about them. Ironically, Mara was feeling the same way.

Surely it couldn't be the cultural differences. Or could it? Perhaps he felt like her humble background did not make her worthy of him and that is why he always wanted her dressed to perfection and driving the fancy car. Well, she was proud of her heritage, so if that was the case, maybe it was time to find out!

Mara clicked on the side of her champagne glass to make a toast. She stood and said with a smile, "Your being here to celebrate this career milestone, during which I can share some of the essence of my beautiful island of Bali in fabrics that tell stories of generations past, means the world to me and I will be forever grateful." Then, raising her glass to Zayn, "And, to you Zayn, as well as your father, Bajir. You had the faith in me to back this dream of mine, and my biggest hope is that as a result of this week I will be able to repay my debt to you both with the interest you so deserve in having the confidence that I would succeed. You have been an impeccable host tonight and I thank you from the bottom of my heart. You are the people closest to me, and for that reason, I want to share with you a decision I have made. At the end of this week, once the dust has settled, I plan to go back to Bali for a time. I have been away far too long and miss my family and all the Balinese wonder that is intrenched in the history of the island. So cheers, my friends. Thank you."

Zayn felt like a bucket of ice had been dumped on him. It was not necessarily in Mara's words, but more her defiant tone. The comment about paying him and his father off bristled under his skin. Had he just been a meal ticket and now that she was successful, she was finished with him? And what about the surprise trip he told her about? He had planned to take her to Slovenia since her friends liked it so much. Now she was just going to leave with no warning or conversation?

Elena knew her brother well, and although he tried to hide his simmering emotions, she saw right through them. Where had all this gone wrong? Back in Marbella, Zayn and Mara had been so happy together working on the design projects. Trying not to let the mood of the evening deteriorate, Elena also got up to make a toast. "To Mara, first of all, thank you for the incredible fashions I will be wearing next season!" Everyone laughed including Mara. "I respect your love of your homeland. I know Zayn and I feel similarly about Fujairah. All of us at this table are a group of nomads really. We bring the essence of our traditions and our cultures with us, but we have learned to make them pliable to accept each other as they are." She smiled at Amir knowing they had gone through this so recently and he squeezed her hand. "I, for one, would love to visit Bali someday and learn about your homeland and meet your family. It sounds incredibly special!"

Looks of surprise and speculation circulated around the table with stirring thoughts of Bali. It was then Annie who got up next to toast. "I loved Bali from the first moment I got there. I have been waiting for the perfect place to take the twins on their first adventure! Mara, do you think we could join you?" Taking Ramone's hand, she asked him, "Come with me, my love?"

Ramone's eyes glistened confirming he loved this woman with all his heart. "To the ends of the earth, *querida*, but Bali sounds good!"

Sarah looked at Hans and he nodded. She grinned ear to ear and said, "Why not? We could come too!"

Mara honestly could not believe what was happening as she sat there in shock, although she found herself holding her breath waiting on a reaction from Zayn.

This wasn't his plan. He thought he had everything figured out. Was he so unwilling to be flexible? Maybe it was just time to tear up the playbook and let fate be the guide. The tension in his body visibly relaxed and he turned to Mara. "Looks like we're all coming to Bali!"

It was then he glanced at his sister and saw the wink that told him this was the path he was meant to take.

CHAPTER 9

Mara studied Zayn with renewed hope, and the look he saw in her eye was exactly what he had been waiting to see. He reached over and squeezed her hand and whispered, "I am coming to Bali and wish to learn more about you and your country."

Annie grinned at Mara who just nodded with a stunned look on her face. Then, for a moment, Mara got serious. "This all sounds too good to be true. But please understand. Bali is not Mallorca with yacht club regattas and tourist attractions. It is a spiritual place encased in tradition and ceremony. If you are up for an authentic experience, I would be honored to share my home with all of you."

El Amir remembered the joy of introducing wonders of the Agafay Desert to Elena and Sarah that enabled them to understand how life-changing certain experiences could be. That subject launched into a discussion about the making of argan oil and both Elena's and Sarah's reaction to Morocco.

Zayn paid the bill and ushered everyone out. "We need to get this rising star home for her beauty rest! She has a meeting with my father in the morning and another show tomorrow afternoon."

* * *

The early morning call from Rochelle confirmed Lucca's prediction that orders would be streaming in from the prior night's show. After a few minutes' discussion about which fabrics would need to have production ramped up, Mara quickly showered and prepared to drive to the Casa Rugiada hotel to meet with Bajir. If the rest of the week went as planned, she might soon be able to pay Zayn and his father back for the investment they made. As far as Mara was concerned, the sooner she was out of debt to Zayn, the better she would sleep at night.

Bajir opened the door himself to his office inside his hotel suite. "Come in, my dear. Please sit down. Would you like some tea?"

It was when she looked over at the tea cart that she noticed Zayn, formally dressed in a suit, ready to pour her tea. "Yes, of course. Thank you."

Bajir took his place behind his desk. "Mara, when you took the stage last night, I could not have been more proud if you were my own child. The fashions Lucca displayed should do exceedingly well."

Mara told him about Rochelle's phone call confirming all the incoming orders. "Everyone is clamoring for a Lucca original."

Bajir nodded. "Which in this case means with a Mara designer fabric. You have seen what the other designers are producing for their shows this week. Do you think the others will be as successful with your fabrics?"

"This evening's show and several of the others might be hit or miss depending on any last minute adjustments the designer has made. In my opinion, the fashion designer who has the most chance of creating a buzz with the audience is Sophia. She is also using my fabrics exclusively, but unlike Lucca's modernistic styles, Sophia's are filled with sophistication and grace. Her show is on Friday evening."

43

"Then I shall plan to be there. There will be production lines to expand in order to keep up with the demand. I have had an earnest conversation with my son." Nodding toward Zayn, he continued. "It seems Zayn would like to buy out my position and finance you and your business exclusively himself. I must say, I am not convinced that is a good idea."

Mara glanced at Zayn as a worried look settled on her face. Reluctantly, Mara realized she would need additional funding to increase production and she could not let the designers down by falling short. But to now more than double her obligation financially to Zayn as her exclusive benefactor, she was torn between her desire to succeed on her own merit and her conflicting feelings about Zayn. Mara was grateful for the support and opportunities that Zayn and his father had provided, but she struggled with the fear that accepting Zayn's offer would only deepen the gap between them by giving up any chance of meeting him on equal ground, both financially and socially. He would always have the upper hand as long as she continued to owe him this debt.

Deep down, what Mara really longed for was a loving connection based on equality and mutual respect with Zayn, but now she wondered if this was truly possible. As Mara struggled with her emotions and conflicting desires, she knew that she had to follow her heart while also protecting her independence and integrity. She needed to have an honest conversation with Zayn about her concerns and make a decision that was true to herself and her values.

Mara looked at Bajir intently. "Bajir, I very much appreciate the support and generosity that you and Zayn have shown me. Your confidence has helped empower me to go beyond the limits I thought restrained me. But to have Zayn as my sole benefactor, in light of our *friendship* outside of business, puts me in an awkward position. Am I to be given a say in this transaction? I think before I can give an answer, I need to speak with Zayn privately. Unfortunately, with all the events of Fashion Week unfolding around us, this is not the best time. I agree that additional funding would be helpful to keep up the production. But I would like to do the math and see if I can manage the additional work on my own. Is it alright with the two of you to leave things as they are for the time being?"

Bajir looked at Zayn for confirmation and got it when he nodded and put away the check. "Mara, you will have our continued support as you need it. Simply let either of us know. The public image you have with my son seems to be opening the right doors. Now, good luck with the rest of the week!"

Mara shook both of their hands, with a lingering look at Zayn, before leaving the suite. She had stood her ground for now but was she ready to pursue her dreams on her own terms even if it meant potentially losing Zayn's and his father's support? There was no question the path ahead would lead to difficult decisions and soul-searching. Right now, however, she had to focus on her work. Ultimately, she needed to find a way to reconcile her ambitions, her values, and her feelings for Zayn if she were to carve out a future that felt true to herself. *Was Bali with all of her friends surrounding her, including Zayn, the right place to do just that? Time would tell.*

CHAPTER 10

Fashion Week continued to dazzle and Mara's star continued to shine throughout the runway shows. Evenings were filled with glamorous parties, endless talk of fashion, and a charming and debonair Zayn at her side. He never brought up the discussion in his father's suite, so she left it alone for now as well. Zayn did try to kiss her a time or two at the end of an evening, but Mara was either too distracted or too accustomed to his superficial attempts at intimacy to respond.

Once the last sparkling light had faded on the latest Milan Fashion Week, it felt more like a beginning than an ending. The designers were clamoring for appointments to work with Mara on custom fabrics for their next lines, and Rochelle, fielding the calls, finally got Mara to stop for a few minutes to discuss her schedule. "Mara, I don't know what to tell them. The designers know you would have to start working on designs soon in order for prototypes and swatches to be produced. Have you decided yet what days you will be gone for vacation?"

Mara fought the worry in the pit of her stomach. This was a competitive industry and she could be forgotten in an instant if she slacked off and afforded herself too much time off. If she were going to forge her own path in this city, she would have to be determined to prove herself every season. What she needed right now was someone to talk with. Zayn and his father had gone back to Dubai. Her friends had all left for their own homes, and it was agreed a tentative date for the Bali trip would be decided on soon so they could all make arrangements to go.

What she really needed was a dose of Annie and it had been ages since she had seen the twins, Salvi and Cece. She made the call and Annie answered on the second ring. After Mara told her she needed a quick weekend getaway, Annie quickly said, "Mara, this is perfect timing. Ramone is still working in Venice and Antonio has gone to join him. Sabine and I were just talking about the weekend. Why don't you get on the next train and you can stay in my guest room? My parents are in town and I know they would love to see you too!"

Mara looked at Rochelle, pushing aside the guilt for leaving, and said, "It is Friday morning and I am exhausted. I am going to visit Annie in Marbella for the weekend. I promise I will come back fresh on Monday and let you know what to tell the designers. For now, just tell them that I took a couple of days off to get fresh inspiration for the next line of fabrics." With as bright of a smile as she could muster, Mara added, "Would you mind calling the train station to make a reservation? I am going to run home to toss a few things in a bag and will head to the station. Just send me a message with what train is reserved."

* * *

The rhythm of the uneventful train ride with the picturesque coastal countryside passing by gave Mara time to reflect on why Annie was the only person she trusted to confide in about her doubts and concerns regarding her relationship with Zayn and her current way of life.

On the surface, Annie appeared privileged with her grandfather's lavish sailing vessel, the *Porto Banus*, seemingly at her disposal to depart for faraway lands on a whim. But Mara had spent enough time with Annie to realize there was much more to the woman who had once been the little twelve-year-old girl who was whisked away from her grandparents in Spain, along with her mother, to a remote area of Maine in the States. They were basically in hiding with her father involved in sensitive British military affairs.

Although Annie saw her father infrequently, she idolized him and worked hard to graduate college with honors to make him proud. Her connection to where she considered home in Spain was enhanced by the summer visits from her cousins, Tomás and Sabine. In a way, her fascination with old-world history and the addition of European traditional elements into her architectural designs was her way of honoring her own culture. That was exactly what Mara was trying to do with elements from her homeland of Bali. Now that Annie was no longer in her architectural position at the prestigious Portland firm and had moved back to Spain permanently, was she satisfied being a wife and mother? Annie was the perfect friend with whom Mara could somehow work through the confusion and doubt she had lurking beneath the surface in her own mind.

The idea of such a large group coming to Bali was reminiscent of the time leading up to Annie's wedding on the island of Mallorca and had Mara's mind spinning with what would inevitably be the duties of hostess and tour guide. She would happily share her country with them but what she needed was to find her way back to her own true self. *How could she do both?*

Looking out the window, she saw the Marbella station approaching. In the distance, Mara could see Annie, with Sabine at her side, each of them holding the hand of a toddler. Mara closed her eyes and took in the energy of what was to come, hoping this weekend would give her the answers she needed.

Annie's warm smile was as welcoming as Mara could hope for but it was Sabine who came forward first to embrace her. "*Mon dieu*! Mara, you look so stylish. I heard how successful you were during Fashion Week and was so sorry to miss it! Auntie Sabine was needed for the children, *n'est-ce pas?*"

It was like a breath of fresh air to see Sabine, such a charming pixie of a girl with her endearing French accent. Mara responded, "The children could not have been in better hands. And look at you! When are you due?" Before Sabine could answer, Mara saw a very shy little girl hiding behind Sabine holding her leg tight. "And who might this be?"

Salvi was the first to step forward and speak up. "Sissy's scared of everything!"

Cece looked at her brother indignantly and said petulantly, "Am not!"

Annie laughed and intervened, taking both of their hands. "You two need to be on your best behavior. This is one of my dearest friends, Miss Mara." Salvi and Cece considered the name and tried it out with countless versions that had the three adults laughing with an easy camaraderie. But it was when Cece shyly reached out her arms to Mara as a request to pick her up that Mara's heart melted, and she knew without question that she wanted to be a wife and a mother.

Annie scooped up Salvi into her arms and suggested, "Let's get these two home for a quick lunch and nap, then we can have some quiet time." They dropped Sabine at her flat with promises to meet the next morning at Don Marco's villa. Annie and Sabine's grandfather and grandmother, Gennie, were the center of the family, and with her parents still visiting, there were usually daily get-togethers at their seaside villa with an abundance of eager babysitters.

Easily swept into the magnetic force that always seemed to surround Annie, Mara made a conscious effort to put her feelings of uncertainty and conflict aside. Now that she was there with Annie, she knew there would be chances to carve out time for honest conversations that would allow her to confide her doubts.

Back at Annie's house, dramatically carved into the hill of Mijas, Mara stood at the door of the nursery smiling as Annie told the twins a naptime story referring to the ABC mural that Mara helped Sarah paint before they were born. This story was about the *mighty elephant who never forgets* representing the letter *E*. Although Salvi's eyelids were beginning to close, he asked, "Mummy, do elephants really never forget?"

Annie slowly stroked the side of his brow. "Yes, darling. It is said that they can even remember events from before they were born! Can you imagine that?" Cece was already asleep and Salvi gave a slow grin as he, too, closed his eyes and let sleep take over.

Mara followed Annie out to the terrace where a gorgeous vista of the hillside and sea beyond along with the aromas of fresh flowers and citrus awaited. There was a large glass container on a table with tea brewed from the sun and Annie strolled over to the overgrown trellis teeming with lemons to pick one to use with the tea. Mara sat in wonder at how natural Annie seemed in this environment. She searched in her mind to contemplate if such a place even existed in her own current world.

Peering at Mara over her cup of tea as she settled into the comfy lounger, Annie scrutinized her friend. Mara had an incredible fashion sense and was dressed impeccably, hair and makeup done to perfection. No wonder Zayn loved showing her off. She was obviously the talk of the Milan fashion world with her recent success. *So, what was the issue?*

Mara wondered where to start. She cleared her throat and began with something neutral. "Annie, you have truly made this flat a home. Anyone can see that you are happy here. I suppose it makes me want to ask if you miss working. You were such a talented architect and you used to talk for hours about how you loved to tackle a new project from every angle, particularly from its impact on history."

Annie thought about it for a moment. "When I lived in Portland, working at the firm, I was living on my own without family or friends close by. My profession gave me something exciting to occupy my time and feel a measure of success. But when I started the sailing journey, my horizons were no longer limited to the confines of Portland. They expanded with every country I visited, every culture I embraced, every friend that I made, and eventually falling in love with Ramone and having his children. I still dabble though. I used my skills when we renovated this flat. Ramone and Antonio are considering building a major shipping facility at the port of Valencia and have asked me to assist with the architectural plans. I would be working with the local contractors and port authority. I'm considering it if I can do most of the drawings from home while the twins are small."

Mara nodded. "One of the things I admire most about you is your ability to accept other cultures different from your own. I admit that because of you I have tried to adapt that same philosophy into my own life. But right now, I feel increasingly disconnected from my roots and the values that shaped me into the person I strive to be."

Appreciating that Mara was opening up to her, Annie wanted to be supportive and lend an empathetic ear. "Mara, it was easy for me. I grew up amidst family from four different countries with their own unique traditions and we seemed to find a way to blend them together. You had never been outside Bali until you went to Australia to work with Kenneth Patrick. Then, all of the sudden you landed in a foreign country speaking French and then English. Your best friends were from two other countries, Sarah from England and Hans from Germany. You had only a short time back in Bali before I came along and whisked you away to Australia and then to Greece. Maybe there just wasn't enough time to transition from your childhood lifestyle that held the simplicity that you cherished to the complex cosmopolitan life you are living."

Mara's eyes began to glisten feeling the truth in what Annie was saying. Annie's encouragement was enough to find Mara pouring out her heart about losing sight of what truly mattered to her. She talked of the internal conflict she was struggling with regarding the cultural and lifestyle differences between her and Zayn. "Of course I am grateful for the success and opportunities that have come my way but I find myself obligated to Zayn and being propelled into a glamorous and luxurious way of living that, to be honest, makes me feel sorely out of place and inadequate. At first, I was flattered by Zayn's attention and the allure of his opulent world, but the lack of intimacy has made me question his intensions and whether the differences between us might be insurmountable in the long run."

Annie took Mara into a long embrace, then looked her in the eye. "I'm happy you came and shared this with me. I get it now. You decide to venture back to Bali to reconnect with your true self and re-evaluate your priorities and even that is taken from you when the whole group, me included, wanted to make a pleasure trip out of it."

Mara nodded miserably, hating this resentment she felt about her friends coming along to Bali.

Just then Cece toddled over rubbing her eyes and climbed up into Annie's lap looking soulfully at Mara. "Why are you crying, Miss Mara?"

The sweet innocence of that little girl brought a smile of joy to Mara, who looked at Annie and said, "I'm good for now. I'm glad it's all out on the table. We can talk more later." Mara smiled brightly at Cece and over at Salvi who was just joining them. "For now, is there a park close by? With a swing?"

When Annie nodded, both children screamed a unanimous, "YAY!"

CHAPTER 11

Now that Mara had shared her true feelings about Zayn and their situation, neither Mara nor Annie seemed in a rush to tackle them. Annie knew Mara well enough to know this was a time when all the pressure from the last months simply needed to be put aside for a few moments. There was one thing she could always count on to give her a better perspective...and she thought it might work for Mara as well. A quick phone call to her grandfather, Don Marco, confirmed his sailing vessel, *Porto Banus*, was in port and that Captain Luis would be thrilled to take them out for the day. Annie's mother, Celeste, quickly agreed to watch the twins. Mara's delighted reaction was enough to let Annie know she had made the right decision.

Mara eagerly anticipated being back out to sea on the 95-foot motorsailor and seeing the captain and crew again. She hadn't seen Captain Luis and his main crew, Roff and Helene since Annie and Ramone's wedding on the island of Mallorca.

Captain Luis was all smiles to greet Mara and Annie from the helm. Roff helped them at the gangplank but there was no sign of Helene. Instead, a young brunette woman came up to introduce herself. "Hello, I'm Karla. May I get you anything to drink as we set sail?"

Roff winked at Annie and she answered Mara's questioning look with, "A lot has happened since the wedding. I guess we have a little catching up to do." Looking at Karla, she answered, "Two glasses of prosecco would be great, Karla."

Under her breath, Mara asked Annie, "Where is Helene? I thought she and Roff were together."

"Let's go up to the bow where we can talk." Annie led the way.

When they were comfortably seated in the cushioned area, Mara prodded, "Well?"

Annie grinned like a young child about to spill the beans with a surprise. "Helene left the *Porto Banus* over a year ago. Remember Simon, Paulo's son, from the Mallorca Yacht Club? It seems he and Helene had a bit of a fling during the wedding. After we left the island everyone thought it was over. Well, I gather they continued to write each other and Simon asked her to come back to the island during her time off. Things progressed and she decided to stay with him!"

"Wow, that is unexpected. I saw Roff wink at you. Wasn't he upset when he found out?"

Annie chuckled. "It turns out Roff met Karla in a regatta in the South of France. Hans Schuman set it up. Remember, he was captain of one of the King's Cup racing boats in Mallorca and Don Marco let Roff crew with him. They stayed friends and when he signed up for the regatta in Antibes, he called Roff to see if he could crew. Karla was also part of the crew, and she and Roff hit it off. I gather Karla was getting pretty jealous of his time away on the *Porto Banus*, particularly in close quarters with Helene. When Helene decided to stay in Mallorca, Roff asked the captain if Karla could apply. With both Roff's and Hans' recommendations, he could hardly say no and she has fit right in with the family. We all just love her, and she is great when the twins are on board!"

Mara graciously accepted her prosecco from Karla with a genuine smile. Mara watched as she left to help release the ropes and get underway, then said to Annie with wonder, "I guess you never know how things are going to work out, do you?"

Annie wisely answered, "No, you don't, and I suppose that brings us full circle back to you, my friend. But wait, you need to experience this. It is my favorite part of sailing!"

Captain Luis had maneuvered the *Porto Banus* out of the channel and into the wind so Roff and Karla could prepare to raise the main sail. Annie's anticipation and excitement were contagious and the atmosphere felt magical as a hush fell over the deck, broken only by the creaking of ropes and the fluttering of canvas. Roff and Karla moved with practiced precision. The moment the sail began to ascend, a gentle breeze stirred, tugging at the edges of the fabric.

Captain Luis shifted his course, and there it was. The ship seemed to come alive, responding to the touch of the wind with a soft shiver that ran through its hull. The sail caught the wind and the yacht lunged forward with its bow slicing through the water. Annie and Mara felt the wind in their hair as they easily breached each wave ahead of them. Annie shook her head. "I love the feeling I get each time I go out to sea. It is as if time has frozen a fleeting moment where there is no past or future, just the present. This is the place for you to listen to your heart and follow your instincts."

Mara closed her eyes, absorbing the soothing sway against the waves, realizing the toll the last year had taken on her sense of self and well-being. She opened her eyes and looked at Annie in earnest. "I was so honored by the faith Zayn and his father had in my talent, and I admit I had never experienced such an extravagant lifestyle before. I think Zayn quite swept me off my feet." Mara smiled. "There is no question he is easy on the eyes."

Annie interjected, "Why do I feel a 'but' coming?"

"There is no clarity with Zayn. We never really communicate on a personal level to discuss our needs and desires. One moment I think he is going to finally break the ice between us, then the next moment the wall is back up. I sometimes feel as if I'm being used in some way and it leaves me feeling subordinate and unequal. As long as he controls the purse strings to my business and the fate of my future, I am going to have this sense of dependency and vulnerability that leaves me feeling used and undervalued, but mostly skeptical about any genuine feelings he might have toward me. Annie, it is time for me to take control of my own destiny."

Annie looked out at the sea for an instant as if to draw some wisdom to share. "Mara, the cultural differences between you are real. You know how I had begun to have feelings for Amir, but his Arab heritage prevented him from marrying a woman outside his faith. Perhaps that is happening with Zayn as well but he doesn't want to lose you. It seems to me that you need to spend some time alone with Zayn to get to the heart of this emotional roller coaster he has you on. Your fabrics are filled with Balinese influence, so I don't think you have lost touch with your heritage. On the surface, Zayn seems like the perfect partner...supportive, attentive, and eager to invest in your vision. It could be something else. Do you even enjoy all the social gatherings and material luxuries? Maybe you need to take time for yourself to re-center and reflect on what exactly brings you joy and fulfillment."

Encouraged by Annie's words, Mara agreed. "You're right, I need to have a candid conversation with Zayn and try to get him to open up and be honest about what he is feeling. I am aware he provides financial security but if the religious differences do not allow us to marry and have a family, I need to consider a different path, or at least a different kind of relationship with him before things get too serious. Annie, I knew I could count on you to be the pillar of support I needed to figure this out."

"Any time, Mara. And just say the word if you decide you want me to cancel everyone going to Bali. Perhaps you need to make the trip home alone to reconnect and seek the guidance and support of your family. Just remember, your true friends will support you no matter which path you choose. Take the time you need and trust that the answers will come to you. After all, you are the architect of your own life, and it's okay to make changes to it to serve your own happiness and sense of well-being."

Mara looked at the friend she so loved and respected. "I loved watching you in Bali and I want to share my homeland with our friends. But I need to settle things with Zayn before I take him home to my country. I will forever be grateful to him and his father for the opportunities they opened up for me, and I am more determined than ever to prove myself in Milan's competitive fashion world. I agree the differing backgrounds are a concern but I am just as worried about a relationship built on an unequal footing."

Annie reached over and squeezed Mara's hand. "You will figure it out, and I will always be here for you."

The weekend sped by filled with family activities that easily included Mara as one of their own. Before she knew it, she was boarding the train that would take her back to Milan to face the decisions that were haunting her. After a final wave to Annie through the window, Mara strengthened her resolve to stand firm in her beliefs to determine whether she was willing to move forward without the financial security and access to social circles that Zayn provided...or if somehow there was a compromise.

Zayn was due back in Milan later in the week and there were plans for the opera Saturday night with a gala afterward. Mara decided to carve out time during the weekend to have an honest conversation with Zayn to determine where their future was headed.

CHAPTER 12

Unbeknownst to Mara, Zayn, back home in the Arab emirate of Fujairah, was facing his own self-doubts. The conversation that morning with his older brothers was a harsh dose of reality. He needed time to think and sort out where his life was heading, particularly when it came to Mara.

Zayn had been walking over an hour, lost in thought, when he finally sat on a bench facing the front of the Sheikh Zayed Mosque, inspired by the original Blue Mosque in Istanbul. Staring at it, he realized it was the only mosque in the city that would even allow a non-Muslim inside. Everywhere else it was forbidden.

Zayn was born into a life of privilege and luxury, always accustomed to having his every need met without question. His upbringing had instilled in him a sense of entitlement, a belief that he deserved the best of everything simply because of who he was. His brothers, Khaled and Omar, had chided him that very morning for his extravagant lifestyle and tendency to chase after the latest trends and fads without considering the consequences.

Was that true? Ever since he could remember, his brothers and sister, Elena, were the pride and joy of the family. They were the ones who excelled in academics, sports, and any task thrown their way. Even Elena was taking on the philanthropic donations of the family business. Zayn realized, sitting on that bench across from the mosque, that their successes had inadvertently cast a shadow over his self-esteem, leaving him feeling inadequate and overlooked.

It wasn't until his father had agreed to invest in Mara's business with him that he had been given an opportunity to shine. But he had never been given any guidance and now it seemed all the success was Mara's, not his. Mara was unlike anyone he had ever met. She was beautiful, talented, and creative, thoroughly captivating him. She challenged his perception of where his life was leading just as he struggled to find his place in the world. He knew his brothers were watchful and protective but they were wrong. Mara was not just a novelty in Zayn's collection, a passing fancy that would eventually fade.

Entranced by her creative spirit and genuine warmth, Zayn saw something in her that money could not buy. He admitted to himself that he was envious of her independence, dedication to her craft, and sense of fulfillment. Although his intentions meant well, he had to admit he'd still used what he knew, money and connections, to woo her.

Was he, in fact, using Mara to achieve something worthy and impress his father? Were his motives as unselfish as he portrayed? That was the hard dose of reality that Zayn struggled with. During their conversation, Khaled had made it crystal clear the cultural and religious barriers that stood between Zayn as a Muslim and Mara a devout Hindu were a serious barrier. That, along with the stark disparities in their social statuses, cast a looming shadow over any chance of a blossoming romance.

Zayn got up and started walking again. He hadn't expected the growing feelings between them, and he was painfully aware Mara felt it as well. Even before the talk with his brothers, Zayn had hesitated to confess his affection for Mara, afraid of the potential consequences. In his heart, he knew Mara would want marriage and a family. Would she really want to pursue a relationship with him knowing there could be no marriage? The thought of losing Mara was unbearable. As their bond deepened, intimacy was so close. *Knowing that, could he simply relegate their relationship to a mere business partnership? Or should he sever ties with the woman who shined like a beacon of hope in his life? Was there a middle ground where love and companionship could coexist without defying societal norms?*

The weight of these questions hung over him. He suddenly knew with clarity that honesty and a candid conversation about the challenges they would face as a couple was necessary, regardless of the result. He knew he could not go to Bali with Mara without some resolution, even if it meant making the heartbreaking decision to let her go.

Now that the decision was made to speak earnestly with Mara, he could not get back to Milan fast enough. They had big plans for the opera and a gala on Saturday. He didn't want to spoil the evening but this couldn't wait. Otherwise, with their relationship ready to progress to the next step, it might be too late.

* * *

Both Mara and Zayn looked forward to the coming weekend with apprehension, concerned about how the other would react. Back in her studio, Mara felt like time shifted back and forth from racing to almost standstill, adding to her anxiety. Zayn messaged her that he would arrive Friday afternoon in time for Mara to pick him up at the private airstrip just outside Milan. In his message, he mentioned wanting some time to discuss a few things prior to Saturday evening's event. Unaware of Zayn's intent, Mara planned to use that conversation to address their relationship.

By the time Friday arrived, Mara was on pins and needles, trying to consider in her mind what she would say to Zayn. Now that her studio activity was winding down for the day, with a couple of hours before she needed to leave for the airport, Mara decided to work on some design sketches to distract her. Rochelle was busy stacking bolts of fabric that had arrived with some of the first production orders from Fashion Week. Bajir had been correct that the increased fabric production required a great deal of upfront financing. There was no question their business relationship added a layer of complexity to the situation. Lost in thought, Mara did not hear the phone.

Rochelle answered, startled. "What? Oh no! Yes, she is right here, Mr. Al Farooq."

The tone of Rochelle's voice got Mara's attention, and she immediately took the phone. It was Zayn. "Darling, there has been an accident. We are all okay. As we approached the Mediterranean, there was a storm the pilot had not anticipated. It seemed to form out of nowhere. One minute I was sitting through the turbulence looking out the window, when a bright flash and a wave of intense heat came through the plane. We were hit by lightning! The nearest place for an emergency landing was the island of Cyprus. We made it down, but the plane is grounded until it can be repaired."

"Oh, Zayn! At least no one was hurt. Will you be able to get a commercial flight?"

"I can get a direct flight from the international airport to Milan, but not until Sunday. I want you to go ahead to the opera. The evening should be spectacular with Antonella Rossi and she will personally be at the gala afterward. I will notify the box office at *Teatro alla Scala* to arrange the tickets to be held for you and for you to have a chauffeur available at your disposal for the evening. I am just so sorry not to be there."

"Zayn, I don't think I should go without you. I won't know anyone."

"There are two tickets. Why don't you take someone?"

"It is so last minute, I can't imagine anyone being available."

"Mara, I won't take no for an answer. You must go. Why don't you ask that designer, Lucca? Go and enjoy! I will make all the arrangements."

"Well, the main thing is that you're safe." Zayn then interrupted her saying the pilot had his father on the other line and he had to go.

Rochelle had watched Mara through the whole conversation and saw that she was dazed from the news. "I heard some of it. Bottom line is Zayn is delayed and won't be here for the opera and gala tomorrow night. You need a date!"

That last statement shook Mara out of her reverie. "I do not need a date."

Rochelle already had the phone in her hand dialing Lucca's number. "He is perfect and will fit right in with his flamboyant manner. And, since he has no inclination toward the fairer sex, you are not in danger of being ravaged."

Mara started laughing at the very idea. It was that unconventional spirit that drew Mara to Rochelle. The phone was already ringing and when Lucca answered, Rochelle shoved the phone toward Mara.

"*Ciao,* Mara! So good to hear from you!" Lucca said in heavily accented English.

With a look of daggers at Rochelle, Mara forced a smile and began. "*Ciao,* Lucca. I realize this is last minute, but Zayn has been delayed getting back to Milan and we had tickets for tomorrow night to see Antonella Rossi at *Teatro alla Scala.* Now that he can't make it, I was wondering if you could join me. If you have other plans, I understand."

Fully animated, Lucca responded with, "To see Antonella Rossi and hear that voice that is nothing short of artistry? Mio dio! How she effortlessly traverses the octaves and pulls the emotions...I would love to go with you, Mara!"

"Lucca, there is something else. After the performance, Antonella is hosting a gala and we are invited. I assume it is quite formal." Mara smirked at a smiling Rochelle.

Lucca became passionate when he said, "You must let me provide a gown for you to wear that is fitting for such a prestigious event! I know your measurements and I have the perfect ensemble. It will be sent over to you tomorrow morning. This will be an unforgettable evening. I must get to work! Thank you, Mara. *Arrivederci.*"

Mara could only sit there stunned at the whirlwind of a call. To Rochelle, she finally said, "I guess he is going, and he is sending over a gown for me to wear."

Rochelle's expression said it all but she added, "Cinderella is going to the ball!"

CHAPTER 13

Anxious about attending the exclusive gala without Zayn, Mara didn't feel much like Cinderella, that is, until she opened the box from Lucca. The stunning three-piece ensemble took her breath away. The whisper-like black silk was cut to perfection and a masterpiece of design. The chemise top was overlaid with intricate copper beading inspired by Mara's homeland of Bali. Its dramatic asymmetrical neckline was a testament to Lucca's style. It fell just short of the waist to give the dramatic beaded basque waistband the attention it deserved. The delicate pattern of beading around the hem of the long skirt also reminded her of her beloved Bali, and Mara felt a surge of pride and gratitude for what Lucca had so thoughtfully crafted. It was perfect for her just as he'd promised.

Once she slipped into the ensemble, her full-length mirror confirmed the elegance and sophistication that exuded from the garment that fit her like a glove, accentuating her curves. Even the slight touch of midriff showing above the waist was the epitome of taste, and the lightly beaded scarf could be worn in a variety of ways. The final touch was the elbow-length copper satin gloves! Looking at her reflection, Mara began to feel a bubble of excitement building in her about the evening. She was about to hear the esteemed Antonella Rossi perform and later have the chance to meet her in person. Maybe she was a princess going to a ball after all. She quickly made a hair and makeup appointment in an attempt to do Lucca's fashion creation justice and enter the theater with confidence and poise.

It was the first time Mara had entered the two-century-old opera house, and there was one exceedingly excited designer by her side. Not only was he going to experience one of the most talented and sought-after opera singers of his generation and witness her enchanting voice, but he was also finally able to dress Mara in a way that showed off her delicate features impeccably. He could not stop staring at her. Mara hardly noticed since she was fascinated by all the ornate treasures on display throughout the theater. "Lucca, look at that painting! It is the architect who did the first renovation. They said at the ticket counter that they have tours. I would love to come back and learn more about its history."

Lucca nodded but had something else on his mind. "You know Antonella is not just known for her incredible voice, but also for her exquisite costumes. I have been told that to see one of her concerts is to enjoy a visual feast in collaboration with the elaborate design of her costumes. Did you know her costume designer is also from Bali?"

That got Mara's attention. "No, I had no idea. Do you think he will be at the gala after the performance? I would enjoy meeting him." Just then, the lights dimmed and flickered, indicating it was time to take their seats.

Both Mara and Lucca were pleasantly surprised to be taken to one of the boxes with an excellent vantage point to see the entire concert. Mara was eternally grateful to Zayn for setting all this up and especially for insisting that she come tonight, even suggesting Lucca as the perfect escort.

Never having been to an Italian opera, Mara was not prepared for the emotional depth Antonella brought to the stage with her rendition of the classic arias. And Lucca was right, the costumes that shimmered under the stage lights added the perfect enhancement to her powerful vocals. The artistry of her voice soared through the grand hall, no question leaving a lasting impact on all attending that night. Mara couldn't take her eyes off Antonella and she leaned in toward the melodic stories of love, tragedy, and triumph woven through her powerful voice.

When the last curtain call had been taken and both Mara and Lucca's hands were red from clapping, the lights came on and guests began their exit. Mara looked at Lucca in amazement. "I can't move. I am positive I have never seen anything like what we just experienced!"

Lucca agreed. "I feel the same way and even with my expectations high, she exceeded them. Thank you, dear Mara, for allowing me to accompany you. And please thank Zayn also."

"We are not finished yet! We get to meet that powerhouse in person. She is such a big personality on stage, what do you think she will be like at the gala?"

Lucca shrugged. "Let's go find out, shall we?"

Mara and Lucca followed the group making their way toward the ballroom. Three sets of double doors were wide open displaying the grandeur of the backdrop for the gala. Once they were checked in at the door, a waiter stood ready to hand them a flute of champagne. Mara leaned in toward Lucca and asked, "Do you see her?"

A young man behind them overheard her question and took the liberty of answering. "Ms. Rossi will be here soon. She is changing into her final costume of the night."

Mara turned to see a devilishly handsome man around her age with crystal-blue eyes and chestnut-brown hair wearing a form-fitting custom tux. His eyes sparkled with a hint of mischief and held hers for an extra heartbeat before introducing himself. With an air of confidence and fascinating appeal, he said, "Welcome. I am Wayan, Ms. Rossi's personal costumier." He took Mara's hand and gave a debonair gentle kiss to the inside of her wrist with his gaze never leaving hers, before moving his hand to shake Lucca's.

Mara felt a flutter in her heart that she couldn't quite explain and was flustered to the point she could not find her voice so Lucca intervened. "It would seem we have something in common. I am Lucca, a fashion designer here in Milan, and this is Mara. She has recently moved here from Bali to set up her own fabric design studio. We just finished a show during Fashion Week where I exclusively used Mara's fabrics."

Wayan's eyes were back on Mara as he appraised her in light of this news although he directed his question to Lucca. "Is this exquisite style Mara is wearing one of your designs?"

Who was this mysterious man? Suddenly feeling an annoyance that the conversation was going around her, she intervened. "Lucca was generous enough to create my ensemble for the evening. It would seem you both have a talent that is undeniable. Did I hear that you were also from Bali?"

Hearing the activity at the door, Wayan apologized and excused himself so he could be at Antonella's side. As an afterthought, he turned to Mara. "I am intrigued to meet someone from my own country here in Milan. We will talk later. Let the line die down a little and I will introduce you to Antonella." There was something about him. The unexpected meeting had sparked a connection between them that was undeniable and spoke volumes even without words.

Mara took a sip of her champagne as Lucca studied her. "It seems you have an admirer."

"Don't be silly. He is probably surprised to see someone from Bali so far from home. But, I have to say, he doesn't have the features of the men I know in Bali." Mara let her eyes roam back toward Wayan when the crowd parted and she saw Antonella. Lucca saw her too and his jaw dropped. Even though each of the costumes worn on stage was a work of art, this vision surpassed them all. Antonella looked like a queen. The gold brocade bodice with a daring neckline stretched to her waist fit her like a second skin. In total contrast was the miles of organza 'fluff' embellished with coordinating gold embroidery that poufed from the bodice and fell to the floor. Topping it all was the gold hairpiece. Mara and Lucca, both in the fashion industry, realized what it took to make such an outfit. Lucca whispered, "He is really good."

Mara agreed but answered, "And Antonella is dazzling. She radiates and lights up the room! Look how effortlessly she mingles with patrons and fellow artists, making each guest feel welcome and appreciated."

Lucca had fame in his own right, and there were frequent pauses to stop to talk with an existing or potential customer of his. Mara watched Lucca, amazed at how comfortable he was and how special he made each woman feel. However, she had to admit, her outfit was getting its share of "oohs and ahhs" as well. That is what Lucca does, Mara thought. He dresses women to feel beautiful and she had to admit it had worked on her. She had never been so aware of men's appreciative stares until that evening, and she basked in the enjoyment of it. Lucca seemed pleased to see it too.

Wayan finally came over and beckoned Mara and Lucca to follow him. They made their way through the hub of guests to a seating area where Antonella lounged on a green velvet sofa. As they were introduced, Lucca reached for Antonella's hand to kiss it like she was royalty. Mara felt as if she should curtsy but instead shook her gloved hand with both of hers.

"I do hope you understand if I don't get up. I honestly don't think I can stand another moment. Please sit down and join me." Antonella smiled and indicated the seats around her. Once they sat, Antonella continued, "Lucca, I understand your latest show during Fashion Week was a grand success and that you exclusively used Mara's fabrics."

Lucca reached over and patted Mara's hand. "Yes, I am certain it was her ingenious sense of design that somehow combines old-world tradition with contemporary sophistication that created fabrics that could be translated into cutting edge fashions."

Antonella nodded and turned to Mara, scrutinizing her from head to toe. "Did Wayan tell you he is also from Bali? What an interesting coincidence. It sounds like you both bring the essence of your homeland to your craft. I met Wayan here in Milan at the Conservatorio di Musica. Our paths crossed when I was searching for a costume for my first major concert. His talent was obvious, but it was his passion for artistry that matched my own zeal for music. Once he designed that first costume, I knew we'd work together from then on and I have worked exclusively with him since."

Intrigued, Mara looked over at Wayan and asked, "Reflecting on the elaborate dress of our people and the variety of spiritual dances, I can understand the basis for your passion. Were you designing in Bali? What brought you to Milan?"

Wayan looked at Mara in earnest, suddenly wanting to share his story. "My sisters were involved in the spiritual dances of our beautiful regency of Buleleng in northern Bali. From an early age, I was captivated by the colorful costumes and accessories used in the ceremonies, particularly the one called the *monkey* dance."

Mara nodded. "Ah, the Kecak Fire Dance."

Wayan was surprised for a moment but quickly realized of course she'd know since they shared the same culture. He continued, "My grandmother was an excellent weaver and she could reproduce many of my early ideas, but I learned to sew from my mother. The other dancers began coming to me for their costumes. I was living a peaceful life with my family enjoying every minute of it until tragedy struck. A devastating earthquake destroyed our home, forcing us to leave everything behind and start a new life elsewhere. I moved with my family to the island of Capri. There were no longer the bright colors and spiritual dances of my homeland. There was a different beauty, though, living by the sea. It was during that time that I expanded my skills."

Antonella had been listening intently. She added, "It was my good fortune that Wayan caught the eye of a recruiter trying to fill a position of costume designer here in the workshops of La Scala. What about you, Mara? How did you get to Milan?"

The first part was easy to convey. "I was working as a batik designer in Ubud and was selected to study under Kenneth Patrick in Australia. He introduced me to silk painting which grew into a passion. He also arranged for me to be part of a designer showcase in Sydney where I worked with a fashion designer to create wearable art. It turned out to be mildly successful, resulting in a few handfuls of orders."

The next part made Mara slightly uncomfortable, but with a sideways glance at Wayan, she continued. "Not long after that, I joined two artists who I met in Australia to do the interior design of an Arab sheik's mega-yacht, which led to the design of his new home in Marbella, Spain. As a result, he and his son offered to finance my studio in Milan. They are very well connected and able to introduce me to the best resources." Mara could see the question in Wayan's eyes, but Lucca interrupted.

"It was at one of the society parties reserved for the most elite that I met Mara, escorted by the sheik's son, Zayn Al Farooq. They were quite the striking pair and I was curious to learn more about her fabrics. Mara has an uncanny gift to be able to work with a designer customizing fabrics that brings his or her creations to life." Mara blushed at Lucca's praise.

"How intriguing," Antonella pondered out loud. As if she suddenly had an idea, she added, "I have a proposition for you two. Tonight was the last performance of this tour. I plan to leave tomorrow for my home in Lake Como where I will spend the next three months preparing for the winter tour. Wayan is planning to come work with me on the costumes to be created for that tour. Lucca, would it be possible for you to bring the line you just featured during Fashion Week? If the ensemble Mara is wearing is any indication of your work, I think I might be interested in acquiring the collection for my personal use when I am not on stage. And Mara, would you consider working on a few fabric ideas with Wayan? With your similar background, I would be curious to see the results."

Lucca was noticeably thrilled and immediately agreed. Mara tried to take it all in. *Lake Como, working with Wayan, designing for Antonella Rossi!* She could hardly believe it. "Absolutely, let us know the details and we will be there." A shy look toward Wayan found him gazing at her, a smile hovering around his lips. During the conversation, Mara felt a kindred spirit in him, someone who shared her love for art and beauty in all its forms. And as the evening unfolded, Mara couldn't shake off the feeling that this chance encounter was just the beginning of something extraordinary.

CHAPTER 14

Both Mara's and Lucca's excitement confirmed the enormity of the offer. They conferred most of Sunday morning by phone about how to properly transport the entire line, how to display it without the models, and what it would mean for Mara to work with Wayan. Lucca brought it up first. "Mara, your fabrics being used on an Antonella Rossi costume could be a major breakthrough for your business. And if she decides to buy the collection, I have to wonder whether she will try to get an exclusive. That would be impossible since we already have so many orders in the house as a result of Fashion Week."

"Perhaps if she likes the collection, she will have you produce a new line specifically for her. Lucca, have you ever been to Lake Como? I have heard it is quite beautiful. I wonder when we'll hear the details?" They hung up, agreeing to let each other know the moment they heard from Antonella.

When the phone rang again, Mara answered assuming it was Lucca with another thought. However, when she heard Zayn's voice, it shook her back to the present and she realized she'd not even thought of him since meeting Wayan. "Mara, how was the opera? I am so sorry I missed it. I have a flight booked and should arrive there mid-afternoon."

It occurred to Mara that if Zayn had been at the gala with her instead of Lucca, none of this might have happened. She tried to re-focus on the conversation she needed to have with Zayn, but she was still too excited to contain it. "Antonella's performance was enchanting and captured my heart. Lucca even designed an outfit for me. At the gala, we met her along with her costume designer. Can you believe it? He is also from Bali! Antonella had heard about Lucca's successful show and wants to see the line in person."

"How fantastic! Will he do a fashion show for her at his studio?"

"Well, no. She wants both Lucca and me to come to her home to show the line. She also mentioned the possibility of my creating some fabrics for her designer to use on the costumes for her next tour."

"It sounds like a productive encounter! When do you meet with her?"

Mara wasn't sure how Zayn would react so she proceeded cautiously. "We don't have the details yet, but her home is in Lake Como. She would like us to stay for a few days and possibly collaborate with her costume designer. We would take the collection with us."

Zayn became keenly aware that Mara had managed the high-society event just fine without him. Her win was good for the company, but he couldn't help admitting to himself that it sparked jealousy as well. He swallowed his initial reaction refusing to discuss it by phone. Instead, he quickly made an excuse to catch his flight. He told her not to bother picking him up and that he would take a taxi to the hotel. Before saying goodbye, they made arrangements to meet at a restaurant near his hotel at seven. Mara was surprised by the sudden chill in his voice, but thought he was simply distracted by the need to catch his plane.

* * *

When Mara arrived at the restaurant, Zayn was waiting for her outside. He was dressed to perfection with an impeccable sense of style, and Mara noted the air of sophistication that emanated from him. She took his hand as he reached for hers and followed him inside.

Once they were comfortably seated, Zayn ordered a bottle of sparkling wine from the province of Brescia in Lombardy. After the wine was poured, Mara began. "I heard from Wayan, the costume designer for Antonella that I was telling you about. They would like us to take the train to the main railway station of Como San Giovanni this Thursday and stay the weekend. This could be extremely exciting for the business!" Mara had been looking for a way to get on an equal footing with Zayn and was hoping this might be a start to more independence. However, she noticed an unfamiliar twitch on the side of Zayn's mouth that made her question her decision. *Why did she have to be so unsure around him?*

With a serious look on his face, Zayn asked, "Mara, there has been something I've been meaning to ask you. We have known each other for over two years. I know we have spent a great deal of time together, but I wonder whether we truly know each other. I think we have done well blending our professional and personal lives. Have you ever wondered whether our relationship could evolve into something more profound?"

Mara couldn't believe he had just led her into the conversation she had been wanting to have with him. "I have to admit, I have questioned a future together but there seems to be some rather large obstacles in the way. What about you? Have you thought about it?"

That made Zayn smile. "All I've done is think about it. Your gentle spirit and radiant beauty, both inside and out, captured my attention right from the moment we met. And your commitment to your talent brings me to my knees that I have not been able to make that kind of commitment to anything substantial."

"Oh Zayn, don't you understand I feel the same way? Around you and your family, I feel a gnawing sense of inadequacy that I will never stand a chance to be on equal footing with you. I am just a girl with humble roots from a family of Balinese farmers."

Zayn nodded in somber understanding that this is what they needed...to lay bare their uncertainties. "When I was home in Fujairah, I sat across from one of the largest mosques realizing it was the only one that even allowed non-Muslims inside, and even then not for worship. My family is very traditional in its Muslim beliefs and I take pride in my faith. I am not allowed to marry outside my religion. Where could this possibly leave us?" Zayn looked tenderly at Mara with a vulnerability in his eyes she had never seen.

Mara was surprised but intrigued. *Could it be that the man who had believed in her from the start was also the one who could fulfill her deepest desires despite this obstacle?* Doubt creeping in, Mara knew she needed to be honest. "In Indonesia, the primary religion is Muslim. However, Bali stands apart with its practice of Hinduism. But the foundation of our belief is not exactly the same as the typical Hinduism, so our religious beliefs are as unique as we are. I don't believe I would ever be comfortable converting to a different faith. It is an essential part of who I am. Even with these looming societal and religious obstacles..." Mara paused know this would not be what Zayn would want to hear. Gathering her courage, she went on, "...there is still the business aspect of our relationship. As grateful as I am, I constantly feel indebted to you and Bajir for your financing as well as the connections you have provided. This opportunity with Antonella would never have occurred without your arranging for the opera tickets and invitation to the gala." Mara wasn't sure how Zayn would react but she knew it had to be said. "Zayn, when you add it all together, the feelings we have might not be enough to bridge the gap between our worlds."

They both sat there, finishing their wine and reflecting on the practicalities of their lives and any potential of a life together. *Was it even possible to navigate the barriers that lay before them?*

Zayn finally spoke. "This is a start. At least we are communicating and recognize the challenges. For now, let's concentrate on ensuring you feel respected and valued beyond the materialistic world we are living in. I will continue to be your escort in public, but outside of our business relationship I will not presume to be any more than that. And, Mara, if we are being honest, I like the lavish lifestyle." Although it hurt to admit it, there were things they might not be able to overcome. He would never want to hurt the woman he had grown to feel deeply about.

Mara studied Zayn sadly. "So nothing changes. Things will continue as they have in a web of pretense?"

Zayn dipped his head, unable to meet her eyes. "Know that I will always care about you, Mara, but until we can find a way around these hurdles, I think this is best."

Mara's eyes glistened as she realized the impact of his words. He'd put the wall back up. There would no longer be a chance of a personal relationship with Zayn. The reality was like a punch to her gut, but somewhere in her heart a voice was telling her *that one door has to close before another one opens.*

CHAPTER 15

Mara took a day to digest what had happened and that her relationship with Zayn would be a platonic one for the foreseeable future. She then called Annie to tell her what happened and that Zayn would not be joining them in Bali. Annie could hear the quiver in Mara's voice and tried to comfort her. "Mara, I understand that you are disappointed with how things worked out. But, hey, you have always told me there are meaningful joys out there waiting. You just have to allow them into your life."

In barely a whisper, Mara answered, "I know. I heard a voice telling me this was right. I need to let the idea of a romantic relationship with Zayn go and not be defined by the past. My focus is forward to the possibilities ahead."

Annie repeated as if it was a chant, "To the possibilities ahead." After a pause, she added, "My guess is that if Zayn is not going to Bali, Elena and El Amir won't be either. Are you okay with Sarah and Hans, and Ramone and me coming? Is it too much to bring the twins?"

Mara loved the idea. It would be her two closest friends and their families. "Yes, of course bring the twins. I actually am really happy to narrow it down to just us. And I think I might have found the perfect retreat for us. I will check the availability. How does the end of the month sound? I'm traveling on business this weekend. Before I go, though, I will check the timing with Sarah. We can discuss the plans when I get back." Mara hadn't wanted to brag to Annie, but suddenly her excitement caused her to blurt it out. "Actually, this could be one of those huge opportunities. I am going with Lucca to Lake Como to work with the opera singer, Antonella Rossi!"

"What? She is a favorite of mine! Her voice reminds me of when I am sailing, the sail catches the wind, and nature takes over. When Antonella sings, she tells stories with her music that take over and tune out all else. I can't wait to hear all the details!" Annie was thrilled for Mara and the possibilities that were already happening for her friend.

* * *

Mara and Lucca secured the large trunk carrying the selection of fashions inside the baggage cargo area and eagerly boarded the train to Lake Como, buzzing with excitement and anticipation for the upcoming weekend. As the train sped through the picturesque Italian countryside toward the foothills of the Alps and the town of Varenna where they would meet Wayan, they discussed their upcoming presentation in addition to sharing ideas for future projects. Wayan would then take them the rest of the way to Antonella's estate in Menaggio, over on the western shore of Lake Como. Mara had to admit she was curious about seeing Wayan again.

Lucca was dazzled by the opportunity before them. "Mara, this is a dream come true to present this collection to Antonella in such a distinguished setting. If she responds well, this could have a far-reaching impact toward our gaining international acclaim and recognition."

Mara knew Lucca was the one bearing the bulk of the weight for Antonella's approval. "She will see the visionary you are.

Lucca, your designs are fearless and you aren't afraid to redefine the rules of fashion. I have a feeling Antonella will embrace dressing in a unique way that sets her apart from the norm."

"My only regret is not having a model available. Even if they are a different size, it is much easier to visualize when actually worn. Simply hanging from a wire hanger will not do the styles justice. Mara, you are close to model size. Would you consider trying them on for her?"

"Oh no, Lucca, I am not nearly tall or thin enough to pull off the look you want. Perhaps Wayan can help us. I am curious about both of them. Wayan was never far from Antonella's side. Do you think they are together? He seems much younger than her, don't you agree?"

"Well, you and I are together yet not a couple. But, Mara, I feel good about our collaboration and see a bright future ahead for us." Looking out the window, he continued, "We're pulling into the station!" They both reached up for a 'high-five' to seal their silent pact that this was an important turning point for both of their futures.

Mara found Wayan in the crowd and their eyes met. His expressive blue eyes stood out from his caramel-color skin and lit up when he smiled, causing that familiar flutter. Wayan greeted them warmly and helped load the trunk and their personal bags into the van. As Mara handed her bag off to Wayan, their hands brushed against each other, and he winked. "The drive to Menaggio will take close to an hour...I didn't want to take a chance with the public ferry. I hope that is alright with you. If you'd like, we could stop for lunch at a charming little restaurant along the way."

He was the perfect host, pointing out the remains of sixteenth century castles, quaint fishing villages, and lavish waterfront homes of celebrities. The massive lake with its crystal-clear water was breathtaking, reflecting the surrounding mountains and little towns stretching from the water up into the hills.

For lunch, they stopped at a terraced café surrounded by stone walls and crimson bougainvillea featuring floor-to-ceiling glass walls where they could enjoy the view of the lake. The salad bar was like nothing Mara had seen before and she created a delightful mix of smoked salmon with kiwi, cherry tomatoes, petite shrimp, papaya, and avocado. "This salad is incredible. Everything tastes so fresh!"

Wayan smiled, pleased with her reaction. "If you like this, wait until you experience the food at Antonella's. Her chef is worthy of a Michelin star!"

Lucca asked, "Wayan, tell us about Antonella. What should we expect when she is away from the theater?"

Warming to his topic, Wayan answered, "Antonella is a masterful artist as you know, but she has many layers. Her performance in Milan concluded a triumphant tour that featured her formidable vocal range and stage presence. This is a time for her to get some much needed rest. Beyond her musical talents, she is a private person. This is her sanctuary where she can enjoy quiet solitude amidst the natural beauty and tranquility of the Italian countryside, finding solace and inspiration to recharge her creative energies. Her villa is quite welcoming, overlooking the lake from the hillside. She must have been very impressed with you. It is not often that she invites someone into her inner sanctum." Wayan looked at Mara and Lucca pointedly.

Mara absorbed the magnitude of that statement and could tell Wayan was protective of Antonella, which made her even more curious about this enigmatic woman. She could imagine how Antonella would feel after such a demanding schedule. Mara often felt the same after Fashion Week. "I assure you. We want to do everything in our power to give her what she hopes for. It is an honor to have been invited. She mentioned my working with you on some collaborations. Do you actually work when you are here visiting or would we work together back in Milan?"

"I think you and Lucca should focus on the collection first. Antonella will let us know how she would like to proceed further."

Mara studied Wayan, realizing that her role in this meeting might still be in question. A slight case of nerves settled in to meet this formidable woman who cherished her privacy yet had the power to make a significant impact on Mara's future.

CHAPTER 16

The approach to Menaggio was like entering a fairytale village. The elegant lakeside promenade with the ornate wrought iron railing was complemented by blooming flower beds and a perfectly manicured lawn as it meandered along the lakefront opposite the colorful row of homes. Wayan continued talking about the town. "Menaggio with its small population of only three thousand, provides a much quieter and laid-back atmosphere than some of the bigger towns like Como and Bellagio. It is easy to understand what drew Antonella to this place. Wait until you see the inside of her home. The views from its location on the sunny hillside looking out toward the Grigne mountains are nothing short of breathtaking and the large picture windows and massive adjoining terrace take advantage of that scenery!"

Wayan turned the van up the hill to the split-level retreat built into the hillside. Oozing style with its deep coral stucco exterior covered with climbing trellises in full bloom, Mara couldn't help but notice the air of functionality that surrounded the property. The well-manicured gardens and imposing statues suggested a meticulous attention to detail, while the subtle hints of privacy made it clear that this was a secluded haven for its owner. Despite its luxurious surroundings, there was a distinct lack of ostentation that intrigued Mara even further.

Their activity unloading the bags prompted the front door to open and a barefoot young woman with no makeup, long, wavy black hair pulled back in a ponytail and cropped jeans came out to greet them. "*Ciao*, Lucca and Mara! Welcome to my special oasis." Both Mara and Lucca stood stunned staring at this wisp of a girl who barely looked thirty. *Surely this was not Antonella!*

Wayan laughed heartily. "Let me introduce you to the real Antonella Rossi."

Observing closer, Mara could see the striking features, delicate yet commanding presence, and soulful gaze that seemed to hold a thousand stories. She stepped toward Antonella to shake her hand. "You're quite beautiful, Antonella. I would have never known you were so young."

Seeing the surprise by her appearance on Mara and Lucca's faces, Antonella exclaimed theatrically, "It is all a grand illusion, is it not? Everyone is stunned when they see me out of costume...I just give the audience what they expect. We can discuss that later. For now, welcome. I have been looking forward to your visit!" Antonella took both of Mara's hands in hers with a most genuine smile.

As Mara settled into a plush armchair, she couldn't help but wonder about the intriguing woman who called this place home. She saw the subtle glance Antonella gave Wayan and his slight nod of the head in return. Intrigued, Mara wondered what secrets lay hidden behind the carefully curated façade of elegance and charm.

* * *

Mara's mind was a jumble of thoughts as she retired to her room to retrieve the fabric steamer. It would be her job to ensure all the costumes were in impeccable shape and without wrinkles

83

to show Antonella. She couldn't stop thinking of the opera star's term for her stage personality as a grand illusion. Mara reflected on her own situation. *Wasn't she doing the same thing when she attended all the high society events on the arm of Zayn? In the end, her image was a pretense as well, wasn't it?*

Once the clothes were hung on the portable racks used on location, Mara left her room to join Antonella, Lucca, and Wayan on the terrace. They were discussing Lucca's collection. Lucca looked up at Mara, then looked at Antonella. "Antonella, will you stand next to Mara? I think you are almost the same size." He whipped a measuring tape out of his pocket to check them both. Lucca announced with authority that left no room for discussion, "Close enough. Mara, you will be my model." Then, as an after-thought, to Antonella he asked, "Shall I presume you are looking at my line for your own personal use? If that is the case, Mara will reflect the correct fit. However, if it is for the stage and the fit would be different..." His voice trailed off.

Antonella's delicate giggle sounded like the tinkle of wind chimes in the breeze. Mara could hardly fathom the difference between that delicate sound and the powerful voice she had heard on stage. Antonella answered Lucca, "They would be for my own use, unless I see something Wayan and I think we should adapt into a costume."

Wayan left the terrace for a few minutes and returned with what looked like a form or corset. Antonella took it and wrapped it around her torso. The transformation was impressive. Her breasts were pushed upward creating a voluminous cleavage, and her rib cage down to her hips was given an extra layer of padding. "The idea was all Wayan's. Directors were finding it hard to connect the way I looked with how I sounded. He felt like the size of my frame was inconsistent with the volume of my voice. I honestly think that the roles I play in each performance are enhanced by the image I present."

Taking off the corset, she handed it to Mara. "I have several hours of rehearsal tomorrow morning. Perhaps you can assist Wayan with his fittings." When she noticed the disappointed look on Mara's face, she added, "Mara, I do hope you will immerse yourself in the entire creative process. Meticulous attention and a keen eye for aesthetics are necessary if we are to create exceptional costumes for the upcoming opera season. I am convinced that the background you share with Wayan can add a unique depth through the fabrics designed and included in each silhouette."

Afraid she had somehow offended Antonella, Mara quickly said she was eager to participate in every part of the process. Focused on the opera star, she missed the look of approval that crossed Wayan's face.

Rosa, Antonella's housekeeper and cook, came to announce dinner was served. Antonella graciously smiled at Rosa and led her guests to the dining room. Once they were seated and they each had a glass of prosecco, Antonella stood up to propose a toast. "Lucca and Mara, I have eagerly awaited your arrival, and I can feel the creative energy in this room. We share a passion for artistry and heritage and my desire is to infuse a new element into both my personal and professional wardrobes. And Wayan, you continue ensuring each season outshines the last. I would like to stay open to all possibilities. Let's consider this weekend an opportunity to weave a tapestry of creativity and inspiration between us that will rock the opera world."

Rosa's home-cooked dinner of bruschetta and chicken parmesan was exceptional, evoking praise from everyone at the table. Antonella said, "On the road, I have so many restaurant meals that when I am back home, I love for Rosa to spoil me with her own cooking."

Mara responded, "I can't imagine what it must be like traveling from city to city with such a grueling schedule. Do you take friends with you? It must get lonely."

Antonella looked fondly at Wayan and put her hand over his on the table, then answered, "I have Wayan with me." Wayan smiled and winked at Antonella. Mara and Lucca chanced a quick glance at each other with an understanding that they got the answer to their question.

Then Lucca, always so comfortable around people, launched into a discussion asking about the schedule for the weekend and access to the studio Wayan used when in residence. On the other hand, Mara sat back trying to understand how she fit into the process as an artist. *She was to help Wayan with costume fittings, steam Lucca's designs, model the clothes, create fabrics... based on what?* Lost in thought, it was Wayan clearing his throat that brought her back to the conversation.

"After dinner, Antonella plans to retire early to rest before her rehearsal tomorrow morning. Why don't the three of us go out to the terrace for an espresso? The night lights over the lake are quite impressive and we have a great deal to accomplish. Does that sound good to you both?" It was as if Wayan had read Mara's mind and was providing the space where they could talk freely about why she was there in a way that Antonella had not been able to explain.

Out on the terrace, the conversation centered around the schedule for the weekend but Mara couldn't help but sense an unspoken undercurrent with Wayan. Upon meeting him, she had felt an instant connection with him, probably a mix of shared love for their Balinese heritage and mutual respect for each other's craft.

However, as the evening had progressed, seeing the closeness between Wayan and Antonella, Mara began to doubt her initial feelings, curious about what exactly Wayan's role was with the diva.

CHAPTER 17

Mara awoke the following morning, thoughts filled with Antonella and fully aware that only a select few knew the truth behind Antonella's carefully crafted façade. She was determined to hold that trust sacred. The relationship between Wayan and Antonella was none of her business. She needed to stay focused on what was important...the enormous business opportunity for Lucca and herself.

However, that did not keep Mara from being curious. At the gala, she and Lucca met the Italian opera diva. What a master of illusion that with the help of heavy stage makeup, padding, and elaborate costumes, Antonella could easily slip into the larger-than-life persona of a glamorous star of the stage.

Mara grabbed a few bites from the buffet of breakfast items Rosa had laid out. Antonella was already rehearsing while Wayan and Lucca were in the studio discussing the designs. Mara went to retrieve the two racks of samples and the steamer, then maneuvered them down the long hallway to the studio.

Wayan and Lucca were at the brightly-lit work table looking at preliminary sketches Wayan had drawn. When Mara entered, Lucca got up to help her with the racks. "Wayan has been telling me a little more about Antonella's tastes, and after looking at his sketches, I have a few adaptations I'd like to make that might work better for her. Mara, once the steaming is done, let's do a preliminary fitting." As Mara steamed, Wayan conferred with Lucca as he studied each style, noticeably impressed with Lucca's craftsmanship and Mara's intricate fabric designs.

"Lucca, you are nothing short of a visionary! Antonella will love the sharply angled cuts and unexpected fabric combinations. It is like each garment is a cross between art and fashion. And Mara, Lucca is correct. Your fabrics add a unique layer of dimension to the collection, with textures and finishes that captivate the senses. Now if you can focus on the cutting edge of each piece in a way that allows her to stand out fashionably but is unrecognizable as the diva that she is on stage, I think you will find her highly responsive."

Tossing aside her good intentions, Mara commented, "Wayan, you obviously know Antonella well enough to know her likes and dislikes. You seem to have a bond that goes deeper than mere costume collaboration." Wayan's momentary look of concern spoke volumes causing Mara a pang of worry that she might have overstepped. *Had she veered too close to a sensitive subject?*

"What I mean to say is that you are there to see her transform before your eyes for each performance." As she tried to backtrack, Mara felt herself stumbling over her words. Wayan's silence only added to her unease, his gaze inscrutable as he seemed to assess her in a new light.

"More than you know," was Wayan's barely audible response. He moved his attention to Lucca. "Lucca, I admit I am excited to see these fashions come to life. Let's get started!"

Each outfit had been fitted to a professional model, but Lucca was used to making adjustments on the spot. Wayan pulled out his sewing machine and they chatted endlessly about every style to make it perfect for Antonella, all the while tugging and pinching each garment Mara tried on, turning her this way and that. The moment that would remain in Mara's memory was when both men were staring at the dress she wore. It was daringly low-cut and Mara was attempting to be oblivious to her discomfort when she noticed Wayan was no longer looking at the dress, but rather directly at her. It suddenly seemed as if he was willing her to look back at him.

Lucca, ignorant of the exchange, said, "I think I can do better with the sleeves to enhance the bodice."

He was about to walk over to Mara when Wayan said, "I've got this." He moved behind Mara close enough that she could feel his warm breath on her neck. Slowly, Wayan reached for the edge of the fabric to tuck it under while his fingers lingered on her shoulder as if in a caress. It was pure reflex for Mara to turn her head toward his hand. They both felt the current that surged between them. Under his breath, he mumbled, "You should have this one." And then it was over.

When they moved on to the next outfit, Wayan's casual manner started to make Mara question whether she had imagined the moment. Even though she attempted to remain nonchalant, her eyes continued to glance at Wayan for some recognition of what happened between them. She saw none. However, the searing feeling still lingered where he'd touched her shoulder and assured her that her mind was not playing tricks on her.

As the preparations for the fashion presentation progressed, even Lucca started to notice that Wayan was avoiding looking at Mara. They needed these fashions to be perfect. *What was going on beneath the surface?*

It was time to bring Wayan's focus back to the task at hand. "Wayan, these last few samples might be perfect for Antonella. Once I get your final feedback, it will take me about three to four hours to make the adaptations. Help me with these last few designs, then you and Mara can discuss her innovative fabrics and how they might fit into your costumes. You have seen what her fabrics have added to my designs. She has a unique talent for translating a designer's vision to fabric."

Wayan answered, "Yes, of course. I am eager to explore Mara's ability to translate my visions."

There was something in the way he phrased that statement. *Was it a challenge of some kind?*

Mara dressed after the final design was discussed and helped Lucca take the two racks of clothes ready for alterations to the far corner where the sewing machine was ready. She then returned to Wayan ready to dismiss any personal thoughts of him and get down to business. The last thing she needed was another relationship like the one she had with Zayn. This time she'd keep things strictly professional.

To Wayan, she asked, "Do you just have sketches for the new costumes at this point or are you already beginning to build prototypes?"

"I thought I would show you a few of Antonella's favorites from this past season so you would understand her tastes. In each new opera, a story unfolds. Antonella wants each costume to fully engage her stage presence in that scene. That way the illusion is perfected and the audience overwhelmed."

Mara stepped over to the large closet and studied the costumes one by one, occasionally pulling one out to look closer. Finally, she said, "These are stunning and the designs are a blend between reality and fantasy. But they are so heavy and Antonella is petite. How in the world does she handle such weight and use her voice in such a magnificent way all at once?" Picking up on a term she had heard several times during this collaboration, she asked, "What if it were possible to give the *illusion* of a heavy fabric, but in actuality it was lightweight." She pointed to a heavy brocade bodice. "I believe I could translate this exact look into a lightweight silk pattern that would take at least three pounds off this design. I would be willing to try it back at my studio if you like the idea."

"Intriguing. I like it and can imagine Antonella would be pleased not to have to carry around all that weight, particularly under the heat of the stage lights."

That gave her another thought, "True, I hadn't thought about the stage lights. I can use that in detecting how the lights will reflect from the fabrics."

Mara's imaginative ideas had met the earlier challenge and upped it, passing a test of some sort so that Wayan began to pool their ideas in earnest. "For the next tour, Antonella will be playing the Ethiopian princess in *Aïda*. There will be one primary costume and six secondary ones. It will mean a great deal of work in less than three months until they have to be ready."

Mara didn't miss the irony of the story of forbidden love between an Egyptian commander and an Ethiopian princess. "I know the story well. My relationship with the son of an Arab sheik just ended because of the differences in our cultures and religions. I would really enjoy working with you on it."

Wayan digested the news that Mara was just out of a relationship. "Normally Antonella has my exclusive attention. She chooses carefully who she allows so close to her inner circle."

Mara held out her hand to shake Wayan's to seal the agreement. He took her hand but instead of shaking it, he began to pull her toward him never lifting his gaze from hers. Once her face was mere inches from his, his eyes drifted toward the lips that beckoned him. Just as they were about to kiss, Antonella walked in and they quickly pulled apart. Her eyes, blazing with daggers, looked at Wayan and she said sharply, "I came to confirm the time of Lucca's presentation." Then shifting to Mara dripping with honey sweetness, she asked, "Will you model for me during the presentation, Mara? I would love to see the individual pieces on someone before I make my decisions."

Lucca overheard Antonella and came over with needle and thread in hand. "We should be ready within the hour and Mara would be happy to model, right, Mara?"

"Of course." With her head held high and the briefest of glances toward Wayan, Mara went with Lucca to ensure everything would be ready.

What did not go unnoticed by Mara was the stern command to Wayan by Antonella. "Come with me now."

CHAPTER 18

Lucca and Mara stared at each other in confusion. He finally asked, "What is going on here behind the scenes? Is he with Antonella and thinking of cheating on her with you? Mara, you need to avoid anything that would cause a confrontation with Antonella at all costs."

Mara was flustered. "We have seen them together. They don't act like a loving couple. It just seems like she wants to keep him close."

Lucca chastised her. "It is really none of our concern, Mara. Let's get this presentation completed, make lots of money, and get out of here."

"I just offered to work back at my studio with Wayan on some fabric ideas. This is really important. There is nothing going on with Wayan and I intend to keep it that way."

By the time they wheeled the racks into the parlor for the presentation, Antonella greeted them with warm, welcoming smiles. Wayan, ever present, went over to the tea cart and poured a sherry for Antonella and himself, then sat down to watch.

Lucca presided, and with each style he presented, he guided Mara to turn or walk to feature the intricate details of the garments, emphasizing the craftsmanship of each piece. He was quick to point out Mara's fabrics in his descriptions, bringing them to life with his words painting vivid images of silk flowing like water, lace as delicate as the fibers of a lotus stem, and sequins sparkling like stars in the night sky.

Under the watchful eyes of Antonella and Wayan, Mara had a strange sense of déjà vu. It was as if she had been in this situation before, with someone scrutinizing her every move. Memories of Zayn's assessment of what she wore, how her hair was styled, and even what kind of car she drove had made her feel like a specimen on display. The familiar discomfort gnawed at her, but she pushed it aside to focus on the task at hand. Since she wasn't required to speak, Mara allowed her mind to wander, escaping into her own thoughts to block out the lingering unease. It was Lucca's words describing her fabrics that soothed her, building a sense of empowerment as she confidently wore each outfit.

She had to admit there was a chemistry with Wayan. But what about Zayn? She was still sorting things out with him, *or was she?* Their earlier conversation had made it clear that a romantic future together was not feasible. *Was she ready to jump back into another relationship, particularly if it might affect her business?*

She had reached the age of twenty-nine without ever having an intimate experience. There had only been two boyfriends, Jonathan from Australia and Zayn, but neither had gone beyond kissing. Wasn't it time for her to explore the intimacies enjoyed between a woman and a man? She couldn't help smiling at the idea, then quickly amended *in Lucca's case a man with a man.* The smile did not linger since she quickly realized both Zayn and Wayan were off limits for such fantasies.

Mara finally got to the dress with the off-the-shoulder tailoring and noticed when Wayan adjusted in his chair but kept a poker face. What she missed was Antonella's lingering gaze.

Antonella nodded, "I must have this one as well. The lines are perfection. By the way, Mara, it looks lovely on you. Perhaps you might get it in another color."

Once the presentation was complete and Mara was back in her own clothes, she and Lucca pulled out the nine styles Antonella had selected, seemingly more than pleased. She then turned to Wayan. "Please get with Lucca to produce an invoice and double the price for each. They have come all this way and customized each one. It is the least I can do. To celebrate, I have secured a boat to take us on a little sightseeing tour of the lake so you have at least a taste of this special area so dear to me."

* * *

By four o'clock, Mara and Lucca were packed and ready to join Antonella and Wayan for the sightseeing tour. They walked along the charming lakefront promenade to the city marina where a tour boat was loading. Mara had expected a private boat for such a renowned star and was shocked to see her board and blend in with the rest of the tourists. Antonella whispered to Mara, "This is the way I like it. I can go on with my life with no one the wiser."

Mara was astounded to see a man accidentally bump into her as he passed and he hardly gave her a second glance as he mumbled, *"Mi scusi."* They found space on a bench toward the back of the boat while Antonella proceeded to point out her favorite highlights. In between commentary, Lucca was excitedly telling Antonella his ideas for his next line of fashions for the fall. That left Wayan and Mara in awkward silence until Wayan suggested they go up to the bow to discuss their meeting back in Milan.

Once they were far away enough not to be heard, Wayan looked at Mara and said, "I want to apologize for earlier. It was foolish of me, and I had no right to make an advance toward you."

Curious, particularly realizing the current between them was just as strong as ever, Mara asked, "Are you in love with Antonella? Is that it?"

Noticeably tense, Wayan answered, "It's complicated. I had no right to put you in the middle of something. Let's get back to our shared love of artistry that tells a story. Our heritage is full of symbolism and I would like to explore that further with the costumes for the upcoming *Aïda*. I plan to be back in Milan working at my studio at La Scala by mid-week. Let me know when you can meet to strategize about the fabrics we discussed."

Mara, more confused than ever, said, "I will have to do it soon because I plan to take a trip back to Bali in the next couple of weeks. I need to see my family and recharge. Unlike Antonella, I am not good with pretense." Although it was unintentional, the last comment came out like a challenge.

She could see Wayan bristle, but all he said was, "I'm not particularly fond of it myself."

Something pushed Mara to want to know more about this mysterious man. "Have you and your family been back to Bali since you left after the earthquake? I remember hearing about how tragic it was. I had just moved to Ubud with my cousins. There were many people from Buleleng who took refuge there."

"Unfortunately, no. After I moved to Milan, I seemed to always be too busy trying to build my business. And, after meeting Antonella, that has proven to be a full-time responsibility."

Mara couldn't help the frustration that crept into her voice. "Interesting choice of words. We'd better get back to Lucca and Antonella."

Antonella saw them and waved, pointing at the gangplank to get off at the next stop. When she reached them, she suggested, "This is Bellagio, one of my favorite towns on the lake. Let's get off here. I will take you to a restaurant on the hill that has magnificent views of the Alpine mountains and breathtaking villas with elaborate gardens and fountains. There will be another boat to take us back in two hours. Then you will see the moonlight reflecting on the water."

Wayan helped both Antonella and Mara down the gangplank, then Antonella possessively took his arm to walk up to the restaurant. Lucca noticed and threw his arm around Mara's shoulder, but when he felt her shiver, he gallantly removed his jacket and put it around her for warmth. Mara smiled in gratitude. She and Lucca had developed a close friendship and she admired his seemingly effortless ability to exaggerate his makeup and create an image his clients adored. Mara thought about Zayn and his family's grand lifestyle. *Was anyone authentic? She wasn't sure anymore, but what she did know was that her friends, Annie and Sarah, were real, and she couldn't wait to introduce them to her homeland!*

CHAPTER 19

Monday morning arrived and Mara was back in her studio ready to work. There was a message from Zayn to call him with an update about the weekend and a reminder that they had a black-tie fundraiser Friday night. He assured her he would be there Friday morning in time for their monthly meeting with the accountant to ensure there were sufficient funds available for Mara to continue to grow her business.

Even with the new understanding of the relationship with Zayn, it appeared that their social life would continue as before. Between that and the strange weekend encounter with Antonella and Wayan, Mara shook her head in confusion. Then, as if in perfect relief to the direction her thoughts were going, Rochelle walked in wearing red polka-dot sneakers, an arm full of bracelets and heart-shaped purple glasses. "Glad to have you back, Mara! I have sorted your schedule to try to fit everything in prior to your trip home to Bali. Wayan called and will be back in his studio Wednesday. I have scheduled two hours for you with him Wednesday afternoon. Is that enough time?"

Mara couldn't help but give her a hug. She adored how her crazy exterior was a total contrast to her efficiency. "I'm glad to be back too. And yes, two hours Wednesday afternoon with Wayan is fine. What is on the agenda for today?"

"You have an initial developmental meeting with Sophia to discuss her thoughts on her new line. I also have on my calendar to remind you to choose a place for your group to stay at while in Bali." Rochelle had her pen in hand.

"I would like three days to go home to my parents' farm and see my cousins in Ubud. Annie and Ramone and the twins, as well as Sarah and Hans, can meet me in Ubud. After two days of touring, there is a wellness retreat that I would like to book that is close to Ubud called *Mundur Kesehatan*. Three days there should be sufficient. Eight days is really more than I can afford to take off, but I need at least that so I will do whatever it takes to work extra hours to make the time there work. Rochelle, I need you to keep me efficient!"

"I'm on it! Go meet with Sophia. I will line up tomorrow's schedule. You will get your well-deserved time in Bali."

* * *

Later that evening, Mara had a chance to call both Annie and Sarah, after speaking with her cousin, Kadek, in Ubud. "Annie, I am so thrilled you are bringing the twins with you and Ramone. Remember Kadek? She is my cousin whose wedding you attended. She can't wait to see you again and has offered, along with my aunt, to watch Salvi and Cece. They are making all sorts of plans from going to the monkey dance, to learning batik, to helping in the flower gardens." At the mention of the monkey dance, Mara's mind flashed briefly on Wayan.

Annie sounded excited. "What an amazing first trip for them! I have to admit they have been on the *Porto Banus* a few times and Captain Luis might have kindled their excitement about a grand adventure! Don Marco has already begun telling them stories of Indonesia and Bali's history."

"Sarah and Hans said they would come to Milan and fly with me since they are so close in Venice. We will meet you in Ubud. There is a spiritual retreat just outside the city that focuses on wellness and recharging. They even have a program for children so I thought we might go there for a couple of nights."

Mara was about to hang up when Annie said, "You haven't said a word about Zayn. Did you two have your talk?"

So much had happened since then, Mara almost forgot she'd promised to let Annie know. "We did. It's strange. Nothing much has changed. We still plan to go to society events to keep me in the right circles, but the difference is that we no longer have to pretend to ourselves that we have a future together. He won't be coming to Bali. Neither will Elena or El Amir." After a moment, Mara added, "Annie, I did meet someone at the opera and then again on business in Lake Como. His name is Wayan, and he was originally from a northern part of Bali. He is a costume designer working here in Milan. It seemed like there was an attraction, but I think he is involved with an opera singer."

Annie was quiet for just a beat and then wisely said, "Bali will be amazing with just us. I have to assume the opera singer you are referring to is Antonella Rossi. Don't chase the dream, Mara. Let it come to you. He is working right there in Milan. If it is meant to be, it will unfold in its own time. Just be open to whatever comes and feels right."

Mara then made the call to Sarah and let her know the details and that Zayn, Elena and El Amir would not be coming. "I am really looking forward to it, Mara. Hans and I are both finishing up an assignment, and he has been asked by my old art gallery in London to feature some of his glasswork! Can you believe it? Mr. Templeton is still there after all these years. I have to admit, I can't wait to catch up with him when Hans goes there for the opening."

Mara quickly said, "Once you have a date, let me know. I wouldn't miss it!"

After the phone calls, Mara poured a glass of wine and got comfortable on her sofa with her legs tucked under her. A wave of gratitude washed over her for these two friends who had become such an important part of her life. Although, after the weekend in Mijas with Annie and the twins when she realized she wanted marriage and a family, she agreed she wasn't going to chase it. She had to have faith that love would show up when it was meant to be.

Mara arrived at the studio the next morning with a renewed sense of hope. She was going to make a concerted effort to put all the confusion of the last ten days aside and move forward. She and Lucca were getting started on new designs, and input on the collection from Wayan had inspired them both.

Rochelle was waiting for her with pen in hand to keep her on schedule. She started with, "Three of the fabrics used during Fashion Week are getting enough order volume to require an additional run of fabric. Unfortunately, the minimums are fairly large and you might end up with a surplus."

"I will call Zayn to push the orders through, but in the meantime, get me samples of all three. I will take them to the meeting with Wayan tomorrow to see if he can incorporate any of the extra yardage in his new designs. We should be able to offer him a decent discount. I will see if he can introduce me to some of the other costume designers. This might be a great avenue for us since, as costume designers, their use of my fabrics would not in any way compete with my fashion designers."

Rochelle nodded. "Great idea, Mara. I will call the weaver in Florence to request several large samples of each of the fabrics."

Mara went to her bookshelf to look at her drawings from last season's collections. She took them to her table to study them side-by-side with the spreadsheets Rochelle had provided with the sales reports. She planned to take them to the meeting Friday with Zayn and the accountant. For now, she wanted to study her designs against the results. Granted, if the audience did not care for the design, no fabric in the world would salvage it, so Mara's instinct had to play into it as well.

She thought about Allison Ford. The woman had done so much for her by recommending her to Kenneth Patrick. That move had literally changed her life. Mara remembered one of her favorite batik dresses that Allison put in the catalog. Mara was so sure that it would be a success that she convinced the owner to produce more. Sadly, it was a terrible disappointment with hardly any sales. When Allison saw the look of failure on Mara's face, she explained. "Mara, it is never wise to lay all the odds on one style. The dress is beautiful. It could be the model who wore it, the stylist who accessorized it, the weather outside that could have affected the photo, or the location of the shot by the photographer. So many things go into it! But I'll tell you what. I will try changing all those things and give it another try."

The second time around, the dress was an incredible success and it ran in the catalog for four years after that. Mara had never forgotten that lesson and looked deeper at the correlation between her fabrics and the designs. Mara was so lost in thought she didn't hear the door open. Rochelle was leading someone in. "You have a visitor. She says she knows you."

Looking at the young woman beside Rochelle, Mara said in disbelief, "Antonella?"

Antonella corrected her with a glance toward Rochelle, "Nella. I thought I would pay you a surprise visit."

CHAPTER 20

With the use of the name *Nella*, Mara realized she was embroiled in a delicate web of intrigue and secrecy. Antonella stood there with her commanding presence and piercing stare, remaining silent until Mara nodded at Rochelle signaling that she could leave. As soon as Rochelle left the room, Mara, feeling a combination of curiosity and unease, asked, "Antonella, I mean Nella, what are you doing in Milan? I thought you were remaining in Lake Como during your time off."

Antonella paced around the studio scrutinizing it. "I thought it important to see for myself the work environment of the fabric designer I am investing in to collaborate with my exclusive costumier."

Mara noted the possessive tone she used to describe Wayan in the way she said *exclusive*. She also had the uneasy feeling that if she weren't careful she would be obligated to yet another investor. Being indebted to Zayn and his father was more than enough for her to handle.

"My studio is nothing fancy, I assure you. However, I am honored to be singled out to produce fabric designs for talented designers like Lucca as well as the opportunity to provide them for the costumes for your upcoming season." Sensing Antonella's unease, she added, "I meet with Wayan in his studio tomorrow to discuss how to proceed. One of the things I am the most excited about is the chance to give the fabrics in your costumes the illusion of being heavy yet are light enough for you to not be weighed down by such cumbersome outfits."

Reluctantly, Antonella conceded. "I have to admit the heavy costumes under the stage lights can be quite hot. I look forward to seeing what you develop. I know you are busy so I will make this visit short. But Mara...a word of caution. I am hiring you to be a professional. My stage identity is held in the utmost secrecy. There will be strict boundaries when it comes to you and Wayan working together both professionally and personally." Then, with a dismissive smile, added, "Do I make myself clear, Mara?"

Mara found herself unsure of where her alliances fell, the tension between the two women palpable, revealing the power dynamics and unspoken expectations that threatened to reshape their collaboration. Mara could feel that Antonella was trying to intimidate her, but she was unwilling to succumb to such tactics. "Antonella, or Nella, we are in a business where appearances can be deceiving. You can trust me not to reveal your private appearance. I'm always a professional when it comes to work, and I consider it an honor to design fabric for you and to be selected to work with Wayan. I will keep track of my hours, and at any time if you do not feel I'm sufficiently doing my job, I will submit an invoice with the accrued hours to date."

In a voice that was a stark contrast from the genuinely happy woman in Lake Como, Antonella said, "Mara, my dear, if there are any indiscretions that cause me to release you from my service, there will be no invoice." With that, Antonella turned and left.

* * *

Twenty-four hours had passed since Antonella appeared at Mara's studio...more than enough time for Mara to experience a range of emotions from confusion to anger to frustration. She approached the entrance to the museum section of the opera with a major debate taking place in her mind about how she should proceed with Wayan.

However, once she entered the museum and saw all of the memorable costumes used over the history of La Scala by opera legends such as Luciano Pavarotti, Cecilia Bartoli, and Enrico Caruso, her mind focused on one thing only. She wanted to be part of this distinguished setting that blended awe-inspiring talent with magically-imagined costumes.

Her mind resolute, she determined that if Wayan and Antonella were the path she needed to take, so be it. Whatever their issue, it would remain none of her business. After all, nothing was going on between Wayan and her, and she intended to keep it that way. Mara found the studios at the back of the museum and proceeded to look for Wayan.

He must have sensed Mara's presence since he looked up in her direction. It was his eyes, simply staring at her, that jolted Mara with their endless pools of Aegean blue. *Why does this man have such an effect on me?* She needed to keep her wits about her. Stepping forward, she reached out her hand, only to pull it back remembering the last time he had taken her hand. "Hello Wayan, I am ready to get to work. As I mentioned, I have three fabric samples that you might remember from the collection. I have enough yardage that they could be used in some of the larger areas that are necessary but not featured." Mara reached for the samples in her case.

Wayan motioned her over to his table where a series of eight designs were spread out. He held the sample swatches out to one, then the other. In total concentration, he pulled his mobile mannequin over to the table, holding up a design in one hand and the samples in the other. It was as if he could squint his eyes and visualize his design in her fabrics. Mara was captivated and hadn't even realized he hadn't spoken until he finally did. "Are you saying these fabrics would be readily available to begin working with them?" When Mara nodded, he continued,

"These would be good to use in large fabric capacities like the first layer of a full-length skirt or a long cape." He made a few calculations and handed Mara a sheet of paper with his yardage requirements. "Put this on my account which is co-signed by Antonella."

After attaching the samples to his cork storyboard, he turned back to Mara. "Now let's get to work on some original designs. You mentioned a fabric with the appearance of being heavy. Do you have a sample to show me?"

"I have a sample from last season but the yardage on it is sold out, so just use this as an idea to get a sense of the weight. Let me know the areas of the costumes where you'd like to use it and a theme for the designs so I can rough out a few sketches for you. I remember the basic story of *Aïda* but not broken down into scenes and the necessary costumes needed for Antonella."

The eagerness Wayan saw in Mara was contagious and he quickly reached for his storyboards to outline the scenes. He began to explain the story behind *Aïda* and how it would impact the costumes. "Antonella will have to pull out a heart-wrenching range of emotions in this opera in which she plays Aïda, the Ethiopian princess. She experiences excruciating despair when her love, Radames, leads the Egyptian army to war against the invading Ethiopians, giving her the impossible choice between her love or her country."

Looking at the first board, Mara began to sketch, then looked up. "Tell me more."

"The Egyptians win the war, and the Pharoah offers Radames a reward for such a victory. With Aïda at his side, he asks that the Ethiopian prisoners be summoned, then Aïda recognizes her father, the Ethiopian king, among the prisoners. He is disguised as a captain and warns Aïda to not reveal his identity as he pleads for the prisoners' release."

Mara stopped her sketching to look at Wayan. "This is not going to end well, is it? Even though I know the basics of the story like many in the audience, her costume has to add to the tragedy so there will not be a dry eye in the theater."

Inspired by Mara's insight, he continued. "In the final scene, a compromise is agreed to that the prisoners shall be released with the exception of Aïda and her father. As an additional reward, the pharaoh offers Radames the hand of his daughter, Amneris, in marriage leaving Aïda and Radames in total despair. The opera is a classic tragedy of love versus betrayal that, in the end, leads to the lovers dying in each other's arms."

Wayan looked at Mara's sketches and he could *feel* the emotions. "These are brilliant, Mara." When he reached for another sketch, his hand accidentally brushed hers. Her instinct was to pull her hand away, but it seemed to be glued to the table. Wayan looked her in the eyes and said in barely a whisper, "I think we are going to make quite a team, Mara."

CHAPTER 21

It was late. The sun had set long ago. Yet Mara sat at her drafting table unaware of time. Unable to contain her excitement, images of Aïda, Radames, the warring countries, and the new bride Amneris floated through her mind and onto one sketch after the other. She thought of Zayn and the boundaries placed on their relationship because of two differing religions. *Would she have ever loved him the way Aïda loved Radames?* In her heart she knew it was never that kind of love. *If she ever found it, how far would she go to keep it?*

Mara slowly flipped through the sketches. Even she had to admit she had poured her heart and soul into them, acknowledging they were some of the best she had ever rendered. She couldn't wait to show them to Wayan! At this late hour, Mara picked up the phone expecting to leave a message. Instead, Wayan sleepily answered the phone, "Pronto."

"Wayan, I am so sorry to wake you. I meant to leave a message. It's just that I haven't been able to stop sketching and really want you to see them! I think they might be exactly what you want."

Wayan sat up in his bed catching Mara's excitement. "You have been at it ever since you left? Get some sleep now. Meet me at Piazza San Fedele. I know a café with the best brioche in the city. Is nine a.m. too early?"

"Not at all. I'll be there!" She smiled, then quickly set her alarm and practically fell into bed exhausted.

* * *

The Piazza San Fedele was buzzing with activity that morning. It seemed to Mara the cobblestone streets had literally come alive with a myriad of sights and sounds. The aroma of freshly brewed coffee wafting through the air mingling with the tantalizing scents of freshly baked pastries, beckoned her to walk faster. Her portfolio was tucked under her arm as she searched the square for Wayan, finally spotting him in front of the imposing San Fedele Church surrounded by street vendors selling crafts, souvenirs, and fresh produce.

Wayan waved and Mara made her way through the crowd to where he was waiting. Breathless, she asked, "Where can we go?"

"It's not far. Follow me." Wayan led her to a narrow alley adjacent to the church. When they reached the café, Mara followed Wayan passed the baker's demonstration to the room in the back with a large table.

Once they had been served their coffee, Mara, a bundle of nerves and excitement, could not wait any longer to unveil her sketches and share her vision for the costumes. "The deeper I delved into the world of Aïda, the more captivated I became by the beauty and complexity of the story. That is why I went to such intricate detail to convey the heart of the character Antonella will play." As she spoke, she saw a spark of respect and admiration ignite in Wayan's eyes. Usually reserved and cautious, Wayan found himself drawn to Mara's energy and enthusiasm. Her fresh perspective and unique approach both challenged and motivated him. Their conversation sparked new ideas and possibilities, pushing both of them to think outside the box and explore new creative methods to merge his insight and feedback with her creativity.

Wayan felt the undeniable attraction he had for Mara the first time he saw her at the gala. But her unwavering enthusiasm and talent had touched something within him that went beyond mere attraction or professional collaboration. As they talked and laughed over cups of steaming coffee, he recognized the fierce determination that burned within her, and by the end of breakfast, he knew that Mara was not just a talented designer. He was beginning to see her as a kindred spirit whose presence inspired him and someone he wanted in his life beyond this particular job.

Deep down, Mara had longed for someone who could see past her walls and truly understand her. Studying him, she wondered if she might have found that unexpected connection she had been yearning for. His presence seemed to unravel her defenses effortlessly, his understanding piercing through her layers of protection with ease. Mara felt a wave of vulnerability wash over her, and when she looked closer into his eyes, she could see a reflection of her own hidden desires mirrored back at her. His understanding smile and the squeeze of her hand ignited a spark of hope to flicker to life within her. He answered her silent question with, "Let's get out of here, Mara."

Wayan took Mara's hand and practically pulled her out of the café. Mara recognized the direction they were taking as leading back to his studio. "Wayan, stop. Please. What are you doing? Antonella says there can be no indiscretion between us."

He slowed down and turned around, staring at Mara as if weighing the cost. Then, he reached for her face with both of his hands and pulled her toward him. "To hell with that!" He kissed her gently at first, coaxing her response. Despite the risks, Mara was unable to resist the magnetic pull between them, abandoning herself into the kiss. Her arms went around his neck, taking in his scent of allspice, the lingering taste of coffee, and his strength as he slid his arms around her back and pulled her to him. Neither of them noticed the portfolio that slid to the cobblestones with papers starting to blow in the breeze.

An older man passing by, wearing his traditional Coppola hat, smiled at the young couple, picked up the scattered pages, and cleared his throat. When he finally had their attention, he kept saying, "Amore!" with a jovial smile and handed the pages and the portfolio back to Wayan.

Mara was about to speak when Wayan handed her the portfolio but touched his finger to her lips to quiet her. "We need to talk." Wayan's hand never left Mara's as they walked back to his studio in silence, each reflecting on the consequences of a forbidden romantic entanglement. Antonella had clearly set a boundary which they had just broken.

Inside the studio, Wayan closed the door behind them and turned to face Mara. Her question was expected. Her heart was racing, desperately needing to know. "Are you in love with Antonella, Wayan?"

Wayan searched for the right words, knowing she deserved an explanation. "It's complicated, Mara. Let me explain. Despite Antonella's undeniable talent, the world of opera has not always been kind to her, facing many challenges on her journey to success. She was constantly underestimated and overlooked in an industry dominated by older, more established performers. Casting directors were hesitant to hire a young soprano, even with such a powerful voice, fearing she lacked the maturity and experience to truly embody the roles she sought to portray."

Mara began to understand the plight of a young woman trying to break into a harsh industry. "So, to prove her worth, with your help she transformed herself into an industry-worthy middle-aged diva to conceal her true identity."

"Yes, that part is true, but there is more to it. Antonella is a woman of deep complexity. There are times she struggles in the real world outside of the spotlight. My role since this began was to be her devoted companion and confidant, but most importantly to shield her from prying eyes to allow her to live a more incognito personal life. She relies heavily on me, Mara, to keep up the appearance of a romantic partner, but I assure you, beneath the surface our relationship is purely platonic. She has my devotion and my allegiance, but she does not own my heart."

Wayan reached to caress Mara's cheek, but Mara pulled away to speak once she absorbed the complexity of their situation. "Where does that leave us? It won't work. You can't disrupt this carefully orchestrated façade, and I am not able to betray Antonella after her offering me such an opportunity and her trust. This was a mistake, Wayan. We need to simply pretend it never happened." Mara placed the portfolio on his workstation and said, "The sketches are numbered. When you decide which ones you'd like me to translate to fabric, call my assistant, Rochelle. She will ensure it gets to my attention. Goodbye, Wayan." Without waiting for a response, Mara turned and strode out of the studio. As she walked away, her eyes began to glisten with the knowledge of another love that could never be, the elusive spark of hope turning to ash.

CHAPTER 22

When her phone rang for the fourth time without picking it up, Mara turned her phone to silent and tucked it back in her bag. Talking to Wayan would not accomplish anything. She told Rochelle to be on the lookout for the costume designer's instructions regarding his fabric selections, then re-focused on the designs she was creating with Lucca and Sophia.

As hard as she tried, however, she found it impossible to concentrate. *How had her life gotten so out of control?* The differences in their cultures and religions had ended any chance of a serious romance with Zayn, yet she was about to meet with the accountant and attend a high society fundraiser with him as if they were a happy couple. There could be no romance with Wayan because of a fabricated romantic relationship between him and an opera star. Yet she had to act as though all was normal around both of them. Mara felt like she was living inside a glass bubble that could shatter to pieces with any wrong move.

Zayn, dressed impeccably as always, showed up at Mara's studio promptly to take her to the accountant's office. Rochelle had produced a spreadsheet with the estimated proceeds from the orders resulting from Fashion Week, along with the costs of manufacturing the extra yardage of fabrics needed. Once they sat with Nico Amato, Zayn's preferred accountant, Mara explained the new work that had been commissioned by Antonella Rossi to use in her costumes for the upcoming opera, *Aïda*. "I believe the designer plans to use some of the extra fabric we had to produce. Ms. Rossi has offered to pay me handsomely for any designs I make exclusively for her. We are waiting to hear back from her designer about which designs they want to have fabricated. If it goes as planned, this could be a very lucrative part of our business."

Nico was making notes. Zayn looked at Mara approvingly. "Nice way to take advantage of a chance meeting, Mara! That is exactly why we attend these functions. There should be some very influential people at tomorrow night's fundraiser. Just keep being the beautiful and talented woman that you are. Before long, women from far and wide will be clamoring for designs made with a Mara fabric!"

In the taxi on the way back to the studio, Zayn took her hand to his lips for a light kiss. "I miss us, Mara. Seriously. I would give anything if things were different. It is not easy to be this close to you knowing I will never be able to have you."

Mara gently removed her hand and met his gaze with a mixture of yearning and resignation. "Zayn, I owe you and your father a great deal. You have given me opportunities I would never have been able to acquire on my own. From the start, our connection has been more than mere business, but we both know the barriers between us seem insurmountable. The pretense of being a couple for the sake of appearances makes our relation-ship that was already complicated difficult for me too. But to be honest, beneath this glamorous façade that I wear when I am with you, I long for quiet moments away from the chaos of the city. That is why this trip to Bali is more than just to visit family and seek inspiration for new designs."

Zayn looked at this woman with so many layers that he had never tried to explore. He realized in his attempt to succeed, he had tried to mold Mara into something she was not. Filled with regret over what might have been between them, he also knew she needed this trip home to Bali. "Take a break, if you must,

Mara. But if you want to go as far as Father and I think you can, the role you play needs to be carefully orchestrated."

They reached her studio and Mara got out of the taxi. She forced a smile as Zayn reminded her he would pick her up at her apartment at seven the next day. The warm smile he gave her back gave her hope that he somehow understood she needed to reconnect with the free-spirited, nature-loving girl who craved the simple joys in life...the rustling of palm trees in the breeze, the laughter of children playing in the villages, and the vibrant sunsets painting the sky with hues of orange and pink. She couldn't wait!

* * *

Knowing well the role she must play, Mara took care with her choice of what to wear that evening. She pulled out one of Sophia's most sophisticated designs that draped her body in a way that revealed nothing but suggested everything. She swept a portion of her hair up in a tidy fashion, letting the other half fall in tendrils around her face and neck. Her makeup was a dichotomy of the sheerest base with overly accented eyes outlined with the pale lavender that played off the color of her dress. Staring in the mirror, Mara tried a variety of necklaces, but in the end chose only a large diamond-encrusted serpent bracelet with two purple amethyst eyes. She looked at her image as an array of contrasts which would provide no one with a glimpse of her true self. It was the perfect portrayal of the mix of emotions that stirred within her that evening.

When she answered the door, she noted that Zayn's jaw dropped in surprise, but Mara showed little response. "You are stunning, Mara! No one will be able to take their eyes off you. Keep this up and you will make it impossible for me to keep my hands off you." That finally got a slight acknowledgement of irony from her.

Mara picked up the deep purple wrap and handbag then looked at Zayn. "Shall we go?"

The taxi dropped them at the acclaimed Excelsior, and Zayn took Mara's arm to arrive at the Grand Ballroom prepared to smile and appear as the happy couple for the high society attendees. However, beneath the charade, they both carried unresolved feelings for each other that didn't just disappear after so much time together. The admiring glances from men at the event stirred a pang of jealousy and possessiveness in Zayn that in his mind he understood was unfair, but his heart was not cooperating which emphasized the conflicting emotions he was trying so hard to hide.

Tables full of silent auction items were woven through the ballroom. Mara wandered over to study a large Murano glass vase that reminded her of a sculpture Hans had created. She mentioned it to Zayn, wondering if it might be a good piece for his family's new home in Spain. He was writing a bid for it when he noticed a photo of Antonella Rossi on an adjacent table. He pointed it out to Mara and curious, they moved over to find that it was a signed photo with a full musical collection of her operatic arias from *La Bohème*. Zayn looked at the photo and commented, "Antonella is really quite lovely. I hate to have missed her performance. I am sure she was incredible."

Mara nodded, then mumbled, "Even more beautiful in person." Catching herself, she more clearly added, "Her voice can evoke such emotion but her costumes add a great deal to her grandiose stage presence. Look, here is a booklet with some of the costumes. It's hard to believe that I am actually participating in the creation of her new designs."

Zayn placed a bid for the entire package. He then wondered aloud, "If this package is part of the auction, I wonder if she is attending?"

Mara had not anticipated that Antonella and Wayan would be at the event, but perhaps that was why she was in Milan this week. Then, it was as if those hypnotic brown eyes had a magnetic force of their own and her head turned to see Wayan's stare scrutinizing her to the point that she felt stripped naked before him. Fortunately, just as Zayn noticed who had her attention, Mara composed herself and waved, forcing a wide smile. To Zayn, she explained, "There is Wayan. Antonella must be close by. Come, let me introduce you."

Wayan touched Antonella's arm to interrupt her conversation long enough to tell her that Mara was coming over to say hello. Antonella followed the direction of his glance and noticed Mara's dress with an envious resentment since Antonella herself had dressed as her middle-aged stage persona. But quickly her admiring gaze moved to the handsome young man escorting Mara, close by her side.

"Mara, my dear, you look simply stunning! And who is your attractive date?"

Mara couldn't tell if she was seriously interested in Zayn, or if she was just pleased to see Mara with another man. "Antonella, please let me introduce Zayn Al-Farooq from Fujairah. This is the man I mentioned while I was visiting you in Lake Como. I worked with two other designers on his family yacht and their new home in Marbella, Spain. Zayn, this is Antonella Rossi and her escort is her exclusive costume designer, Wayan."

Zayn gallantly took Antonella's hand for a kiss, then shook Wayan's hand missing the exchange of looks and unspoken words between Wayan and Mara. "Ms. Rossi, I am a huge fan and am so sorry I missed your concert. My plane went down and I was stranded in Cyprus. However, I understand that Lucca taking my place was quite fortuitous and that their time in Lake Como with you and Wayan was well spent."

When Antonella engaged Zayn in a conversation about the lightning strike that hit his plane, Mara tapped Zayn's arm and excused herself, explaining she was going to powder her nose. She retreated to the restroom without a glance at Wayan and, once inside, began to pace the lavish ladies' room stirring up a whirlwind of inner turmoil that threatened to consume her. How could she find herself caught between two men, both forbidden to her, and now they were both here in the middle of a conversation? She couldn't offend Zayn, but try as she might, the intensity of her feelings toward Wayan was undeniable.

Mara pulled herself together best she could. Heading back into the ballroom, she saw Wayan leaning against a column waiting for her. She couldn't say she was surprised. After all, she hadn't returned any of his calls or messages. Determined not to have a confrontation, she resigned herself to speaking with him, if only to make it clear they could not embark on a relationship. When she approached him, he took her arm. "Come with me, Mara."

He guided her through an open door leading to the garden. Mara had a fleeting moment to notice Zayn and Antonella were still deep in conversation. Wayan took her to the side of the garden that was more remote and held her shoulders at arm's length. Then, running a hand through his hair in frustration. "Mara, you, that dress that has my imagination going wild...you tempt me beyond my endurance. You can't keep avoiding me!"

Mara sighed with her own sense of frustration. Her voice held a hint of weariness as she spoke, burdened by the weight of deception and hidden truths that threatened to tear her apart from within. "We can't do this, don't you see? Our very existence is based on falsehoods. Every word we speak and action we take is all part of the charade. My being with Zayn is a lie, your being with Antonella is a lie. But they are lies we both must maintain." Then, swallowing a half sob, she added. "You and me not being together is a lie too. It is all just one deception after another. I can't do this."

"Yes, you can." He took his fingers and traced the edge of the fabric of her dress under her arm to where it fell to her waist putting the slightest curve of her breast on display. There he lingered, causing ripples of fire to course through her. "This is far from over, Mara. You go back and I will bring drinks."

As if things weren't complicated enough, Zayn greeted her with a warm smile and put his arm around her. Antonella pointedly asked Mara if she had seen Wayan. Trying to remain nonchalant, Mara answered, "Yes, he was in line at the bar. I believe he was ordering drinks."

Antonella, pleased with discovering Mara had a serious boyfriend, said, "When Zayn and I were talking, we happened to find out we are staying at the same hotel! We thought we would make the rounds here at the fundraiser to put in a few more bids, then we could all meet at the hotel in the lobby bar for a nightcap before retiring."

Once they moved to the auction items, Mara whispered to Zayn, "Retiring? She thinks I am staying in your room?"

"Don't worry. Just come back to my room long enough for them to get settled, and I will order you a taxi to take you home." Mara found Wayan's eyes, locked in a moment of shared under-standing, as he returned with the drinks he'd promised.

CHAPTER 23

Antonella and Wayan were seated at the mahogany-embellished lobby bar first. Antonella leaned over to Wayan. "I wish I could remove all this makeup and change into my own clothes. Mara has already seen me without all the extras. But I felt Zayn out to see if Mara had shared my little secret and he seemed unaware. I am happy to know she has a sense of loyalty." A flush of guilt washed over Wayan as he realized the thoughts he was having were far from loyal.

Once Zayn and Mara joined them, Zayn signaled the waiter to bring over a bottle of their finest port. As they sipped their wine, the conversation naturally came around to their common subject of Mara's fabrics. Zayn directed his question to Wayan as he patted Mara's hand. "You should have seen the Fashion Week shows Mara participated in. Her fabrics literally made the designers' fashions come to life!"

Antonella immediately responded, "I can certainly vouch for that. Lucca came with her to my home in Lake Como and brought the fashions that he presented during the event. He and Mara and Wayan were able to customize a handful for me to wear when I'm not performing. I haven't seen the fabrics Mara has designed for my costumes yet but Wayan assures me they are spectacular."

Wayan added, smiling at Mara, "They certainly are, and Mara's talent is inspiring. The more I told her about the upcoming opera, *Aïda*, the more enthusiastic she became about what she might offer. I have selected five sketches to have engineered to fabrics. Then I will be able to share them with you, Antonella."

Feeling the need to somehow shake off the numbness that had fallen over her, Mara joined in. "Yes, those sketches are at my weaver's workroom being fabricated now. They should be ready in about seven to ten days."

Wayan explained to Zayn, "I have been able to incorporate some of Mara's existing fabrics while featuring her new designs. There is a great amount of fabric in each costume so they tend to get quite heavy. I must admit I am looking forward to seeing the costumes made with the fabric she says can be feather light but look like a heavy brocade!"

"Well, I don't know much about that, but if Mara says she can do it, rest assured you will get it."

The conversation wound down, and they all agreed to call it a night. As they got up from the table, Wayan subtly slipped a note to Mara. She glanced at him with a question in her eye. When the elevator stopped at Antonella's floor, she and Wayan got off. The sideways look from Wayan signaled Mara to read the note. Wayan said goodnight to Antonella at her door, but Zayn asked Mara to join him in his room. When the door to Zayn's room was closed, he pulled her into an embrace. "This was much harder than I expected, Mara, I care about you deeply."

Mara had lost her superficial smile. She walked over to the window to look out upon the city and glanced down at the note. "Zayn, please, would you call me a taxi? Pretending that we are something we're not gave me a horrible headache and I want to go home and take a long bath to relax." Zayn tried to push aside the image of Mara bathing. Resigned to what could never be, he walked Mara out to the waiting taxi and kissed her hand, then hugged her.

"Take care of yourself, Mara. We don't have another event for a few weeks and I know your Bali trip is coming up soon."

She looked up at Zayn, seeing the man she had counted on for the last two years, knowing any hope of a future with him was gone. She stepped into the taxi, and out of the corner of her eye, she noticed Wayan in the shadows of the building watching them. Leaning her head back, rubbing her temples, she knew without a question. He would follow her taxi. His car had been parked at the curb and the headlights that shined through the back window merely confirmed the path they were headed down was inevitable with no possibility of stopping it.

Mara unlocked her front door and walked into her ground-level apartment, leaving the door slightly ajar. It was dark with only the light from the street lamp illuminating the interior. She knew, no she could feel, the moment he entered the room and Mara turned to see his silhouette. As they stepped toward each other slowly, it seemed appropriate to be surrounded by shadows as they both yearned to find the light in the other.

Everything was moving in slow motion, both of them eager to savor each moment. Wayan reached for the clip holding her hair, unfastened it, and let it fall to the floor. He then took her face in his hands and brought it to his, seeking her lips in a sensuous kiss that heated slowly only to ignite into an urgency that demanded the kiss go deeper and deeper. Wayan had been thinking about the silky softness of her skin and the shape of her body since their short time in the garden, but nothing prepared him for the paradise that awaited him.

There were no words between them. There was no need. They knew where this was going and the consequences that would follow them. There was a palpable electricity in the air along with that familiar magnetic pull that transcended mere physical attraction. Clothes tossed aside and naked, Mara led Wayan to her bedroom where he swept her up into his arms before gently placing her on the bed. Mara then reached for a match and lit two bedside candles slowly letting the light and the delight of seeing and touching Wayan's body surround her.

Hands were followed by lips in a journey of discovery and desire. When Wayan moved on top of her, he wanted nothing more than to explore the deepest depths of her. Until he suddenly stopped, the reality that she was untouched sinking in. Mara pulled him toward her. "What is it, my love?"

"This is your first time?"

Mara, aroused and ready for this man who had stolen her heart, replied, "Yes, and it's perfect."

Humbled to the very core of him, Wayan felt a surge of love and admiration for this woman, that he would be the first to unlock her innermost secrets. They reveled in each other's bodies to experience a completeness neither of them had ever felt before. The late hours of night soon gave way to the early hours of dawn and they dozed, intertwined as one.

Wayan slowly awoke and slid out of the bed. In the bathroom, he found a bottle of oil which he brought back to the bed. Mara was lying on her stomach. Wayan lowered the covers, pushed her long raven hair to the side, and straddled her. He poured drops of oil into his hands and rubbed them together, the friction causing them to heat up. Then he took those warm hands and stroked, rubbed, and kneaded her body, languid and pliable under him, from her neck to her toes. It was as if Mara was in a trance allowing every inch of her body to wake up once again to his touch. He gently turned her over and began the same on her front. Yet, when he got to her breasts, oiled and gently lit by the early dawn, the enticing peaks summoned his kisses, fully engaging Mara which led to making love once again.

They dozed, not rousing until the sound of Wayan's alarm on his phone. Reaching over to Mara, he kissed her. "I don't want to leave but I have an event scheduled that I have to attend. I promise I will call you first thing tomorrow and see you tomorrow night."

Mara instinctively sat up and pulled the covers higher, suddenly shy. "You are going to Antonella?"

"No, Mara. I am going to an event where she will be. This is a commitment I made that I must keep."

"Of course. Nothing has changed."

"Are you kidding, Mara? Everything has changed! We will figure it out. Don't worry." Wayan kissed her with the passion they had discovered during the night to assure her this was the case.

He quickly dressed, leaving her his t-shirt which he tossed at her with a smile. She pulled it over her head to walk him to the door. He kissed her again. "I will never forget this night, Mara."

"Nor will I. Goodbye, Wayan." The door closed and Mara turned the deadbolt, proceeding to the kitchen to make herself a cup of tea. Sitting on the sofa in Wayan's shirt, his familiar scent of deep musk with a hint of allspice lingered. She had the shirt but not the man. Mara suddenly knew what she needed to do and sprang into action. She made the necessary phone calls and packed her bag. *She was not willing to live in the shadows.*

CHAPTER 24

Rochelle was going through the instructions Mara left her, setting her list of priorities when the phone rang. "Hello, Rochelle? This is Wayan. Is Mara available?"

Rochelle looked at her notebook. "She isn't here. The fabrics you are waiting for should be ready by the first of next week."

"Thanks, Rochelle, but do you know when she will be back at the studio?"

"Mara is gone, Wayan."

"What??!!" Where is she?"

"She left for Bali late last night. Her plans changed suddenly and she moved the trip up." Rochelle assumed she would be fielding a lot of these calls with designers looking for her.

"Seriously, I need to reach her. Do you have a forwarding number of where she will be staying?" Wayan felt as if the walls around him were caving in. "I have to talk to her."

Rochelle looked back at her notes. "She is going to her parents' farm. She says they do not own a phone, and her phone will not have service until she is back in Ubud to meet her friends." Now Rochelle was curious about Wayan's reaction.

"Rochelle, you have to help me. I need to know the exact location of her family's home. It is important that I reach her." He paused, then said, "It's personal. She will want to know this."

Rochelle thought for a moment. "I know. She has some letters from her mother somewhere. I will see if I can find them then call you back."

"Hurry. Do you know if she flew into Ubud? She might have phone service at the airport."

"Yes. That I do know. I booked her original flight. She re-booked it yesterday but the destination didn't change. I'll go look for that address now. *Ciao.*"

Wayan called the airline to verify a flight departed Milan last night for Ubud and it was confirmed. He made a reservation for himself for the same flight that night. He would be only one day behind her. Rochelle called with the address and he determined how best to get there from Ubud. The village where Mara's parents lived was just beyond *Campuhan Ridge*. He could take the *kura kura* bus most of the way and then walk. The only thing left was the hardest...the call to Antonella.

The conversation was a difficult one as he expected. Would Wayan's attraction to Mara be the downfall of the elaborate charade Antonella had worked so hard to maintain? A rage of jealousy surged in her as she saw the pieces of her intricate puzzle start to shift. Her first inclination was to intervene and try to stop the budding romance. Next, it was to cut off Mara's work on her designs. But then she thought about the long-time companionship and support Wayan had provided her, and Antonella couldn't imagine what she would do without him. Perhaps she was at a new crossroads. Was she ready for her image to be exposed? She thought not. By the end of the conversation Wayan assured her they would find a way to make it work if she would just give him some time to explore the possibilities with Mara.

* * *

It wasn't like Mara to run away from a problem. By the time the plane landed in Ubud, she was more confused than ever. She had played along with the growing web of lies and deception, so entangled in it she seemed to be losing track of what was real. Yet she believed that in the middle of her world of secrets and illusions a genuine bond had formed between Wayan and herself. She had loved collaborating with him on the designs for the *Aïda* costumes. Mara found no explanation for the way they seemed to be drawn to each other and she had been unable to stop that simmering attraction from boiling over, revealing the intense attraction that had been brewing between them. One single night had sparked the end of an era for Mara, with a passionate coupling like nothing she had ever dreamed of. Yet he left her bed to go to Antonella. *Was this all part of the façade? Did he expect them to launch into an affair that could upend their carefully constructed lives?*

Mara had panicked over the consequences of that forbidden encounter and its potential effect on both Zayn and Antonella. She arranged for her cousin, Kadek, to pick her up at the airport and give her a ride to the farm. The calls Mara placed to both Sarah and Annie had naturally gotten their support when she explained she was going early to visit her family and would meet them at the end of the week back in Ubud. Although curious at her sudden departure, it was clear Mara did not want to elaborate so neither Annie nor Sarah questioned her. They would find out soon enough, and Mara was pleased about the spiritual wellness retreat, *Mundur Kesehatan*, that she had reserved for them with a resident healer.

As the plane touched down, Mara looked out the window at the familiar Balinese surroundings. Taking a deep breath, she allowed a sense of peace to wash over her somehow knowing that in the tranquil beauty of her homeland, she would find the clarity and authenticity she had been yearning for. She had left the glittering lights of Milan behind her. Now it was time to start her journey to rediscover her true self within the simplicity and serenity of her family's farm.

Kadek was there waiting, her warm smile a welcome sight after the long flight and mix of emotions. After their initial greeting, Kadek stood back as she seemed to sense something was troubling her cousin. Her observant eyes fell upon the symbolic prayer necklace Mara was wearing. Kadek asked, "Isn't that the prayer necklace Annie gave me at my wedding? I remember giving it to you when you left Bali."

"It was an important gift, both from Annie to you, and you to me. I always keep it close, but for this trip I feel I need to wear it." After a pause, Mara added, "Annie will be here at the end of the week and I know she is looking forward to seeing you again, Kadek. Since she gave you the necklace, she is now married and has twins! She is bringing them along with her husband, Ramone. My close friends, Sarah and Hans, are coming too. You probably remember me talking about them. They were art students with me in Australia. Both of them are quite talented!"

Kadek knew her cousin well and could tell there was more going on with Mara. "My dearest cousin, are you alright?"

During the drive along the familiar route and landscape she loved, Mara found herself sharing a little about the pressure and glamour of working within the fashion elite of Milan. "It is time for me to get back to my roots and the simple life that we love."

Suddenly curious, Kadek asked, "Are you staying this time, Mara?"

Mara's eyes glistened with a single tear remembering the night with Wayan. "I honestly don't know, Kadek. Hopefully, I will find the answers I seek during my time here. Now tell me, how is the family?"

Kadek did not pursue the subject further. Instead, she spent the time on the scenic drive telling Mara all the updates about the relatives.

The overgrown palms began to thicken; carved spirit stones lined the road; and a pair of macaque monkeys clamored to the top of one of the stones for a proper vantage point. Mara absorbed it all, knowing the road would narrow and the memorable view that she loved would soon open to the countryside displaying miles of rice terraces with thatch-roof houses scattered among them and narrow walkways intersecting the perfect grid of fields.

Kadek maneuvered the small car to a grassy area when the road became too narrow to continue. She helped Mara with one of her roller cases. Mara managed her backpack and the second roller case, now realizing she had drastically overpacked. As they began to walk the path, with a water-drenched rice paddy on each side, Mara allowed herself to listen. The quiet was such a contrast to the constant sounds of Milan that an overwhelming sense of peace fell over her. The path led them past farmers tending to fields in different states of harvesting who glanced up and waved, then through various houses and huts with colorful floral gardens.

Mara and Kadek both picked several different flowers as they approached her family's fields and placed them on the small temple altar at the corner of the path and first terraced rice paddy. This standard ritual was common among the farmers with a carved stone shrine strategically placed throughout each farmer's land.

Through some silent communication that always amazed Mara, her mother came out to greet her, drying her hands on her apron. Mara called to her mother, "Ibu! *Om Swastiastu.*" The Balinese greeting was actually a blessing and her mother repeated it back to her, reaching out her arms for an embrace.

Ni Luh hugged her daughter with tears of joy running down her cheeks. She then looked at Kadek with gratitude for bringing her daughter to her. "*Om Swastiastu, Ni Kadek.*" Mara and Kadek had long ago dropped the formal addition of "*Ni*" to their names, but it was used here in the countryside. Ni Luh ushered them inside and to a small room with two palettes. It was understood Kadek would spend the night before driving back to the city the next day.

Mara changed into a yellow cotton shirt with a sarong skirt made with one of her designs just in time for her father's arrival from work in the fields. He removed his sandals and rinsed his bare feet in the foot wash at the front door, then took a sarong from the hook and wrapped it around his dirty trousers. Emotion welled up on his face the moment he saw Mara. He placed his palms together in front of his chest and bowed. *"Om Swastiastu, Ni Made."* Somehow her father, using her given name, gave Mara a grounding that she was indeed home.

"Om Swastiastu, Bapek." Mara practically ran to hug him tight, allowing the feeling of love and comfort he offered to penetrate her layers of confusion. "I have missed you so very much, Bapek. It was time for me to come home."

"I want to hear all about it, my child. Go help your mother in the kitchen and we will have a long talk after dinner."

Kadek walked out of the kitchen to greet Mara's father, her uncle, *"Om Swastiastu,* Putu." She hugged him. To Mara she said with a wink, "Ni Luh is making your favorite chicken satay and says she has something to show you."

Mara smiled, following her to the kitchen filled with the smells of coconut oil, fresh lemongrass, and roasted peanuts. All of the ingredients for the marinade were on the large counter. In her youth, Mara would spend at least half an hour grinding the peanuts and other ingredients into a paste. She raised her eyebrows at her mother who reached under the cabinet and brought out the food processor Mara had sent them. Kadek explained that she had taught Ni Luh how to use it and she was now quite an expert!

Mara went closer to watch. Her mother tossed the large shallots, garlic cloves, herbs, spices, and peanuts into the processor and closed the lid. Within seconds, which would have taken so long by hand, she had the perfect texture of liquid paste. Mara could see how proud her mother was of such an accomplishment and gave her a big squeeze. "Ibu, let me help." Mara scooped the paste over the chicken pieces, turning each to fully coat them.

She then covered the bowl with a cloth and put it in the refrigerator to marinate while they prepared the rest of the dinner.

Mara thought of all the fancy dinners Zayn had treated her to, but she honestly wouldn't trade this one night for all of them put together. She loved the rich flavors of her homeland which blended a mixture of sweet, spicy, salty, sour, and even bitter, in a way that was completely unique. Her father joined them while the charcoal was heating. The only thing that would have made the evening even more perfect was if her brother and his wife, as well as her grandmother, were there with them. Her brother, Gede, lived by the coast in Canggu and worked at one of the resorts there. It was actually one of the places she thought about taking Annie and Sarah but it didn't reflect the culture of the island as well as Ubud. Luckily, her grandmother, *Nenek*, lived in Ubud with her aunt so she would see her later in the trip.

Ni Luh asked Mara, "We are most pleased you have come early, my darling girl.

What caused you to change the date? Are your friends still coming?"

Smiling at both of her parents, she answered, "Yes, they will be here at the end of the week. I have come early to spend more time at home with you both. I hope that you will come to Ubud Sunday to meet them. Kadek met my friend, Annie, three years ago. She is now married and has twins. Salvi and Cece are their names and they will be here too. You must remember my speaking of Sarah. She came to Australia early to help me learn English in order to study with Kenneth Patrick." Both of her parents were smiling and nodding at the memory of Sarah, but mostly about the blessing of good fortune for Annie to have had twins!

Then to Kadek, "Are you sure you can pick them up at the airport on Friday? Sarah and Hans are booked on the flight I was originally on. It arrives a few hours earlier than Annie's flight."

Kadek quickly agreed. "I will be back to pick you up that morning in plenty of time to make Sarah's flight. Then we will have time to take them to your guest house and come back to the airport for Annie and her family."

"Perfect." Mara relaxed. Now all she had to think about was her time with her parents on the farm for the rest of the week. All the chaos was behind her, and Zayn and Wayan were oceans away.

CHAPTER 25

After dinner was finished and cleaned up, Ni Luh fixed a pot of her homemade *jamu*, the herbal beverage Mara grew up with, and another comfort of home. Her mother used a unique combination of ginger, lime, turmeric, and honey that was delicious and perfect after a big dinner.

Putu patted the seat next to him for Mara to sit. Kadek pulled up a chair for *Ni*

Luh and tossed a cushion on the floor for herself. Putu began, "Ni Made, you have been gone a long time. Now that you are living in Italy, would you tell us about your life there?"

Looking at the family she loved, Mara began, "I am grateful for the blessings that have been bestowed on me. My sketches have been able to be transferred onto fabric with success." Pointing at her sarong, she added, "This is one of them."

Kadek, in particular, studied the intricate patterns within the design. "It is beautifully crafted, Mara."

"Thank you. I am sure you all remember that after I worked for the Arab family in

Spain, they offered to invest in my work and set up a studio for me in Milan. Their son, Zayn, is very handsome and I thought we were serious about a future together. He has been an import-ant reason I have met influential people and been included in the right circles to help my business succeed. It unfortunately has become clear to us both that his being from the Arab Emirates and a devout Muslim and my being a Balinese Hindu made a future marriage and family together impossible. Since we made that decision, it has become awkward between us to attend the necessary events and pretend to be a happy couple."

Kadek reached over to touch Mara's hand. "Do you love him? Is that what is troubling you?"

Mara sighed. "I thought I did, but there is more to it than that. I met someone else through my work. I have been asked to collaborate with him to create fabrics for the costumes of a well-respected opera singer. She has the most beautiful voice and the tour she will do next is the opera *Aïda*. You must all see an opera. It is like our ceremonial dances with a story of strug-gle, love, and tragedy with soulful voices and music added to tell the story. There is nothing exactly like it!" Mara knew she had gotten off her topic when she realized her parents had most likely never even heard of an opera.

It was Kadek, ever insightful, who brought the subject back around. "So, cousin, where did you meet this new man?"

Suddenly uncomfortable, Mara willed herself to stop think-ing of his kisses and the feel of his bare skin. *Impossible. How to tell them the basics and leave it at that?* "The opera star's name is Antonella Rossi...her costume designer who I am work-ing with is Wayan."

Putu interjected, "I don't understand. Wayan is a Balinese name. I thought you said you met in Milan?"

Another sigh from Mara. "That is where it gets complicated. His family is originally from Buleleng on the north end of Bali. After a terrible earthquake, their home was destroyed and they had to evacuate. They moved to Capri, an island off the coast of Italy. It was his design talent that brought him to Milan just as mine did."

Mara's mother studied her daughter, then said, "So, even though you are far from home, the spirits have brought you someone of your own culture."

"Ibu, mother, I was beginning to think the same thing. However, I believe his relationship with the opera star is more than what I originally thought. It has become obvious to me it goes beyond a working partnership. It seemed like my life was getting consumed in lies and deception and the difference between the lies and reality were confused. I needed my family and homeland to allow honesty, sincerity and gratitude to be my priority in life. That is why I came early. I couldn't wait another day."

* * *

Mara walked Kadek to her car early the following morning, sorry to see her cousin leave. They verified Friday's pick up, then Kadek hugged Mara. "I hope you find what you are searching for here, my cousin. I made something for you after you went to sleep last night. It is in the drawer next to your palette. And Mara, keep that necklace around your neck. You can be proud of your culture and your heritage. There is no need to define yourself by others' expectations."

The tumultuous world of high fashion was far removed from the familiar rhythms of rural life and unconditional love of her family. Mara stopped for a loaf of bread and a bag of fresh coconuts at a lean-to open air market, smiling at the small children playing. Mere existence here was so much simpler. She hoped that would be the understanding her close friends found when they arrived for their visit.

As she got closer to the house, she saw her father in the field, already hard at work. He looked up and waved. She waved back with a wide smile. Her mother had a large bushel of coconut leaves and was about to weave the leaves into platters for the daily offerings of fruit and flowers to the various shrines. "Ibu, where can I be of most help today?" Mara knew they operated the different paddies in a rotation system to enable them to harvest the rice year-round.

Her mother looked at Mara in appreciation. "They have finished plowing and raking in the far corner paddy. It is ready for seeding. There should be bales of thatch close by that your father put there yesterday."

"You know I love that job! That means I will see the beginning of the small seedlings before I leave Friday morning. It happens so quickly that it is like a tiny miracle." Mara got some work clothes from her mother and went to change. When she was in her room, she remembered Kadek's surprise and opened the drawer with a smile of recognition. She lifted out a string of fresh lotus blossoms intermingled with white sage incense sticks. Mara attached it to the ceiling rafter at both ends. They used to make these all the time when they were young for good luck and to ward off evil spirits. She planned to light the incense later to take full benefit of the blessing shared by her cousin!

Mara grabbed one of the triangular *capil* hats used for sun protection. Even in the intense heat, she wore long sleeves and trousers to avoid a major sunburn. The calf-height boots were next to be able to move around in the water-soaked mud. Burlap bags were stationed near the readied paddy and sealed to prevent the birds from enjoying the seeds inside. Mara opened the first bag and used a large scoop to begin a methodical spreading of the seeds, followed by pushing them down into the mud. It was a tedious job to be certain the seeds were spread properly in order to produce the healthiest seedlings that would then be carefully moved in small sections to the next larger paddy. There they would have room to grow to the size and fullness required to harvest.

When all the bags were empty and the seeds spread, Mara studied carefully to be certain each seed was properly covered by the mud. Her mother brought her, and the rest of the workers, some *pisang rai*, similar to a coated banana fritter rolled in coconut and drizzled with brown sugar syrup. The last step for the seeding was to loosen the bales of thatch and spread the dried reeds over the entire paddy to protect the precious seeds from the birds.

Mara was exhausted, drenched in sweat, but looking back at the perfectly seeded paddy she knew her father would be proud. Nodding in satisfaction, she gathered up the empty bags and rope to make her way along the paths back to the house. In the distance, she saw a man with a large backpack walking toward her house. For a moment, she thought it might be her brother, Gede. She couldn't see how it was possible, though, since she had spoken with him right before she came and he wasn't able to get time off from the resort. Maybe he was able to get away after all. It would certainly make her time here perfect!

Mara sped up her pace, her hope building as she remembered the string of lotus blossoms hanging in her room. When she was close enough to realize it wasn't Gede, but rather some local, she let out a small sigh and slowed her pace. Mara forgot about the man when she saw her father close by. She saw that he was weeding using a clever, a handmade tool that fit between the rows of growing seedlings. She called out, "Are you almost finished? I was thinking of changing into my swimsuit and walking to the waterfall for a swim to cool off. Would you like to join me?"

"I need to check on one more section that should be ready for harvest this week.

How did the seeding go? You always were an expert at that important first stage."

"It went well. All done. I'll be swimming if you need anything." Her father tipped his hat. Now that she was walking toward the house again, she looked around but there was no longer any sign of the man. *Strange that he would be on their property.*

Anxious to get out of the nasty clothes and dive into the cool water, she opened the front door and headed to her room to change, calling out, "Ibu, I'm back!"

She didn't expect a reply but her mother surprised her with, "Ni Made, please come here." Mara had rinsed off her feet and was barefoot. Although she didn't want to wait another second to undress, she would not disobey her mother and walked toward her. "You have a guest."

Realizing her eyes must still be adjusting from the sun, she looked closer in confusion. Standing there in person was Wayan, looking as handsome as ever, who ironically was the man from the pathway. Staring at him in disbelief, it suddenly occurred to her how she might look. With a sick sense of humor, she thought *what a far cry from the sophisticated woman from the night of the fundraiser!*

Wayan stood there calmly, smiling at her. "Ciao, Mara."

CHAPTER 26

Mara was taken aback to see the familiar face of the costume designer standing before her with sincerity in his eyes. Confusion and a sense of intrusion swirled within Mara as she struggled to make sense of his unexpected arrival. "W-What are you doing here, Wayan? This is my home."

"Mara, believe me, I am well aware this is your home since I have pulled nothing short of a miracle to arrive here only twenty-four hours after you. Considering our last night together, you left rather abruptly, don't you think? And without a word of explanation." Then, remembering Ni Luh's presence, he asked in perfect Balinese,

"Why don't you introduce me to your mother?"

Despite knowing Wayan was originally from Bali, Mara was still surprised by how easily he dropped into the language. "Ibu, this is Wayan, the costume designer I am working with in Milan. Wayan, this is my mother, Ni Luh."

Ni Luh studied the young man standing before her, his hands clasped together at his chest in a traditional gesture of respect. "*Om Swastiastu,* Ni Luh." Wayan's voice was soft yet filled with a quiet strength. "I am pleased to make your acquaintance." Ni Luh listened intently as he explained the suspicions her daughter held toward him, associating him with the world of luxury and deceit that often tainted their industry. She saw and heard the resolve in his words as he expressed his earnest desire to prove his loyalty and sincerity. "Trust is a rare commodity there and I am here to ensure your daughter understands that I am determined to break those barriers. If you will allow me the chance to stay, you will find me willing to work hard and contribute to the family."

As she considered his request, Ni Luh's look of confusion softened as she looked at her daughter so flustered by this young man. "I will speak with my husband. For now, you may put your things in Mara's brother's room." To Mara, she said, "You were planning to go swim. Wayan has had a long journey. Why don't you change into your swimsuits and go to the waterfall? It sounds as if you have much to discuss. I will speak to Putu as soon as he returns from the field."

In the privacy of her small room, Mara changed into a modest, one-piece black swimsuit with her pareo wrapped around her, tucked in at her breast. She pulled her hair up into a top knot and secured it with a long hair pick. So many questions were racing through Mara's mind. *How did he find me? What would Antonella say? Had she misjudged him?* And, most importantly, *WHY was he here?*

Nervous and wary, she grabbed her straw bag and slung it over her shoulder to walk to the waterfall. Wayan was waiting for her at the front door wearing board shorts and a surfer t-shirt. She walked past him without a word and started down the path.

Wayan caught up to her. "Is this the way it is going to be with us, Mara? You run away anytime you're unsure of me...of us?" Mara said nothing. "Ah, well, I guess I will have to do whatever it takes to prove that you can count on me...always. I am where I need to be. I want to discover you and your upbringing. And, Mara, also for you to discover me...the true me who has fallen under your spell."

Mara finally looked at Wayan, a glimmer of hope igniting within her, and asked the question that most haunted her. "Does Antonella know you're here?"

"Yes. Even though she had her suspicions, she was shocked. I told her how I felt about you and that I was going to do whatever it took to win your heart and deserve your trust. It might disrupt her carefully fabricated identity, but I assured her I would help any way I could. She needed to understand that you are my priority." Wayan took Mara's shoulders and turned her to face him. "In the end, I convinced her I was coming here to prove I am serious." He pulled her into an embrace, willing her to believe in him.

Getting close to the waterfall, the path narrowed surrounded by lush, jungle-like greenery. It then opened up to a majestic waterfall pouring down the side of the mountain into a crystal-clear pool of water below. They were the only ones there at the moment. Mara dropped her pareo, released her hair, and grabbed a bar of herbal soap from her bag. The water was glorious, moving her to dive down again and again. Wayan felt like he could watch her for hours. Then, shaking himself into action, he came into the water after her.

The water not only removed the soil and sweat, but it also soothed her doubts.

She swam over to where the waterfall cascaded into the pool and stood under it, allowing it to wash her hair. Wayan was mesmerized watching her. The magnetic pull that was undeniable between them was as strong as ever. It lured him to stand beside her under the weight of the falling water. Wayan pulled Mara to him, enclosed by the waterfall, reveling in the feel of her body close to his.

Mara caught her breath, only to choke on the water. Pulling her head out to cough, she shoved him. "Are you trying to drown me?"

"Far from it!" He reached for her and coaxed her into a kiss. Their natural chemistry took over and the kiss deepened. Things would have progressed, but a small family arrived and began playing in the water.

Mara, content to tread water and talk, said, "I can't believe you have come all this way and that you are right here in front of me!"

"Don't forget, Bali is my homeland too. I want to take time to get a reminder of its culture while I get to know you better, and I want to meet your friends. They are still coming, right?"

"Yes, but not until the weekend. You are planning to stay?" Mara was amazed he would simply drop his work to find her.

Wayan shrugged and nodded. "If your parents will allow me to stay, I am here to be by your side as you find your way back to your roots and determine if, and how, we plan to maneuver back into the rat race that awaits in Milan. All I ask is that you give me a chance. Let's use this time wisely to see if we have a future together."

For so long Mara had wanted to hear those words from Zayn, but here was Wayan, a man she'd only just met and already he was able to open his life to her.

The walk back to the house was much more relaxed and their conversation flowed easily. Wayan asked, "Are there many waterfalls in this part of the country? In Buleleng, our home was near the coast, rather than the mountains, so I never saw waterfalls."

Water was a subject sacred to Mara. She warmed to the idea of sharing about it. "Lake Batur supplies our water as well as the subak irrigation system used throughout the rice terraces. There are many waterfalls created as the water travels down from the mountain peak. Water has a powerful energy that is both purifying and holy. It keeps us alive and allows us to grow food so we can eat. My father can explain more about how the subak irrigation works exactly. I know the water moves by way of canals, channels, and even drainage ditches, through a series of temples starting with the floating temple of Lake Batur. It is my hope to take my friends there while we are in Ubud and possibly do a water purification ceremony."

Wayan nodded. "I would like to see it. I remember hearing about it, but I was very young when my family left Bali. On the island of Capri, there was nowhere for us to keep up with the old rituals. I look forward to reconnecting with my Balinese roots just as you do yours."

Amidst the sounds of nature and the scent of fresh earth, Mara began to see a different side of Wayan, contemplating the possibility of a new beginning. Maybe, just maybe, if she allowed her roots to ground her and her instincts to guide her, she might find a way to re-shape her future that would include love, design, and authenticity. Perhaps her mother was right when she'd pointed out the amazing coincidence that Mara and Wayan had found each other so far from their homeland. Could this be destiny?

* * *

Freshly showered, Putu was anxiously waiting to meet the young man who had gone to such lengths to see his daughter. That he was originally from Bali gave Putu some relief. He had never cared for the man Ni Made had been seeing for such a long time. It concerned Putu and his wife that Zayn had never bothered to meet her parents. He understood the talent his daughter brought to this world, and he was waiting to meet a man worthy of her. Ni Luh had warned him not to have his expectations set too high. She had faith that Ni Made would be able to determine if a man were truly worthy of her heart.

Mara and Wayan reached the house, and Mara handed Wayan a sarong to wrap around his waist. He then asked, "Mara, I have arrived uninvited. Is there anything I should know about your father before I meet him?"

She loved her father dearly. "His name is Putu. He is a gentle, but wise, man who is a respected figure in this rural community.

He has spent his life tending to the family's rice fields. I think he would have loved to pass down the traditions of farming to my brother. Sadly for my father, Gede had no interest in farming and is happy working in tourism at a coastal resort."

Wayan shook off the fleeting thought of his own father and responded, "I look forward to meeting him."

Mara thought it only fair to ask, "I would like to put on some dry clothes, but if you would rather me stay while you get to know each other, I'm happy to."

"No, go ahead and get dressed. I want to be certain I'm not a burden."

That statement appealed to Mara and she went inside ready to introduce him and leave them to their conversation.

Ni Luh was preparing dinner in the kitchen, however, Putu was in the living room with a chunk of wood and a blade whittling. "Bapek, this is Wayan, the man I have been working with in Milan. He is originally from Buleleng. He surprised me with his arrival and I apologize for being unaware he was coming. He was not able to reach me on my phone to ask if he could stay here until Kadek picks us up on Friday." Turning to Wayan, she added, "Wayan, this is my father, Putu."

"Om Swastiastu, Putu." Mara left to go change and Wayan could see the subtle twinkle in Putu's eyes. Wayan continued, "As you know, Mara left ahead of schedule. I am afraid that my behavior had something to do with that. Sir, I care about your daughter more than she realizes. I could not let her think my feelings were not genuine. I realize I have arrived unannounced and uninvited, but I am willing to do whatever you need to be able to stay here and make things right with her."

Putu admired the young man's tenacity and wanted to learn more about him. "Wayan, tell me what you remember from your time in Buleleng. The earthquake must have been a difficult time for your family."

Wayan was relieved that her father wanted to get to know him. "I was only thirteen when the earthquake hit. We lived near the coastline and I was learning to surf. My father was a silversmith. He had such talent for creating intricately designed architectural elements that were used in temples throughout the area. He was the creative force behind my fascination with costumes. My sisters used to come to me to make their costumes for the various ritual dances. Once I learned to sew, I loved doing it, even at that young age. I was never exposed to farming so I am quite interested to see how it all works."

"Proper rice cultivation can be an art as well. I would be happy to have you in the field with me tomorrow to show you our traditional methods." After some thought, he continued, "I remember hearing about that earthquake. I heard there was much fear about a tsunami. Many people evacuated to Ubud. Our population grew almost overnight, which meant more mouths to feed. What made your family go to Italy?"

"You are right. My family was extremely concerned about a tsunami, but it honestly amazed me that so many people were out on the beachfront areas watching like it would be a fun thing to see. We were fortunate it never happened. But our home was old, and it collapsed during the earthquake. Afterward, my father wanted to continue to work with silver, and he was approached to work with an Italian jeweler who specialized in silver. The jeweler had been searching for a silver craftsman to do filigree. It sounded intriguing and challenging to my father and he accepted. So we moved to Capri, a beautiful island off the southern coast of Italy."

Putu was thoroughly enjoying getting to know Wayan and loved that his Balinese was fluent, but at that moment, Mara joined them in the living room. "I just checked with Ibu and she says she could use some help in the kitchen. Bapek, do you mind if I steal Wayan to help?"

Putu nodded and, to Wayan wisely said, "We shall see if your actions align with your words. Show us your sincerity through your deeds, and trust shall follow. For now you are most welcome as our guest and I look forward to introducing you to the art of rice cultivation tomorrow." Then to Mara, "Ni Made, there is a field ready to harvest tomorrow. Will you participate in that area?"

Mara smiled because she loved to see the process go through its cycle. "Yes, absolutely. Will there be time to start the drying process?"

"This particular paddy is not huge. Let's see how it goes. The priority for tomorrow will be to remove the seedpods from the plants. I will check on you mid-afternoon to see if you need help."

Mara motioned to Wayan to join her in the kitchen. Grinning, she said in a soft voice, "You and Bapek seem to be getting along well. I think my mother wants a turn!"

Wayan turned Mara to him. "I do not want to take time away from you and your parents. You are here to reconnect with them. Mara, I'm serious. I want to fit into your life."

"As long as it's honest between us, Wayan. I can't take any more pretense."

"Understood." A slightly wicked smile emerged. "The hardest part is keeping my hands off their daughter in their sight."

Mara had kissed him at the waterfall, but she wanted to make it clear she still had reservations about his being there. "I want to be honest too. I am not here on vacation. I am here to reconnect with my family, my homeland, and my roots. I don't want to confuse that journey. Can you understand that?"

Wayan ran his hand through his hair. "When I stepped on that plane, I knew I might be interfering. But you need to understand that you can count on me. As you discover yourself, I want more than anything for you to explore yourself with me. I care about you, Mara, and I want to help you regain your balance."

Mara squeezed his hand in appreciation and led him into the kitchen where the smells of curry, fresh coconut, and saffron filled the air. "Ibu, we are here to help! What can we do?"

"Ni Made, the chicken curry is cooking. Let's add some mixed vegetables, saffron rice, and corn fritters."

Wayan looked over at the counter where a pasty white substance appeared to be fermenting in a bag. "Could that possibly be *tempeh*? I haven't had that since I was a child." Reminiscing, he continued, "My grandmother, Nenek, used to soak the soy beans for several days, and my job was to get the skins off before adding the yeast to cause them to ferment. When they were ready, she would slice them very thin so they looked like crackers and sauté them in a savory-sweet sauce until they were golden brown."

Ni Luh raised her eyebrows in thought. "I do not think I have tried that. The tempeh should be complete by tomorrow night's dinner. Do you think you could make it for us?"

"I am not sure what went into the sauce. I do remember her taking the leftover sauce and serving it over rice. It would be a pleasure for me to try and feel like home. Ni

Luh, will you help me with the sauce?"

Mara silently watched the interchange between them, acknowledging to herself that his fluent knowledge of the language made such a difference. She tried to imagine Zayn here in these poor surroundings unable to communicate. She might not know what she wanted yet, but seeing Wayan getting along so well with her parents, she was beginning to understand what she didn't want.

They retired soon after dinner. It would be an early morning and they needed their rest. Wayan was about to go to Gede's room when he turned and went to Mara, taking her hands. Right in front of her parents, he raised them to his lips staring at her with an intensity that offered all his promises that came from his heart.

Putu looked over at Ni Luh and reached for her hand to squeeze it with a nod of approval.

CHAPTER 27

Just after dawn, there was a light knock on Wayan's door. It was Ni Luh with a neatly folded work shirt and trousers in her arms, and a capil hat on top. She handed them to Wayan and told him breakfast was almost ready. He quickly dressed and slathered sunscreen on his face. Looking at the hat, he realized the sunblock would soon be gone with the heat of the day and the hat would be needed for sun protection.

These next two days with Mara and her family were crucial to finding a place in her heart. He was thankful there was no phone service here on the farm. That way, it was impossible for Antonella to reach him. He understood clearly that she was not pleased when he told her he was following Mara to Bali. He also knew without a doubt how Antonella could be when she was upset. Wayan cringed to think about it. Such a mesmerizing angelic diva on stage. Very few knew there was a dark side to her that rarely surfaced. Wayan sent a prayer to the spirits that this would not be one of those times. For now, he had to believe this was the best path and to focus on Mara, her family and friends, and the art of rice cultivation.

Mara was already in the kitchen enjoying a smoothie with coconut milk and mixed fruit when Wayan joined her. She could hardly believe he was there and found herself wondering if she could find love and trust once again. She was seeing a different side of him. Gone was the polished costume designer on the arm of a famous opera star. He was showing her a side that was genuine, caring, and seemingly devoted to her. She realized she had misjudged Wayan and wanted to make it up to him. Some of the rituals planned for the time in Ubud with her friends would be perfect to do together.

For now, Ni Luh served Wayan two eggs and a bowl of porridge filled with flax seed, raisins, and nuts. Putu was already in the fields as he was every morning at first light. He had instructed Mara to give Wayan a tour of the different stages involved in a rice harvest before leading him to where he was working.

"Are you ready for today? It is not easy work. Be sure to wear your boots. There might be the occasional snake that wanders through the paddies."

That got Wayan's attention. "You're not serious, right?"

Mara smiled at this man who had no idea what he was about to get into but was willing to try. "Well, you are going to be working with a sickle, so your hands will be in the mud too." To her mother, she added, "Ibu, would you please give Wayan a pair of gloves to protect his hands." She handed him some heavy-duty rubber gloves that reached to his elbows.

Wayan mumbled, "What have I agreed to?" Mara's spontaneous laugh was enough to have Wayan laughing with her.

"Okay, let's get this started!" He carried his boots and gloves with him to not be cumbersome during the tour.

Mara began by taking him to the area where she did the seeding the day before. Wayan noticed she brought a few small pieces of fruit and picked some flowers along the way. She stopped in front of a stone shrine carved with the face of a monkey, then laid the fruit and flowers on the platter on top. "Balinese farmers needed to expand rice production back in the ninth century because of the growing population. In order to do that, they had to find a way for the water in the hills to dependably irrigate the countryside. It was brilliant really. Tunnels were carved by hand, and rice paddies were terraced to take advantage of the water from the crater of the volcano high in the mountains as it traveled down to the sea by simple gravity."

Wayan thought about it, then reflected, "Throughout time, mankind has had to step up to build or invent something to fill a need." Mara nodded.

"They called the original system subak, and it relied on the elaborate methods of moving the water and the rotation of the production phases to create a harmonious ecosystem that would keep the field in proper condition to yield the finest crops of rice. I suppose even the snakes are important. When I was little, we used to go out to the rice field at night with an oil lamp to catch eels. Kadek, my cousin, and I would listen to the sounds of the frogs and make up stories about all the fireflies."

"Ah, I have seen firefly images in your fabrics! It makes me want to go back and study your designs more closely." Wayan imagined Mara as a little girl with her sketchbook and could start to understand how she saw nature through an artist's eye.

"It is hard to imagine that I have not picked up a sketchbook since I got here! I think you have gotten me a little sidetracked!"

Wayan took her hand and looked at her as though he could get her a lot more sidetracked!

Mara cleared her throat. "Let me continue. In order for the water to be fairly distributed between the farmers, a primary water temple dedicated to the lake's deity, *Dewi Danu*, was built and the water temple priests took over managing the subak system. The water temples throughout the fields are all part of the ritual technology that monitors the rice growing cycle."

Fascinated, Wayan asked, "So *Dewi Danu* is the deity the farmers depend on?"

"In our culture, water and rice must exist in harmony. *Dewi Danu* is the goddess of the crater lake, and *Dewi Shri* is the goddess of rice and fertility. In this area of Bali, we believe if the goddesses are angered or neglected, water won't flow which means rice won't grow. The priests work with the farmers to maintain an equitable system, and if any farmer tries to take advantage, they are quickly fined. There is a water temple close to Ubud that I plan to take everyone to on Saturday. It is known for its holy spring water. I will see if everyone wants to experience the water ritual by cleansing in the water there inside the temple. It is more of a purification ceremony."

Wayan asked, "After we finish working today, can we go to the waterfall and you tell me about your friends who will be here?"

They reached the paddy where Mara had seeded the day before. "Of course we can!" She reached down into the mud to pull out a seed to show Wayan. "See how the seed is already breaking open? In a few days they will begin sprouting, and in twelve days they will be ready to move to a bigger area to finish their growth cycle."

They passed another field with several workers busy with long tools. "At this stage, the seedlings are dug up carefully so the roots are not disturbed. When they are re-planted in the bigger paddy, they are broken into clumps, each with about four or five sprouts, then spread equal distance from each other in even rows. You will see the workers busy weeding in between the rows."

They moved to the next paddy. "This group has now doubled in size in just twenty days." They followed the path to the next field. Mara pulled one of the large plants apart so the middle stalk could be seen. "This group is around sixty days old. You can begin to see seed pods on the leaves and small white flowers begin to grow at this stage. By around one hundred days that small seedling of four sprouts has produced well over a hundred seed pods! I will be coming back to work in the next field where we will be taking groups of plants and hitting them hard against a large stone so the rice with its husks falls off the plants. There will be piles and piles of these but they will still be damp. We then spread them out to dry in the sun for two days. Tomorrow, you and I will be taking bags full of the dried seeds to the local mill to remove the husks by machine.

The rice that we bring back will be gleaming white and perfect."

Wayan could easily see the passion Mara had for this process and was shocked his parents never took him to an area where he could learn about it. Mara reached the paddy where Putu was working and left Wayan there to work beside her father.

As she returned to her designated area, Mara hoped she had explained the process in a way that made Wayan appreciate it as much as she did. She once again thought of Zayn and how he would have reacted to all of this. In the end, it seemed much better that they had broken up before this trip so she wouldn't ever have to find out if he would have looked down on their lifestyle despite what he claimed.

CHAPTER 28

Putu, a hard-working man with weathered hands from all the years of working in the rice fields, observed the interaction between his daughter and the young man who had come so far to see her. A look of both curiosity and concern crossed his face. With what Mara had shared on the night of her arrival, he was worried about his daughter's life back in the fast-paced world of high fashion and questioned if Milan was the right place for her to settle down. He also had an intuitive sense of unease about Wayan's sudden appearance and the impact he might have on her decisions.

Despite Putu's reservations, Wayan's easy charm and seemingly genuine connection with his family softened the old man's heart. But, as Wayan joined him and they began to work on the harvest together, Putu found himself silently studying Wayan. His keen intuition could not help but wonder if there were hidden secrets behind this young man's warm smile.

Throughout the day, Wayan worked hard and talked of his appreciation for the Balinese traditions and shared how impressed he was with Mara's ability to translate them into her designs and fabrics. By the time they finished for the day, Putu wondered if his initial suspicions of Wayan were misplaced. Mara had worked hard and accomplished so much. Putu wanted nothing less than the best for her. Unsure of what the future held for his daughter and the enigmatic costume designer who had found his way into their lives, he planned to give them ample time alone so he could hopefully shake the feeling that there was more to their story than met the eye.

* * *

After the workday, Mara hurried back to the house to change into her swimsuit. When she saw her father deep in conversation with Wayan walking back to the house, a warm feeling fell over her that she finally had someone she could bring home to her family. Even with the ill-fitting clothes and fatigue from the work and the heat, she could feel that now-familiar pull between them as she watched him. Wayan wasn't classically handsome and sophisticated like Zayn. He had a more rugged look with an impeccable physique that was wildly attractive to her.

Mara thought about Annie and Sarah, and especially Ramone and Hans, wondering if they would all get along during their time in Ubud. Her last conversation with them was about Zayn. Mara chuckled. A lot had changed. Neither knew she had her first intimate experience before her quick exit from Milan although she had mentioned Wayan to Annie. She tried to remember if she had told Sarah she was working with Antonella Rossi's costume designer. Now, here he was working in the rice fields with her father. It all seemed surreal.

Wayan entered the house to see Mara had already changed into her swimsuit, but upon a closer look he saw the desire in her eyes and made haste to go change himself. On the way out, Wayan called out to Ni Luh. "I haven't forgotten the tempeh! I will finish it when we get back."

Ni Luh popped her head out of the kitchen and answered in good humor. "I will have it sliced and ready for you to work your magic."

Wayan grabbed Mara's hand and practically dragged her out of the house, down the path, until they were out of sight. Then he drew her to him for a kiss that, as it deepened, ignited a passion in them both. They began to move again, anxious to make their way to the waterfall deep in the jungle. The air was heavy with the scent of frangipani blossoms, and the sound of rushing water beckoned them as the setting sun cast a golden glow over the scene before them.

Wayan helped Mara climb up a rock formation close to the waterfall. Sitting on a smooth, moss-covered rock, they let the cool mist from the waterfall wash over them, soothing their tired bodies. In the hazy twilight, the electricity between Mara and Wayan was palpable, crackling with unspoken desires and longings. Wayan leaned Mara back, hungry to feel her bare skin against his. Their hearts seemed to be beating in time with the rhythm of the waterfall. But just as he was pulling down the straps of her swimsuit, a family arrived at the waterfall, their loud voices shattering the moment of intimacy. Disappointment and frustration caused them to quickly readjust, then Wayan stood up to dive off the rock into the pool below letting the cool water temper his desire.

Mara climbed down from the rocks, resigned to join Wayan in the water allowing her hands to clasp his under the water in silent solidarity. As the family frolicked in the water, oblivious to the emotional tension around them, Mara and Wayan exchanged a knowing look, a promise of future moments to come, the connection between them undeniable.

Holding hands on the walk back to the house, a lingering frustration hung in the air between them. Wayan finally spoke up. "Mara, I will not disrespect your parents in their house, but I am not sure how much longer I can keep my hands off you. Let me ask you something. I have not made a reservation at the retreat you are staying at in Ubud.

These are your friends. Are you sure you want me there?"

This time, it was Mara who pulled Wayan toward her for a sensuous kiss. Huskily, she said with a shy smile, "Yes, I want you there, Wayan. I want them to get to know you. About the reservation...I was wondering how you would feel about sharing a room with me?"

Wayan lifted Mara up and swirled her around. "Are you kidding? Of course I want to stay with you!" Then, as an afterthought, he added, "I will need to check in with

Antonella. I will have already missed a week of work."

Mara nodded. This didn't thrill her, but she understood and was happy Wayan was honest with her. "Bapek asked if we could take a load of rice that is sufficiently dried to the mill to be de-husked. Once we drop it off, there will be several hours before it is ready. We could find a place to do some work to catch up. I could bring my sketch book."

"Or we could find somewhere private?" Wayan gave her a mischievous smile.

It either didn't occur to them, or they chose not to think about it, that they were both falling behind in their work in Milan each day that passed.

* * *

Wayan loaded the burlap bags of husked rice onto the old pickup truck that was parked beyond the paths at the road. Mara made notes about the number of bags and weight of each. Behind the wheel driving toward the village mill, Mara felt the bond with Wayan growing. Not only were they getting to know each other, they were gaining an understanding of how the vibrancy of their common heritage had influenced both of them artistically.

Conversation flowed easily between them with Wayan's hand comfortably draped over the back of Mara's seat. The topic drifted toward the Ubud retreat and its rituals that were planned. Mara explained, "There will be the water purification blessing ritual and yoga meditation. That will be followed by an antitoxin massage for couples that ends with the couple's flower bath. This will all happen on Monday. The purpose is to cleanse any lingering pain or misgivings. It induces a great deal of soul searching to help the individual find the true path to happiness. Saturday will be filled with sightseeing and the traditional Kecak show and dinner. Sunday, you will meet my grandmother who is my inspiration and an expert weaver."

Wayan was focused on time alone with Mara, but the topic of weaving caught his attention. "I have done my share of weaving. I look forward to learning from your grandmother. You call her Nenek, as I do my own grandmother."

Mara loved her grandmother deeply. "Yes. When you meet her, you will first notice her eyes. They are the color of rich mahogany reflecting a depth of wisdom and kindness earned from years of cultural heritage and experience. Nenek moves gracefully yet with a sturdiness and determination that comes with working on the family farm most of her life. She moved to Ubud about five years ago to live with my aunt, my cousin Kadek's mother. My grandfather had passed and the family wanted an easier lifestyle for her. I'm not sure she agrees. It is Kadek who will pick us up in the morning to take me to the airport."

"I look forward to meeting all of them. Tell me about your friends who will be there."

Mara smiled. "The four of them are my closest friends. I have known Sarah and

Hans since I was eighteen when we were studying art in Australia under Kenneth Patrick. The course was taught in English. Hans was from Germany and didn't know any English. Neither did I. The school asked Sarah to come early to teach us enough English to get by, so we arrived in Byron Bay a month early. It gave us a time to bond and we have been close ever since. Hans has become a masterful glass artist working on the island of Murano. Sarah is a brilliant painter who specializes in animals that seem to come to life on her canvas."

Wayan listened intently as Mara talked of her multicultural friends. "I met Annie through Sarah here in Bali while she was on an international journey. The only way to explain Annie is that she is a force of nature with an insatiable thirst for history and architecture! Annie had been given this prayer necklace from Thailand during her journey. She selflessly gave it to Kadek, a complete stranger, during her wedding that Annie happened upon. Later, after Annie and I became so close, Kadek passed the necklace on to me. I then met Ramone through Annie. He was a well-known bullfighter in Spain. Annie had her suspicions about him that caused a rocky beginning between them. Once she began to fall in love with him, she was filled with fear each time he fought in the ring under such dangerous conditions. A series of events, including his father's murder, made Ramone rethink his profession and quit the circuit. He and his brother are now in the shipping business. I was part of Annie and Ramone's wedding to provide a Balinese blessing that would bring a spiritual element to the wedding that Annie was searching for. They are bringing their twin toddlers with them! They are adorable and most likely like their mother, up for a grand adventure."

Wayan admired Annie's selfless gift of the prayer necklace to an unknown bride. He empathized with Annie's initial doubts about Ramone, realizing Mara most likely had her share about him. And the transformation of Ramone from daring bullfighter to devoted family man in the shipping business made him reflect on the innate capacity for change and growth within us as individuals. Wayan was suddenly curious to meet this couple and their twins. He then asked, "What about Hans and Sarah? Are they married?"

"No, they love each other deeply and probably will marry someday, but Sarah is such a free spirit, a piece of paper is not what is most important to her. Honesty is what is highest on her list. They had a major hiccup early in their relationship that caused her to distrust Hans and avoid him for several years."

Wayan had unconsciously removed his hand from Mara's seat. The conversation had left him struggling within himself. He knew there was an important part of his complicated relationship with Antonella that he had not shared with Mara. It was a chapter in his life he would prefer to keep hidden from her, especially now that he was finally gaining her trust. Would revealing his past risk losing the bond that was growing between them?

The pinging of his phone startled Wayan out of the turmoil he was feeling. One ping after the other had Mara saying, "We obviously have phone service here in the village. Someone is certainly anxious to get in touch with you!" Mara's nagging suspicion that it was Antonella left her puzzled with an unwelcome sense of insecurity.

Wayan's mind was spinning even as the pinging wouldn't stop. Clearly, Antonella had been trying to reach him, flooding his phone with messages and calls, with increasing frustration and agitation after each missed attempt. He finally turned off his phone.

Mara pulled the truck up to the mill and turned off the engine. Looking at Wayan, she said, "I thought you said you told Antonella you were coming to Bali."

"I did. She is not used to my being away for any length of time." The hair bristled on Mara's arms, trying to sort through the meaning of that comment. The tension between them was intensified by the looming threat of Antonella's intrusion into their peaceful sanctuary. However, it was Wayan's brooding silence that threatened to unravel the delicate fabric of trust that had grown between them.

Wayan needed this time with Mara to solidify their relationship. Now Antonella was about to jeopardize it. He took a breath and said with a determined tone, "Let me help you with the bags and then I will call Antonella to find out what is so urgent."

Mara appreciated Wayan's sincerity and wanted to encourage him. "Wayan, it will be fine. I know you came here suddenly in the midst of a major project. If you have to go back to Milan, I understand. We will be at the airport tomorrow and can drop you there."

Wayan was miserable. He was certain if he gave in to Antonella's demands, she would always retain the upper hand over him. The question that he couldn't answer was, would revealing the truth about his past jeopardize his relationship with Mara, or would keeping it hidden only delay the inevitable confrontation with Antonella?

CHAPTER 29

Wayan solemnly returned to the rice mill to find Mara talking to the operator of the machine that was efficiently removing the husks from each perfectly white kernel of rice. The rice was pouring into a large barrel. He looked at Mara astounded. "This is incredible. The rice looks brilliant!"

Since Wayan had spoken in Balinese, the operator smiled and gave him a reply. "The grain goes into the machine. The removed rice is the fruit of the plant that provides us with sustenance to live. It is a blessing that we dearly appreciate."

Mara added, "When I seeded the other day, I used some of the rice still encased within the husks. Once it connects with the wet mud, it germinates and becomes the seedlings that give us the new grain." She looked closer at Wayan, trying to decipher what was beneath his interest in rice. " We won't be needed here for a while. There is a scenic ridge path nearby. Do you feel like going for a walk?" Wayan smiled at Mara and silently nodded.

As they walked along the path toward the Pura Gunung Lebah Temple, their surroundings became filled with lush greenery with sounds of the jungle and running streams. Wayan had not shared anything about his call to Antonella, but Mara seemed content to take his hand and enjoy the sights and sounds afforded on this unique walk along the Campuhan Ridge. They walked in silence with the occasional monkey scurrying across their path.

Meanwhile, Wayan's thoughts returned to the call with Antonella. In the end, he promised her he would return to Milan by Tuesday. That would give him the weekend in Ubud with Mara. Did Mara really need to know the sordid details of his past? He had never meant for it to get so tangled. Wasn't it enough that she knew who he was now? But, although he hated to admit it, Antonella still had him at her beck and call. She would not respond well to Mara disrupting that situation.

Walking hand in hand with Wayan amidst this peaceful environment gave Mara a much-desired sense of peace, as if daring her carefully guarded walls to come down. It was one of the many things she loved about Bali and she was deeply moved to have Wayan by her side. It was then, not knowing if he would be leaving before meeting her friends, that she finally asked softly, "Wayan, you haven't mentioned the call. Was there an emergency back in Milan?"

Wayan couldn't find the courage to disrupt the easy camaraderie that had formed between them. "No, I had forgotten to tell Antonella there was no phone service on the farm. She was just worried. I explained everything was fine and I would be back in Milan Tuesday. What are your plans for returning?"

"Sarah and Hans are leaving with me on Wednesday. I have to get back to work. Annie and Ramone decided to stay with the twins through the weekend in Canggu by the coast to prolong their visit." Mara thought about the timing and added, "Your fabric samples should probably already be at your studio. Once you make your selections, we will order you some sample yardage so you can experiment." The conversation that ensued became animated with enthusiasm regarding how the fabrics could be used in the upcoming *Aïda* costumes.

For now, Wayan was content to force any thoughts of Antonella from his mind. Even in the heat of the day, the path, a favorite for both locals and tourists, was getting crowded. Mara and Wayan both yearned for a moment of privacy, well aware it had been lacking the last few days, leaving so many things between them left unsaid. Mara saw a cove ahead which she recognized would be more secluded. They ventured off the path to a hidden alcove with an unspoken understanding between them, their hearts and souls entwined in a dance of anticipation and desire. As their lips touched, they surrendered to the fiery intensity of their feelings and wrapped themselves in each other's arms, the world melting away as they explored the magic of their connection.

Finally, Wayan pulled back with his face mere inches from Mara's. "We have never talked about that last night in Milan. You allowed me to be your first, Mara. That humbled me beyond words and a swell of feelings for you exploded from my heart. When I found that you were gone the following morning, I was hurt and confused. I knew I had to find you and to see if you felt the same way and why you ran away without talking to me."

Mara took a deep breath, recognizing her vulnerability. "Wayan, there was obviously chemistry between us from the first time we met. But it was the intensity and overwhelming passion I felt when you walked through my front door after the fundraiser that made me feel as though what was transpiring between us was inevitable. It scared me to think I could experience love and desire in a way I didn't think possible. I was no longer on steady ground. When you left me for Antonella, I felt unsure of how to process it all or where I stand when it comes to her. I think now I understand why trust is so important to Sarah. Trust doesn't just happen in one night. I still don't understand how deep your relationship with Antonella goes."

"Mara, my feelings for you are genuine and growing. I don't want Antonella, or anything else, to get in the way of that. From that morning after you had stayed up all night working on designs for my costumes, I knew we were destined to create something extraordinary together, both in our art and in our relationship." Wayan kissed her again. "We have these next few days in Bali together. Let's use them wisely, and like the rice you planted, let's try to plant those seeds of trust between us."

Wayan's words kindled a spark of hope in Mara, and she could hardly wait for the next part of the trip to begin. Unused to the ache of physical desire unfulfilled, Mara's mind and body were both anxious for the chance to lie next to Wayan again, with all the passion she had stored up over the last week finally able to be unleashed.

The barrels of rice were already loaded into the truck when Mara and Wayan returned to the mill ready to drive back to the farm, each of them filled with a sense of eager anticipation. Something had changed between them that day. Both Ni Luh and Putu noticed it when they returned to the house, giving one another a knowing smile.

Mara knew this might be the last time she would see her parents for a while and asked them again if they might come into town on Sunday. They sadly declined since they were in the middle of harvest, and Sunday was market day where the first of the rice barrels would be sold.

When Mara went to help Ni Luh in the kitchen, Wayan took the opportunity to spend a few private moments with Putu. "You have been most kind, sir, to allow me to stay in your home and understand a little more about Mara's upbringing. You have raised an amazing woman and I have the deepest respect for her. I feel she has stolen my heart. If the time should come, I would like to ask your permission to seek her hand. There is still much to resolve between us before such a thing happens, but with you so far away, I would like to know if you might find the idea acceptable."

Putu gave Wayan a scrutinizing look so intense that Wayan felt he was looking directly into his soul. "Take care with my daughter, young man. She is unskilled in the ways of love and might confuse feelings of the body with feelings of the heart. If you take one from her, be willing to take the other. Be true to her and to yourself. When you hold her in regard above all else, you will know you have my blessing."

Looking back into her father's stare, Wayan knew he could never ask for all of her until she knew all of him. A tear came to his eye in acknowledgement as he said, "Yes, sir." Despite the possibility of losing Mara, Wayan knew in his heart he had to confront his past and fear of rejection. At some point very soon, he would have to overcome his reluctance to fully open up to her.

Parked at the airport, there was some time before the flight arrived with Sarah and Hans. Mara could tell that Wayan was still brooding and she tentatively asked, "Wayan, something has been bothering you all morning. What is going on? Hopefully, by this time, you know you can share whatever it is. Maybe I can help in some way."

Since his conversation with her father, the fear of jeopardizing his growing connection with Mara was in an intense inner battle with his desire to share the demons that haunted him. How could she accept him if he couldn't accept himself? Putu had unknowingly pointed out the truth and that he'd have to share all of himself, including the parts he had kept hidden for so long. "It is complicated, Mara. Things are not as they seem. I have made some bad choices in the past."

Mara was taken aback and stunned. "What do you mean? Tell me, Wayan. What is not as it seems? What choices?"

Her reaction struck fear in Wayan. Driven by a mixture of panic and selflessness, Wayan said, "I think I should leave. None of this is fair to you. I never expected to fall so deeply for you. I can't make it worse by getting close to your friends. Let me go into the airport. I will find a flight back to Milan."

Mara's fiery determination and unwavering honesty confronted Wayan. She took both of his arms and practically shook him, forcing him to look at her. "You say you care about me. Is that a lie? If so, perhaps you should leave. I believed everything you told me. I came here to get away from the lies and the images that I have been swept up in, but I let you in and now I find you weren't open with me."

Her words cut through his excuses and forced him to confront the truth he had been trying to avoid. "No! My feelings for you are not a lie. You have shaken my world. Your talent and your beauty had already captured my heart. But to meet your family and see your love of your heritage, our heritage, Mara, has made me realize that there are things in my past that I regret. I don't want to complicate things for you. Let me go, Mara. It's best...for your sake."

Although Mara was alarmed by what he was saying, Wayan's misery was clear, making her even more determined to get to the bottom of this. "I have told you that I felt our coming together was inevitable, as if we both had to travel far from our own country to find each other. I care deeply about you too. I gave myself to you without hesitation. You can trust me, Wayan. No matter how sordid the situation is. If we have the possibility of a future together, you will have to trust me. I also have to be able to trust you. Whatever it is, there is no question it still haunts you. Let me help you work through it."

"All I can say is that I have a past with Antonella and owe a great deal to her. Our relationship is complex. It has not always been platonic." Wayan tensed, waiting for Mara's reaction.

The unexpected revelation sent waves of shock through Mara, threatening to unravel the fragile threads of trust that had formed between them. She ignored the roar of the incoming flight and asked, "And what is it now?"

Torn between not wanting to betray Antonella and wanting to assure Mara, Wayan replied. "Platonic but complicated. She depends on me in many ways. I am not sure how to fix it, but Mara, I know I want to be with you."

"So you are involved with both of us?" Mara tried to summon the wisdom of her ancestors, her Hindu faith so unique to Bali, as well as her inner strength. *Was the foundation she and Wayan were forming unable to withstand the past? Was it actually in the past?*

As he looked into Mara's tear-filled eyes, Wayan knew he had a choice to make. He could walk away and leave behind the woman who had shattered his walls and claimed his heart, or he could stay and fight for the love that was blossoming between them.

Mara's heart overflowed with compassion for the conflict that she clearly saw on Wayan's face and reached out. "If you decide to stay, you are here at the right place and the right time. The retreat and rituals ahead will help you bear the burdens you carry, and you can count on me to be there every step of the way to support you. In return, do not trifle with me, Wayan. Do we have an understanding?"

The sincerity of Wayan's sensual kiss gave Mara the answer she sought.

CHAPTER 30

Sarah and Hans had eagerly anticipated their trip to Bali. As they stepped off the plane and entered the airport, Sarah put her arm in Hans's. The flowers, the smells, the exotic décor...it was like nothing they had ever seen before. Sarah said to Hans, "I sense something powerful in this place, like we are supposed to be here. Can you feel it?"

Hans looked around them with all his senses on alert. "It is like there's a soft humming of energy surrounding us. It feels good, don't you think?"

Sarah saw Mara coming toward them from a distance. There was a man with her but it wasn't Zayn. He looked like a local. As Sarah looked closer, a different memory came to her of Mara at an airport with a man. When they had all met on the island of Mallorca for Annie and Ramone's wedding, Mara arrived with a ruggedly handsome man she had met in Australia, Jonathan, a marine biologist. When they came down the stairs of the plane, Sarah remembered thinking how mismatched they were. It turned out she was right. Jonathan saw Mara as a precious specimen.

Sarah had been skeptical of Mara as a couple with Zayn throughout the time they worked together on his father's yacht and new home in Spain. Although they seemed to get along well, they always seemed unsuited to Sarah, lost more in the idea of a relationship but with no clarity or intention. Perhaps it was her artist's eye that scrutinized the honest emotions in her subjects that allowed her to see their innermost truths that made her question their true feelings.

But this man beside Mara...Sarah tried to put her finger on it. There was something vulnerable about him. There was no denying his good looks. Then she looked back at Mara. That was where the difference was. It was Mara who was different, effortlessly embracing the spirit of the island and exuding a sense of peace and contentment, far away from her hectic Milan life. There was also a protectiveness.

Yes, that is what it was. *How intriguing.*

Sarah noted Mara's casual introduction, a total contradiction from the way her gaze lingered on him. "This is my friend, Wayan. I might have mentioned him when I told you about going to Lake Como to work with the opera singer, Antonella Rossi, and her costumier. He is also from Bali and when he found out I was coming, he decided to join me."

Sarah and Hans witnessed the unmistakable spark in Mara's eyes whenever she looked at Wayan. They both wanted to see Mara happy and fulfilled. Sarah commented with enthusiasm, "Hans and I saw Antonella's performance of *La Bohème* in Venice last year. She is incredible! Wayan, what is it like working for such a famous opera diva?"

Mara looked at Wayan and asked, "Wasn't that the opera that was just featured at the fundraiser? The pictures were amazing!"

Wayan nodded. He was used to the fascination of Antonella by her fans. "*La Bohème* was one of her favorites. She has such a large personality on stage, that once she leaves the public eye, she no longer has to play such a lofty role. I would be most pleased to join you here in Ubud if you would allow me. Your friend has made quite an impression on me." His smile toward Mara spoke volumes.

"Any friend of Mara's is a friend of ours." Sarah reached up to hug Wayan, then Hans shook his hand.

Recognizing the potential connection in them worth pursuing, Hans added, "We are happy to have you join us, Wayan."

Wayan's heart overflowed with gratitude and his hand went to his chest in symbolic thanks, not only for Mara who had refused to judge him and instead had offered him refuge, but also for her friends who did not hesitate for an instant to offer him friendship. The look he shared with Mara told her what she needed to know. He planned to stay and was ready to sort through his past to find his way to a future together.

Sarah tried to put her finger on it. She had hugged all three of Mara's men. *What was it?* Then it occurred to her. Jonathan was always distracted. His focus was everywhere but on Mara. Zayn was formal. It was more about what she wore, who she knew, and what car she drove than her true self that he was interested in. Wayan was different. He was right here and present, fully engaged. His touch of Mara's elbow, the look of tenderness exchanged between them...Sarah warmed to the prospect of them as a couple and set her mind to do whatever she could to ensure this man was on the right path, and that it led to her dear friend, Mara.

Sarah took a moment to pull Mara to the side before leaving the airport in case there might not be another possibility. "Mara, as you know I have remained friends with Zayn's sister, Elena. I was speaking to her about this trip, and she mentioned you have a large event planned for next weekend with Zayn. Are you two still together? How does Wayan fit into all of this?"

For a moment, Mara looked blank then remembered. "Ah, yes! It is the Grand Bal de Salut when all the young debutantes are introduced to society. Between Lucca and Sophia, they have made the dresses for many of these girls...many with my fabrics. Regarding Zayn, he and I had a long talk and feel the differences in our religions and backgrounds make a serious relationship impossible. We care about each other, so we have agreed to continue to attend these events that could potentially further my career."

Sarah prodded, "And Wayan? I see the blush on your cheeks!"

Mara confided, "Sarah, it has all happened so quickly! Our chemistry is like nothing I have ever experienced before. I left Milan suddenly, as you know, and once he found out he followed me here to Bali and even found my parents' farm! He's been here with my family since Tuesday. I am hoping you and Annie will have a chance to get to know him and uncover any reasons not to move forward with him. Sarah, I am falling for this man but our lives are complicated back in Milan."

Sarah put an arm of comfort around her friend. "You can count on us for support and whatever else you need. Hans and Ramone care deeply for you too. They will give their insight on Wayan. Let's just give our time here the chance to unfold as it is meant to."

* * *

Arriving at the intimate guest house, aptly named *Suksma*, Balinese for *gratitude*, Sarah and Hans were mesmerized by the beauty and tranquility of its traditional Balinese style. Mara led them to the inner courtyard of the complex where individual casitas with high thatch roofs each faced the courtyard. There was a lush pond filled with lotus and water lilies, with a carved temple-like water feature in the center. Mara explained, "You will find our architecture combines nature, tradition, and texture. That is what fascinated Annie about Bali, as an architect. Walls are minimal and the design is created by blending a mix of wood, rattan, bamboo, jute, and carved stone. There are always an abundance of flower gardens and ponds."

Looking around, Sarah gave Mara an understanding smile. "Over the years, I have seen many of your sketches and doodles. Now I know where many of them came from!" This got a chuckle of acknowledgement from Mara.

Wayan was slowly wandering throughout the courtyard, feeling a wave of inspiration wash over him. "It has been so long since I was in Bali. Now that we are here in Ubud, I remember what a perfect haven it is for artistic exploration." To Hans and Sarah, he added with a growing excitement about their acceptance of him. "Here we are, four artists surrounded by inspiration! Just look at the way the sunlight filters through the palm trees! Even everyday moments should be interesting."

Mara smiled at Wayan, pleased to see his earlier somber mood lightened. "You will find a fusion of past and present reflected in the enduring beauty and power of art that is created here. However, we have Annie and Ramone joining us soon, along with their pair of rambunctious twins!"

The host and hostess approached them with cool, wet cloths to clean their hands, then served each of them the traditional welcome snack of *pisang rai* and ginger tea. Hans looked at Mara for an explanation and she laughed. "They are ripe bananas with rice flour, grated coconut, and brown sugar. They are quite tasty. Use the bamboo shoot to eat them."

After the refreshments, the host welcomed them in halting English to confirm the count. Mara quietly explained that Wayan would be sharing her casita. That got a raised eyebrow from Sarah, but nothing was said. The pair of hosts led Hans and Sarah to their casita where they received two traditionally handmade sarongs and slippers. Their bags were already in the room waiting for them. Mara and Wayan were taken to their room directly across the inner flower garden and given the same sarongs and slippers. The entire scene before them provided a serene backdrop that seemed to effortlessly transport them to a realm of calm and rejuvenation.

Annie and Ramone were due in about an hour so the two couples agreed to freshen up and meet in the lobby to discuss plans to explore this magical land.

When the door to their shared casita closed behind them, Wayan realized there were words left unsaid regarding how entangled he was in the complicated relationship with Antonella. He watched Mara moving about the room suddenly shy, holding on to the fragile hope that their feelings could withstand any storm waiting back in Milan. He knew they were at a crossroads by his staying with her, sharing both the casita as well as her closest friends.

Mara felt it too. They were venturing into unfamiliar terrain, both physically and emotionally by his staying with her. She turned to Wayan as if searching for confirmation that their connection could stand the test of secrets yet to be revealed and vulnerabilities yet to be fully exposed.

The expression in Wayan's eyes assured Mara, and when he held his arms open to her it was completely natural for her to lean into them knowing she belonged there. They would find a way through this...they had to.

CHAPTER 31

The plane was making its approach to the Ubud airport. Annie and Ramone shared a smile of anticipation as they gently nudged Salvi and Cece to awaken them. Although Annie was born into a line of seafarers and adventurers where chasing horizons and discovering new lands was the norm, she possessed a gentle heart and a keen curiosity about the world around her. She was always eager to immerse herself in new cultures, learning languages and traditions with a voracious appetite for history. Her love of adventure was matched only by her devotion to her family, whom she adored with a fierce protectiveness.

Ramone, a former renowned Spanish matador, after years of facing down charging bulls, decided to hang up his cape and take a different path in life. Alongside his brother, he started a successful shipping company. With Annie by his side, the couple decided to combine their skills and passion for travel by expanding the company to include international routes. They were currently in the midst of a new route from Venice to the port of Piran in Slovenia.

With the birth of their twins, Annie and Ramone knew they wanted to instill in them the same sense of curiosity and wonder for the world while they were still young. Their trip to Bali was a chance to introduce the children to a new culture and way of life, as well as spend time with their close friends, Mara, Sarah, and Hans. Sarah and Mara had both been a great source of inspiration and knowledge about the world when Annie met them during her first international journey.

As they landed in Bali, the children looked wide-eyed out the window of the plane, the entire family was filled with excitement for the adventures that awaited them. With an au pair scheduled at the intimate resort to care for the children, Annie and Ramone were free to experience the magic of Bali with their friends, immerse themselves in its culture, learn about the spiritual traditions of the island, and also create lasting memories as a family.

* * *

Mara and Wayan joined Sarah and Hans at the bar in the lobby for a local Bintang beer. All four were now adorned with their gifted sarongs and slippers left for them in their rooms, ready to fit into the cultural norm. It was not long before Annie and Ramone arrived with the twins, creating a scene of joyous reunions and excited chaos. Although Annie understood Zayn would not be joining them on the trip, she was surprised to see Mara with someone else. He was introduced as Wayan, a costume designer Mara knew from Milan but looked like he was a native Balinese. *Was this who she'd run away from? How had he joined their group?* Annie's curiosity was on full alert!

However, before she could ask any questions, Annie's attention was drawn to the twins. The host had brought them a plate of banana snacks and juice. Despite their young age, they both interacted with the host with a sense of independence and curiosity, trying the snacks and eager to make new friends.

The host then introduced them to Aisha, the au pair assigned to look after the children. To Annie and Ramone's relief, she was a vibrant young woman with a flair for creativity, and she jumped right in when she saw Salvi and Cece were eager to explore. Her warm brown eyes glimmered with enthusiasm as she described all the fun activities she had planned for the children, from making a flower wall to learning a traditional Balinese dance!

Ramone scooped up his children with the love and affection he had for them clearly evident on his face. "You are both to mind your manners with Aisha and enjoy this beautiful new place." Both Hans and Wayan felt a tug at their heart to see this intimate exchange between Ramone and his children, something deeply rooted in a father's love that was missing in their lives.

Annie sat with Aisha going over the twins' schedule, handing her the bag with all their supplies, while Hans began to set up the double stroller provided by the host. Ramone set them in the stroller and Aisha enthusiastically took them to see where they would be making the flower wall. The twins were smiling and waved, saying a few words in their secret twin language. Annie and Ramone shared a sigh of relief that the warm hospitality of the staff, and particularly Aisha, would ensure their children were in good hands.

With Salvi and Cece off to play, the adults were finally able to take a breath. Mara suggested Annie and Ramone freshen up where they'd find the sarongs that were in the casita waiting for them. The host showed them to their room overlooking the enchanting courtyard. Annie stopped for a moment at the door to take it all in. Looking at all the lush greenery and hearing the soothing sounds of the water feature bubbling from the picturesque temple, she took a deep cleansing breath feeling a sense of peace wash over her.

Once she let all the tension from travel and the arrival settle, she turned to Ramone. "I have a feeling, my love, that surrounded by our friends and children, this is not just a vacation. Something tells me this could be a transformative journey for all of us. There is something magical here. And, by the way, who is Wayan and why is he here?"

* * *

Annie and Ramone rejoined their friends at the bar to savor the local brew while Mara explained what she had arranged for the time there in Ubud. They had been looking forward to this trip with Mara but her words reminded them of its importance to their friend. She described the weight of conflicting worlds where the glitzy façade of Milan's fashion industry contrasted with the authentic traditions of Bali.

Annie, with her compassionate nature, felt a surge of empathy for her friend. She admired Mara's courage in breaking free from her work and taking this journey home. Ramone knew Mara as a strong and independent woman but he had also seen a vulnerability in her over the years.

"I was not expecting Wayan to join us or even come to Bali." Mara reached over to take Wayan's hand. "However, now that he is here, joining this diverse group of friends, I ask you to accept him into our group."

As Mara introduced Wayan as a new addition to the group, Ramone could see the uncertainty in her eyes, wondering if her friends would accept this unexpected twist in their plans. Annie, always ready to embrace diversity and include a stranger as if they were a friend, smiled warmly at Wayan, acknowledging Mara's pleas for acceptance. Ramone silently nodded his head to total support.

Annie looked at Wayan with renewed interest. It was not like Mara to jump into anything so fast. She couldn't help but think there was more to their connection than design and mutual heritage. As one of her closest friends, she planned to get to the bottom of this new relationship and Wayan's intentions, even if it meant sticking her nose in where it might not be welcome. Putting her interest in Wayan aside for the moment, she turned back to Mara to listen.

Mara continued, "This afternoon, since it has been a travel day, I will give you an overview of Bali's rich culture and vibrant artistic community. As most of us are artists...Annie, I consider your architecture an art form, and Ramone, you too, created an art form as you held your frequent dance with the bulls. Each of your unique stories and experiences will add to the tapestry of this adventure. Dinner tonight will be next door at one of my favorite restaurants. Then, tomorrow we will get to know this city by scooter. Our itinerary will include the sacred Monkey Forest, an eleventh century underground temple, and one of the most beautiful waterfalls on the island where you can go for a swim if you would like."

Ramone asked, "I would like the children to see the Monkey Forest. Would it be possible for them to join us, then come back here with Aisha?"

Mara quickly answered, "Taking the car might be a challenge. Just be patient driving, with the traffic, and we can meet you there. The area is quite beautiful and there are over a thousand monkeys living in the sacred forest. They are safe, but they are wild animals. They can get a little aggressive, especially if they think you are carrying food. On the other hand, there are monkeys everywhere so the children will certainly be seeing them even during their planned activities."

Annie gave her attention to Ramone. "Perhaps it is best that we leave the children here, my love. Aisha has beautiful plans for their activities, and we will be here for them in the afternoon."

Wayan spoke up, "Whatever you decide, you can be sure I will help as needed." Ramone nodded at Wayan in appreciation.

Mara was grateful to Wayan for making an effort to fit into the group. She went on, "Tomorrow night is the traditional Legong dance outside the temple with its colorful costumes and highly expressive dance movements. The music should be captivating and the dance unusual and entertaining. Wayan, you should naturally enjoy the costumes." She caught his eye and smiled.

Wayan agreed. "I haven't seen it performed since my youth, and I am naturally excited about seeing the costumes they use here! I am looking forward to it."

Smiling with a secret as yet undisclosed, Mara added, "There might be a surprise in store." Everyone was curious but Mara moved on. "Then Sunday, we go make silver jewelry at my cousin Nuri's silver shop, then enjoy time with my family. Sunday afternoon, we move over to the retreat where we will experience multiple restorative rituals. Is everyone ready to get this journey started?" Everyone enthusiastically said "yes" and toasted with their beer!

Mara led the group into the tropical garden under the shade of the towering palm trees, eager to share the spiritual essence of Bali, motioning Wayan closer. "This hotel mirrors the traditions and customs of our community. Families and close neighbors live a communal way of life, bound by shared responsibilities and a profound sense of belonging. The cluster of small houses where the various family members live always surrounds a central temple or shrine that holds a sacred aura specific to the family, reinforcing our belief in the deep connection between the physical and spiritual worlds. Wayan, was it like that in Buleleng?"

Wayan answered Mara's question to the group. "Yes, very similar. As children, we were taught about our culture filled with rituals, ceremonies, and customs that have been passed down through generations by our extended family who moved far beyond our parents and grandparents." Wayan thought for a moment, recognizing the significance. "It is those daily rituals that honor our ancestors, attract prosperity, and keep evil spirits at bay."

Mara ushered them closer to where the twins were following Aisha next to the flower wall gathering what looked like a treasure hunt for things to add to their baskets. "Each morning, we would wake and begin to gather a coconut leaf to hold vibrant color flowers and soft grass, creating a fragrant offering to the gods. This was not just a tradition, but a way of life...more of a reminder of how all things are interconnected and the importance of gratitude."

Aisha was showing Salvi and Cece how to place the flowers and grass on top of the coconut leaf and carry it carefully to the shrine where an area waited for their decoration. Both children were walking very carefully not to spill their precious gift. Once they placed their blessing, Cece ran back to the piles of florals with Salvi right behind her. She grabbed flowers and brought them to all of the adults making a special event of each gift. Not to be outdone, Salvi brought the coconut leaves. Mara nodded at Aisha who brought over a tray of fresh grass.

Wayan was the first to assemble his arrangement and place it on the shrine. "It has been so long since I have experienced this ritual that I had almost forgotten the overwhelming sense of gratitude that comes with it."

Annie was next. "When I was last in Bali, the thing that truly stayed with me was how happy the people are. Mara, I remember you telling me that it was their gratitude that, even in the hardest times, kept their spirits high." The rest of the adults each placed their individual blessing on the shrine and the twins clapped in gleeful approval.

Mara then said, "You have already learned much about Bali. It is not just a place. It is a way of life that weaves the threads of tradition, faith, and love. That is what I have been missing while away from here."

In that moment, Wayan gazed at Mara and thought he had never seen such beauty and inspiration, his pride for his home-land swelling, but especially for this woman. He walked toward her, his movements guided by an irresistible force, as if no one else was there. His eyes were only for her. Mara, feeling that familiar magnetic pull that she had felt since that first night at the gala, held out her arms and took Wayan into her embrace.

The fervent kiss that followed deepened with unspoken feelings and desire, leaving no doubt to the other couples that Mara and Wayan were far more than just friends. Annie, in particular, was taken aback by this sudden display of affection, shocked by the unexpected turn of events.

As Mara tried to compose herself in the midst of this unexpected moment, a whirlwind of emotions flooded her, not sure which unsettled her most. *Was it her friends witnessing her raw desire for someone they thought of as a stranger? Or the incomplete picture of Wayan's involvement with Antonella?* Aside from that, there was unquestionable joy at being able to share her mutual culture with Wayan on a deeper level.

CHAPTER 32

Annie normally had no problem sharing an opinion, but Mara's out-of-character public affection threw her into a stunned silence, her overprotective instincts kicking in as she realized the depth of Mara and Wayan's connection. Not wanting to say anything she might regret, Annie needed a few moments alone to collect her thoughts and excused herself to check on the twins.

Sarah, on the other hand, was trying to come to terms with this new dynamic within their close-knit group. To Mara, she said, "Maybe we should talk." The shy, worried look Mara gave Wayan made him immediately contrite that he had acted so impulsively.

While Sarah and Mara headed toward the lotus pond, Wayan's desolate demeanor made Hans and Ramone sympathetic to the spot he found himself in. Ramone suggested, "Why don't we go back to the lobby?"

Hans agreed. "Sounds like it's time for another beer."

Wayan nodded with a lowered head. "I apologize. That should have been left for private. I think this has all come as a sudden surprise to both of us." They sat down in an area surrounded by vibrant tapestries with a hint of burning incense. A plate with the typical blessing elements was on the table in front of them.

Hans pointed at it and smiled at Wayan. "Maybe this will lighten things up!" Once the beer had been delivered, he raised his glass. "I, for one, think it is great you two found each other and I"ll be rooting for you. But Wayan, you need to realize that Mara is our friend too. I have known her since we were both eighteen, starting art school in Australia. The two of us, along with Sarah, did everything together. We were by Mara's side when she painted her first design on a stretched piece of silk. She's family, Wayan. What affects her affects all of us."

Ramone agreed. "I didn't really know Mara until she arrived in Mallorca for Annie's and my wedding. I was struggling and going through a rough time. My father had recently been murdered and my brother was in a wheelchair. That's also when I met Hans and found out he had a past with Sarah and Mara. Hans and I had a chance to get close on that trip, but it was Mara's caring grace that gave me strength and she conducted a Balinese blessing at our wedding that will be in my heart forever."

Hans reflected on that time. "Yeah, that overnight hike through the Tramuntana Mountains up to the pilgrimage took everything we could muster. Strength, endurance, courage...all of it was needed to make it up the increasingly higher mountains to the finish line. But I will never forget that night. I was cramped up and could hardly walk, but this man here refused to give up on me. A bond was formed between us and that is how we feel about each other. It is an added bonus that the women are also close. Wayan, you have suddenly arrived on the scene and have taken all of us by surprise, that's all."

Wayan could sense that, although fiercely protective of Mara, they were giving him an opportunity to enter their inner circle. If he were to deserve that trust, he had to be as open as possible without compromising either Mara or Antonella. "There was something between Mara and me right from the beginning. Her delicate beauty belied a strength I saw in her.

Perhaps it was our both being so far removed from Bali that beckoned me, but I found myself wanting to protect those stars that shined brightly in her eyes and that innocence that could so easily become jaded in the industry we work in. I could tell the cutthroat nature of the fashion world and the image she was forced to portray had left her feeling drained and disillusioned. It was when she began sketching some of her authentic Balinese fabric designs for me that she lit up. Mara actually stayed up all night excitedly creating them and called me in the middle of the night expecting to leave a message about showing them to me the next morning. I answered the phone and her enthusiasm rekindled my own creative spirit. When I saw the actual designs, I was overwhelmed by her talent."

Hans interjected with a smile, "So you have been collaborating? It sounds like you were connecting on several levels. Finding someone who can share your artistry can be an intoxicating feeling."

"Exactly! I think the intensity of our feelings scared Mara and made her question whether they were also just an illusion. That is when she suddenly left without saying a word. When I found out, I couldn't function. I had to follow her to prove our connection was real. I left my work and Antonella in the middle of creating the costumes for her next opera. None of that mattered. I simply knew I had to remove any shadow of a doubt that what we felt was genuine. Our time on the farm with her parents in the peaceful surroundings was the perfect remedy to melt the barriers between us. It seemed as if a new chapter was beginning as she lowered her guard to allow whispers of hope echo through the rice fields."

Wayan could see the look of support in Ramone and Hans's eyes and appreciated it beyond words, causing him to add, "For several years, I have been so caught up with costumes, the operas, and Antonella that I have not had the chance to build any sincere friendships. I deeply respect your feelings for Mara's well-being and willingness to give me a chance. It would be my greatest wish that we become friends." Their nods and pats on Wayan's back gave him the answer he sought.

* * *

Annie saw Sarah and Mara heading toward the lotus pond. With hugs to Salvi and Cece, she left them enjoying a tea party with Aisha to join her friends and get to the bottom of what was going on with Mara. As she approached them, she heard Sarah saying, "Mara, you have us all gathered on this beautiful island of yours. The last time I saw you was at Fashion Week, and you were still with Zayn."

Annie saw the uncomfortable look on Mara's face and interjected with a side glance at Sarah, "Sweetheart, we knew you were struggling with Zayn's opulent lifestyle. When we spoke, you were planning to have a conversation with him to see if you might work things out. Did you have that conversation?"

Mara absentmindedly rubbed the tension in her neck, gazing at one of the perfect lotus blossoms reaching out from the pond, and took a deep breath. "It turns out Zayn was having the same reservations but mostly about our religious beliefs. We still care about each other, yet there has always been a piece missing. Basically, there has been no intimacy, and what I mean by that is not just physical but also emotional. We could never really share our innermost thoughts and dreams, or at least it didn't come naturally. Things are different with Wayan."

Sarah reminded Mara, "Aren't you going with Zayn to the event this weekend? I am still not seeing where Wayan fits into this picture."

Mara could see the love and concern for her in their questions and had to admit she would most likely be doing the same thing if the roles were reversed. "Although I care about Zayn, the challenges posed by our differing religious backgrounds and upbringings brought us to a difficult decision, one that I knew in my heart was necessary for my own happiness and personal growth moving forward. However, because Zayn is also a business partner and feels these functions that he takes me to can further my career, we have agreed to continue to go to these events together."

Annie tried to absorb what Mara was saying. "And Wayan? How does he feel about you continuing your relationship with your longtime boyfriend?"

Annie's words stung Mara, and she stared harder at the blossom for inspiration to formulate answers in her mind. "None of this was planned. It was sheer coincidence that Zayn's flight was disrupted and not able to arrive in time for the opera and gala to meet the star, Antonella Rossi. It was Zayn's idea for me to take Lucca in his place. Lucca insisted he make me the most beautiful dress for the occasion, and that is where I met Wayan with Antonella. That meeting led to an invitation to Antonella's home in Lake Como, and subsequently to working with Wayan on fabric designs for Antonella's upcoming opera! Crazy, right?"

Annie shook her head in amazement. "You girls know how I feel about coincidences."

Sarah and Mara both chuckled and said in unison, "THERE ARE NONE!"

Annie smiled. "Right. For that reason, I have to believe this was not just a chance encounter. What are the odds that you would meet someone in the Milan fashion industry from the same culture as you thousands of miles from home?"

Sarah nodded. "Probably about the same odds as Hans sailing in a regatta on the island of Mallorca and meeting Annie because he needed a replacement for an injured crew member. Then, Hans becoming a friend and getting an invitation to the wedding that I was able to attend after my Barcelona exhibition! I hadn't seen him, and we hadn't spoken for over two years."

Annie loved the concept of destiny and added, "And what about the whole drama surrounding Ramone's father, Salvador. He planned for Antonio to woo me into his plot of revenge against my father, and thankfully Ramone stepped in instead. Everything could have turned out differently and not in a good way."

Both Mara and Sarah remembered Ramone's role in saving Annie and her father, defying his own. Mara finally verbalized her budding feelings about Wayan. "Do you know that feeling when you meet someone for the first time and your eyes linger just a second or two longer than normal? That is how it was with Wayan from the night we met. Neither of us were expecting it. Whether the immediate connection that was fueled by our shared passion for our craft was the cause, the chemistry between us was undeniable. There was a magnetic force at work that was almost hypnotic, and I felt that it was inevitable that we should be together."

Sarah asked, "So you invited Wayan to join you on this trip and even meet your parents?"

Hesitating for a moment, Mara decided to share the reason she left Milan so abruptly. "The night before I left Milan, I attended a fundraiser with Zayn. Wayan was also there with Antonella. Zayn was captivated by the opera diva, which left time for Wayan and me to have a few private moments. With him, I felt a spark of something hard to describe. When he pulled me into the shadows, it was like for the first time in my life I felt truly alive, with the promise of a future I had yet to discover."

Taking a deep breath, Mara continued, "It turned out Zayn and Antonella were staying at the same hotel, so they arranged for the four of us to have a nightcap at the bar there. That is where Wayan slipped me a note that asked if he could follow me home. I wasn't able to read it until I got up to Zayn's suite since he was still trying to make it look like we were a couple. But I did read it and when Zayn got a cab for me, I saw Wayan standing in the shadows and subtly nod."

Mara could see the surprise in both Annie and Sarah but pressed on. "That night, I allowed myself to believe in a new-found sense of joy and possibility in my life. However, that was shattered when the following morning Wayan left me for an event with Antonella. I couldn't just stay there so I left for home earlier than planned. When Wayan found out, I can't imagine how he did it but he followed me to my parents' farm! He arrived only twenty-four hours after me and has been trying to show me the honor of his intentions. He was amazing on the farm. I am sorry our kiss was such a surprise."

Annie and Sarah shared a glance, understanding the enormity of this new relationship in Mara's life and were unified in their response. Annie said, "The shock is over and we are ready to embrace Wayan as one of our own as long as he is good to you, Mara."

Sarah added, "Why don't we get back to the men before they think we have whisked you away!"

CHAPTER 33

As dusk settled in and the group reunited in the main salon, the friends found themselves drawn together in their acceptance of Wayan, along with their mutual excitement and determination to make the most of their time in Bali. Dinner was served family style, consisting of an Indonesian sampler of delicacies such as chicken curry, Balinese vegetables, pork and chicken satay skewers, saffron eggs, sauteed coconut, tempeh, and corn fritters. Mara announced when everyone was seated and the twins were in their high chairs, "I ordered this assortment called the *Nasi Campur* so there should be something for everyone."

Salvi reached for an egg and gave it to his sister to try first. Cece tasted it tentatively at first, then quickly decided she liked it causing Salvi to get two for himself, much to everyone's amusement. The waiter brought them each a plastic bowl of rice and they both said *merci*, French for thank you, which sounded more like *messy*. When he glanced at Annie and Mara in confusion to understand if they were asking for something else and Annie explained, the waiter laughed and continued to bring plate after plate.

Mara was pleased to see that Wayan seemed to have bonded with Ramone and Hans. He was sharing stories about the silver pieces his father made to add to the intricate temple architecture in the Buleleng area as well as the vibrant traditional dances that his sisters loved and begged him to make their costumes. Both Ramone and Hans seemed eager to immerse themselves in a world far removed from their familiar surroundings. Bringing Wayan into the conversation, they eagerly discussed plans to visit ancient temples, witness traditional ceremonies, and engage with local artisans.

Meanwhile, the women were engrossed in a conversation of their own as Mara shared some of Bali's spiritual essence they might discover. Annie painted vivid images of her time in Bali, describing the lush landscapes, the vibrant culture, and the mystical energy that seemed to permeate through the island. She spoke with passion that was infectious, fueling Sarah's curiosity and igniting a desire to connect with the island's energy that she had felt ever since she stepped off the plane. Mara knew her friends well enough to understand they sought experiences that would nourish their minds and souls. After all, that was why she was here too.

Dinner was winding down and the sleepy twins crawled into their parents' laps immediately falling asleep, yet no one seemed overly eager to leave the table. Another round of tea was poured, and the friends began to discuss the upcoming retreat. Mara explained, "There will be opportunities to participate in a variety of sacred rituals and practice a unique form of meditational yoga. Most importantly, though, you will have a chance to engage in heartfelt conversations with local healers and spiritual guides who can offer you wisdom and guidance on your own inner journeys."

Sarah again felt that surge of energy that she perceived when they landed at the airport. "Does everyone feel the sense of purpose as to why we are here? This magical night marks the beginning of a profound adventure that can not only enrich our minds and souls but also forge deeper bonds of friendship." She encouraged them to take the hand of the person next to them on either side forming a circular bond. "This is a moment of unity. Wayan, that includes you. Let's make a silent vow to support and uplift one another in the days ahead to embrace the teachings of Bali with open hearts and minds."

There was not a dry eye at the table. Wayan squeezed Mara's hand, so deeply moved to have been accepted by her friends. They knew they were all travelers on this journey, mutually agreeing to approach each new experience with an open heart and an open mind, eager to learn what mysteries Balinese culture had to offer.

* * *

Each couple retired to their private sanctuary, closing the door behind them to allow the nurturing environment within to envelop them. Annie and Ramone lovingly set the twins down on their pallets with a cuddly stuffed animal next to each of them. Annie looked up at Ramone with love in her eyes. "I never imagined it was possible to love you any deeper but, my love, you are my soul. I now realize this new journey is not just about finding ourselves but also finding out about each other in ways we never imagined."

Ramone took Annie into his embrace. "*Querida*, I will forever be by your side wherever life's journey takes us. Here in Bali with our children, I am ready to learn. We are embarking on something that feels transformative and my deepest desire would be to create a Balinese younger sibling for Salvi and Cece."

Reaching up to kiss this man she adored, Annie smiled with a twinkle in her eye. "I would love nothing more, my love."

* * *

Hans closed the door to their room and solemnly took Sarah into his arms. "Sarah, speaking with Wayan earlier made me once again realize how fragile life can be. I cannot imagine what life would be like if I had not found you again on the island

190

of Mallorca. I loved you from the moment on that bus when I looked up at that shy, freckle-faced girl with the ponytail. All I wanted was to hold you and protect you to keep all the agony of your youth in the past. Look at you now. You are a beautiful, talented artist who has collectors clamoring for a Sarah Wilkinson original painting. I love you, Sarah, beyond words."

A single tear fell down Sarah's cheek. "It is heart-wrenching to think that if we had not had a second chance at love, we would have lived a half-life and not even realized it. Life can be fickle with one wrong turn. Remember what the minister said at Annie and Ramone's wedding? He said something like, 'Miracles do happen. Don't miss what is right in front of you.' The thought of not having you by my side every day for the rest of our lives is more frightening to me than becoming your wife and the mother of your children."

Stunned, his eyes moist with emotion, Hans reacted with a joy he could hardly contain. "You're ready to marry me, Sarah? You would make me the happiest man in the world!"

Sarah couldn't help the loving smile she gave him. "Let's say I'm willing to give this process here in Bali a chance to see if we get the positive affirmation to take such a big step." Hans already had Sarah's clothes off and tossed aside, with his quickly following, in order to get the two of them under the covers so he could fully show Sarah just how in love with her he was.

* * *

Mara and Wayan had been anticipating this time alone together ever since he arrived in Bali. Now that the door was closed behind them and they were finally alone, the enormity of their emotions took over. *What were they doing?* Suddenly, the bond they shared felt fresh and fragile.

Mara tried to express how she was feeling. "Wayan, I have to think our meeting was serendipitous, perhaps reminding us of this place that has shaped us with a deep sense of reverence

191

for life. Now that we are here, I feel a quiet sense of peace and belonging that eluded me in the fast-paced urban lives we left behind. It is not just a spiritual, or even physical, journey, but rather a homecoming."

Thoughtful, Wayan reflected, "Do you think it is possible that fate led us to each other in search of something deeper, more meaningful? What if what once defined our lives isn't enough? Is it possible this homeland of ours has beckoned us here to reconnect with our own inner selves in order to establish a strong and genuine foundation for a relationship between us?" Wayan took Mara into his arms and kissed her, awakening the desire in them both. "There is no rush. For now, let's cherish the shared experience of being together in this magical place."

Although more attracted to Wayan than ever, Mara was flooded with relief. "I remember after Kadek's wedding, my aunt told me something I forgot until just now."

"True love unfolds slowly and organically, like a delicate flower blooming under the soft caress of the tropical sun."

Suddenly, with the pressure of physical intimacy off the table, they both wanted to take things slowly and savor each moment. The journey toward spiritual awakening was more about cultivating a deep appreciation for each other and the shared experience they were about to embark on.

As they drifted off to sleep with Mara chastely nestled in Wayan's arms, he remembered Putu's words:

"Take care with my daughter, young man. She is unskilled in the ways of love and might confuse feelings of the body with feelings of the heart. If you take one from her, be willing to take the other. Be true to her and to yourself. When you hold her in regard above all else, you will know you have my blessing."

CHAPTER 34

Waking up next to Wayan, having met him so recently, was a new intimacy for Mara in spite of their one night of lovemaking. He sensed her movement in his sleep and adjusted to hold her closer. Tucked in his arms, Mara was filled with a sense of gratitude and contentment, knowing she had found a kindred spirit. She loved that he brought a fresh perspective and a deep appreciation for Bali's diverse culture to her friends. She also realized she would never have been able to share the deep connection to her roots with Zayn and now saw clearly that it mattered to her.

Wayan's eyes slowly opened and relished seeing the early morning version of Mara without any ornamentation or pretense. He had seen enough of that for a lifetime. In this whisper of light, he knew this woman next to him was the most beautiful he had ever seen and he cherished the idea of their having a life together. "Good morning."

Mara smiled in return. "Good morning to you. Are you ready for a day of exploration?"

"More than ready. I really enjoyed getting to know your friends last night. I think they will respond well to the underlying philosophy of our culture. I wonder, though, about the twins. It might all be a little much for them to take in."

"I have said that the best way I know how. In the end, it is Annie and Ramone's decision whether they come. Aisha is wonderful with them and they seem to love her already so that gives them a great backup plan." With a quick kiss on the cheek, Mara started to get up but Wayan coaxed her back.

"That is no kiss to start the day, my lady." The sensuous kiss Wayan gave her deepened when he felt her response, causing them to forget for a moment the pressing need for a shower and to get dressed for the day. However, a knock on the door had Mara scurrying to the bathroom with a motion to Wayan to see who was at the door.

With a smile he couldn't contain, Wayan put on the robe laid out and went to open the door. It was Ramone. "Hey, good morning. Annie and I wanted to let Mara know that the twins are remaining here today. Aisha has a full day planned for them. Just let her know we will be taking a scooter along with you and will see you at breakfast."

Wayan closed the door to their room as Mara emerged from the bathroom. She had been thinking about how she was going to begin the day and wanted to clear up something with Wayan first. "Wayan, I wanted to let you know that I plan to bring up Zayn and his religious culture as compared to ours here in Bali. I hope that won't bother you but I think it is important to share."

"Now that you mention Zayn, I have been meaning to ask you if he even knows about us. Since you went to his room after the fundraiser, I assumed you were still playing a role. That is why I waited. But every moment that went by and you didn't come out was torture that you might still be with him."

Deciding she should be honest, Mara said, "He doesn't know anything about us and I do have an event scheduled with him this weekend. You are still attending functions with Antonella, right? Our lives in Milan are a bit complicated right now."

Wayan nodded at the complexity of their situation. "Let's hope these few days give us some clarity about how to transition into our lives back in Milan." With her agreement, Wayan took Mara's hand to join the others and begin their journey.

* * *

The three couples gathered around the scooters. With Wayan and Mara leading the way, the group set out on their adventure, taking in the sights, sounds, and smells of the vibrant town. Mara's laughter set the adventurous tone as they rode the scooters through the bustling streets, while she shared tidbits of local lore, pointing out hidden gems along the way to the sacred Monkey Forest.

Once they arrived, Mara paused to the side of the entrance to give them a little background. "The influence of Hinduism has left an unmistakable mark on the island's art, architecture, and way of life. The majestic temples, vibrant ceremonies, and intricate dance performances were all derived from the deep-rooted Hindu culture. However, during the spice trade period, over fifteen centuries later, Islam brought a new layer of diversity to Bali. Most of Indonesia embraced Islam during this time but Bali held on to its predominantly Hindu beliefs. The coexistence of these two beliefs here in Bali has been infused with mutual respect. As a matter of fact, the basis of the unique Hindu religion that developed in Bali was built on an inclusive social foundation, with its people open to a diversity of beliefs and cultures. That is why, when I was seeing Zayn who is an Arab Muslim, I did not see the religious differences as a hindrance." Mara glanced at Wayan to see his reaction.

It was Wayan who added, "When our family moved to Capri after the earthquake in Buleleng, the outlook was much different. The people there did not understand our culture, and often my father would talk to me of *Menyama Braya*. He taught me it was a local wisdom typical of the Balinese people which promotes peace, unity, and harmony between people regardless of any differences in religion, race, or class. I never forgot that. For that reason, you will immediately feel a kinship with Balinese people who embrace each other equally. As a multicultural group yourselves, you are already several steps into this principle." Wayan's voice was filled with sincerity and kindness, touching the hearts of Mara and her friends. His words resonated with them, reminding each one of the importance of inclusivity and acceptance in a world often marked by division and prejudice.

Mara and Wayan could see the comprehension sink in on the others' faces. Sarah looked over at the entrance and asked, "So where do the monkeys fit in?"

Mara guided them through the entrance with the large stone statues. "The Monkey Forest here in Ubud has a significant place in history deeply entwined with Balinese culture. Beginning in the fourteenth century, this forest has been regarded as sacred. You will see temples intermingled with the ancient trees. It is said spiritual forces are maintained here with over one thousand mischievous macaque monkeys that live here and are considered sacred guardians in our folklore. They symbolically represent both protection and mischief, creating a unique connections between humans and wildlife."

Sarah thought about all the wild animals she had seen and painted in Tanzania and even the Barbary monkeys she had painted in Morocco. One of the monkeys ran past her and jumped onto Hans's shoulders. With a laugh, but gentle reminder, Mara warned. "This is not a zoo. You do not want to stare straight at them or they will think you are being aggressive. Hans, he will quickly tire of your shoulder. Right now, he is determining if you have anything he can grab from your pockets." Hans chuckled and shoved his hands in his pockets, causing the monkey to quickly lose interest and move on to climb to the top of a statue.

Sarah asked, "So we are somehow connected to the animals?"

Wayan smiled at Mara in support. She answered, "Think of it as connecting to the natural world. We call this Hindu doctrine *Tri Hata Karana,* or basically three ways to reach spiritual and physical well-being. It is all about living harmoniously with other humans, with the natural environment that includes both animals and plants, and the supreme God. You will learn more about this at the retreat."

They strolled through the forest, watched the mischievous monkeys, and studied the temples. Annie commented, "I never got here during my prior stay in Bali. Mara, this is really special. Thank you for sharing it with us!"

Ramone took picture after picture, loving all the monkeys and the scenery. Once they finished, Mara said, "Let's take the scooters up to a majestic waterfall I think you will love. We can get some refreshments there and take a swim if you'd like."

As Wayan got on the scooter for Mara to climb on behind him, he turned and whispered, "I am loving every minute! Thank you for allowing me to remember all we hold sacred."

Mara put her arms around his waist to hold on and squeezed. "Me too. I SO needed this! I'm happy you are here to share it."

Soon, they heard the sound of rushing water echoing through the lush surroundings. They took the scooters as close as they could, then walked the rest of the way toward the sound. Then, at the last turn of the path, there it was. The group stopped in their tracks in a state of awe and wonder at the towering cascade of water and natural beauty surrounding it. As they stood there, Mara explained, "In Balinese culture, water has a major significance as a symbol of purity and life itself since all living entities need it to survive. While we are at the retreat, you will be able to experience a water purification ceremony which I think you will find most transformative. The lesson here is to respect and cherish the precious resources of the earth."

Annie had made a call to Aisha and talked to the twins. When she rejoined the group, she laughed and said, "They are having so much fun! They are making puppets and plan to do a show for us this afternoon." Once they knew there was no rush, they enjoyed a beer and chicken satay followed by a refreshing swim at the bottom of the waterfall. Annie, relaxing to know her children were in good hands, poked Ramone in the ribs. "If I'm not mistaken, I remember you taking me to a really pretty waterfall!"

At the memory, Ramone swept Annie up into his arms and walked with her into the water, "Yes, *querida*. I remember."

Hans had climbed up the rocks to dive into the pool and Wayan went with him, leaving Sarah and Mara alone. Knowing they could speak in confidence after so many years of friendship, Sarah asked, "How did it go last night? You and Wayan seem really comfortable with each other."

Mara shared her relief. "Everything was moving so fast in Milan. We decided to slow things down and grow into the relationship. I think it is working. He is really special, don't you think?"

Sarah smiled at her friend. "Yes, he is. I liked him from the moment I saw you together at the airport! Hans and I are in a good place too. I haven't made any promises about the future, although I am hopeful the time here in Bali will give me the clarity and confidence to take a leap of faith and get married. I have to admit that I love the prospect of building a future with Hans filled with love, laughter, and adventure!"

"What? That would be amazing. I sincerely hope your experience in Bali will give you what you need to make such a big decision." Mara's support filled Sarah with gratitude for having such a caring and understanding friend by her side. They both knew that no matter what the future held, they would always be there for each other.

"For now, let's just keep it quiet." Then, with a mischievous smile, Sarah added, "I don't want Hans to get his hopes up too high!"

Mara shared stories of the significance of water in Balinese culture, of its cleansing and healing properties, and of its connection to the flow of life itself. While she spoke, they listened to the gentle rush of water and felt the cool mist on their skin. Finally, Mara said, "The last stop on today's adventure will culminate in a serene temple where we will participate in a traditional ceremony to embrace the concept of *Tri Hita Karana*. I will guide you through the rituals and prayers that honor the Balinese tradition of spirituality and devotion."

When they entered the eleventh century temple built into the side of a cliff, Mara reminded Annie and Sarah to cover their shoulders. Inside the temple, together they explored hidden passageways and secret chambers. Mara's passion for her craft was evident as she pointed out the intricate patterns and ornamentation adorning the temple walls, explaining the significance of each motif. Wayan, in turn, admired Mara's talent and dedication as he discovered the subtle influences of her fabrics' designs in the temple's architecture.

Annie, always fascinated with anything to do with history or architecture, got close to Mara and said, "You know this is my favorite! I could spend days in these historical buildings." Mara smiled as they ventured deeper into the temple knowing their journey was just beginning.

CHAPTER 35

After an unforgettable day, the friends maneuvered their scooters back to the guest house and arrived to the rhythmic beats of gamelan music softly echoing through the air. When Salvi and Cece saw them, they gleefully squealed with laughter and ran to meet Annie and Ramone, grabbing their parents' hands to come see what they had made. Aisha explained how they had crafted colorful puppets decorated with textured fabrics, buttons, and sparkling beads inspired by the traditional Balinese characters that would be featured later in the dinner performance of the Legong dance.

The children proudly showed off their puppets, capturing the hearts of each of the adults. It was Aisha who suggested they display their newfound artistic skills as the twins, with the help of Aisha and one of the workers, managed to use their tiny hands to act out a playful puppet show. Their delighted audience cheered and clapped, touched by the joy and innocence of the twins' performance.

Wayan tried to ignore the continuous vibration of the phone in his pocket which was threatening to intrude upon this idyllic setting. His gaze shifted from the children to Mara who was enjoying every aspect of the show. He reached for her hand and squeezed it affectionately. Finally, to his relief, the vibrating stopped and Wayan was able to give his full attention back to the puppets, smiling with the knowledge that the twins had just made their first costumes. *Wasn't that how he had started?* He remembered working with his grandmother for hours making puppets to be used in the children's version of the ceremonial dances.

Unwelcome thoughts of Antonella drifted back into his consciousness, bringing with them a harsh dose of reality. Why did he have a nagging feeling that all he had worked for professionally was nothing more than a mirage, a fleeting illusion that could vanish into thin air at any moment? Being around Mara, her friends, and these beautiful children, with their easy smiles and relaxed manner, only served to highlight the contrast to living in Antonella's shadow subject to her whims, needs, and demands.

Wayan knew in his heart he wanted a future with Mara but life was complicated for them outside this bubble of common culture. *Would they both consider leaving all they had built behind to seek a simpler life here in Bali?* He was certain that choice could never really be an option. They both loved what they did and were good at it. The opportunities in Milan were unequaled. If only there was some guiding light that could lead them to a brighter future that combined both ambition and authenticity.

After the puppet show ended, Aisha took Cece and Salvi to get some coconut ice cream as a reward for putting on such a wonderful act. This gave the three couples time to freshen up for dinner. Wayan agreed to shower quickly and meet Ramone and Hans for a beer while the girls got ready. Inside their room, Wayan gave Mara a lingering kiss before heading to the shower, leaving Mara with a few moments to collect her thoughts. It was then she heard the muted vibration of Wayan's phone. The light had flickered on, indicating a message was waiting. It was not her intention to pry, but she was unable to resist the temptation to glance at the message. Not surprisingly, it was from Antonella.

Wayan, sono disperato e ho bisogno di te! The producer from La Bohème is here in Lake Como and I am certain he recognized me. I can't go out anywhere for risk of being seen. I told you of my interest in the girl yet you follow her to the ends of the world. You are breaking me, tesoro mío. Come home to me.

Stunned to read that Antonella desperately needed Wayan, Mara was also confused by her "interest in the girl." *Was Antonella referring to her? What did that mean?* Mara heard Wayan finishing in the restroom, doubts swirling in her mind about the nature of his relationship with Antonella. She put the phone back on the table, her mind racing with what to do. The dinner show would be starting soon and she still needed to get ready. She hated the idea of ruining the evening for everyone and understood it would be inevitable if she confronted Wayan now. Mara took a deep breath. She had invaded Wayan's privacy by reading the message. Perhaps her best course of action was to hold her personal struggles at bay, see how he handled the message, and if he brought it up.

Wayan came out with a flirtatious smile. "The shower would have been nicer if you were in there with me!"

Mara blushed at the comment, still flustered by the message, and grabbed her clothes, saying, "I will hurry." She then quickly closed the door behind her.

Strange...Wayan thought he detected a coolness that wasn't there before his shower. He was about to join the men and thought to pick up his phone. When it lit up, he saw the stream of messages from Antonella, each sounding more desperate than the last. For a moment, he wondered whether Mara had seen one of the messages and that was the source of the change in her demeanor. In the end, he decided Antonella should not interfere with their evening and turned the phone off, setting it back on the table before finding Ramone and Hans at the bar.

* * *

Ramone was in the lobby with the twins who were still proudly clutching their treasured puppets when Wayan joined him. Hans was close behind. To Wayan's surprise and delight, Cece toddled over with her puppet attempting to climb up into his lap. Salvi, not to be outdone, scrambled up into Hans's lap. Hans grinned at the sight, thoughts of a family with Sarah on his mind. He then asked Wayan, "Can you tell us a little about the dance we are going to see tonight? Was it performed in your part of Bali?"

Wayan warmed to the topic, pointing at Cece's puppet. "My grandmother taught me to make puppets at an early age. It was like magic to see the inanimate scraps of fabric with a few accessories come to life as the puppet developed its own personality."

He asked Cece for her puppet and began telling the story through the puppet, much to the twins' wonder. "The story of the Legong dance dates back to ancient times when the village was being threatened by a neighboring kingdom. The village elders decided to call upon the spirits to protect their people and bring prosperity to the land."

Wayan swooped the hand puppet over to pluck a flower and reached it up toward the sky. "A group of talented young girls was chosen to channel the divine energy of the *Dewi Sri*, the goddess of fertility and prosperity. These girls were trained rigorously by the village's most skilled dancers and musicians, perfecting their talent and embodying the grace and elegance of *Dewi Sri* herself. The Legong dance was performed as a tribute to the goddess, a symbolic representation of the bountiful harvests and prosperity that she bestowed upon the village."

Mara quietly joined the group, along with Annie and Sarah. When Wayan looked over at her with a silent question of whether to proceed, she glanced at the awestruck twins watching the puppet's performance and nodded her approval.

"My sisters were selected to learn the specific movements and gestures that have become essential in the ceremonial dance that is filled with intricate footwork and hand gestures that each have a specific meaning. Think of the Legong dance as a way for the dancers to use their bodies to weave a story based on traditional Balinese stories and myths. It is believed to bring blessings and good fortune to all who witness it so we are in for a big treat to see the dance performed!"

Salvi and Cece both ran over to Annie, in unison asking, "Can we go? Please!" Annie looked at Mara, still amazed by Wayan's rendition about the Legong dance.

"If your parents say yes and you are very quiet during the dance, of course you may go." Mara's smile belied the hurt and confusion simmering beneath her composed exterior.

The group arrived at the outdoor venue of the age-old temple where the ruins were bathed in warm lighting, creating a stage at the far end with dining tables arranged, each positioned to get an intimate view of the dance. Each table's centerpiece was a palm leaf platter filled with flowers and fruit creating a blessing bowl like the children had made the day before. They were delighted and Annie could tell that having made their own blessing bowls, and then the puppets, the projects had affected them. Aisha joined them to help occupy the twins, but they were completely entranced by the entire scene. Annie's loving glance at Ramone told him how happy she was to be sharing this experience with their children.

Although Mara was smiling and engaging with her friends, Wayan could sense the subtle differences that told him something was amiss. When his gaze met hers across the dinner table, he noticed the shadow of worry in her eyes and the tension that lingered in the air between them.

As the Legong dancers twirled and leaped in a mesmerizing display of artistry and grace, Mara found herself caught up in her own dance of emotions and obligations. Fear and uncertainty gnawed at her, clouding her judgment and stirring up a storm of conflicting thoughts and feelings. She was torn. Should she confront Wayan about the message from Antonella and risk shattering the evening with her friends, or should she bury her doubts and maintain the illusion that all was fine between them. By the end of the evening, however, what she did understand was that if she and Wayan were to have a chance at a future together, there needed to be honesty and transparency in her budding relationship, no matter how uncomfortable or daunting it might seem.

CHAPTER 36

After the show, everyone was tired and ready to retire for the evening, knowing they had a full day ahead of them with Mara's family. As Mara and Wayan walked back to their room, it was as though a shadow had fallen between them, a distance Wayan couldn't quite pinpoint but he felt keenly. Not wanting this shift that had been simmering all evening to follow them into their room, he asked Mara if they could walk a little.

Following the path toward the lotus pond, Wayan mustered the courage to address what was bothering her head on. "Mara, I can't help but feel there's something between us that is not being discussed." His voice was soft but there seemed to be an urgency to it.

Mara's gaze flickered toward him. "What do you mean, Wayan?"

"I mean the tension that's been hanging between us ever since I got out of the shower earlier. I am getting to know you pretty well, Mara, and I can sense it." Wayan paused, steeling himself for her response. "Have you read the messages from Antonella?"

Mara's eyes widened slightly, a pang of guilt coursing through them before she looked away. "I...I might have seen one or two," she admitted her voice barely above a whisper. "I didn't mean to pry, but the phone lit up while you were in the shower and I picked it up, seeing the stream of texts."

A knot formed in the pit of Wayan's stomach, knowing the desperation and threats in those messages trying to get him to come back "home" to Lake Como. His eyes searched Mara's, seeking a glimmer of understanding, a spark of hope that they could maneuver a path strewn with obstacles and challenges that tested their resilience.

"Mara, I never meant for you to question my intentions. After meeting you, I could never go 'home' to Antonella. My definition of the word 'home' goes far beyond physical places or professional obligations. With you I have found a sense of belonging and contentment that I have struggled to find elsewhere. You have become my anchor, my sanctuary, my home. Antonella has her demons, and I have allowed myself to fall into her web of lies. I can't do it any longer. Being here in Bali with you and reconnecting with my youth has meant everything to me." Taking both her hands in his and lifting one to his lips to kiss it, he added with evidence of his sincerity all over his face, "I love you, Mara, with all my heart and soul."

Mara looked deep into Wayan's eyes searching for the authenticity she desired, knowing they lived in a world that often blurred the lines between reality and illusion. "I am not sure how we should maneuver the dynamics of our lives in Milan but, from the time we met, I felt like our lives were somehow connected and our destinies intertwined. I am in love with you too, Wayan."

Wayan stood up and pulled Mara into his embrace. "Then it is time. Let me show you the full passion of my love for you that will leave no doubt in your mind about my feelings for anyone else but you."

Throughout the night, Mara and Wayan surrendered to the passion and intoxicating allure of newfound love, their bodies entwined in a primal embrace. Although the complexity of their lives in Milan threatened to disrupt the happiness growing between them as a couple, naked in each other's arms, they knew that whatever lay ahead, they would face it together...united not just by love, but by the courage to face their demons head-on. What they had found here in the serene landscape of Bali was not just a physical return to their origins but also a metaphorical quest for inner truth and a genuine connection.

* * *

Annie and Sarah glanced at each other with a knowing smile when Mara arrived at breakfast with a glow about her and Wayan close by her side. Sarah whispered, "Someone had a good night!"

Mara shot them both an innocent look that basically said, "I have no idea what you mean!" What followed was easy laughter and good spirits as anticipation for the day ahead with Mara's family filled the room.

Hans had his arm casually wrapped around Sarah when he announced to the group that one of Sarah's earlier paintings had re-sold for an enormous sum of money. "Do you remember the *Birds of Prey* collection Sarah painted in Africa? She exhibited them in Barcelona right before Annie and Ramone's wedding in Mallorca." Annie and Mara nodded, curious, and Hans continued. "Well, the Peregrine Fund bought the entire collection and have just re-sold one of them to a collector!"

Annie asked, "I remember seeing the photos from the exhibition. They were magnificent! Which one sold?"

Sarah smiled at the genuine interest from her friends. "It was the secretary bird. He was so strange looking and definitely my favorite! I would love to know who it was that bought it but the article said the purchaser's name was withheld as private."

Mara was truly excited for her friend. "That is amazing news, and hopefully it raised funds for such a lofty cause. Perhaps you will find something to paint today?" To the group, she said, "Today you will meet my grandmother, Nenek. Also, my cousins and aunt will be there. But, first, I thought I would take you by the batik studio where I got my start. Then, later in the afternoon, we will make our way to *Mundur Kesehatan*, the retreat where we will stay for two nights. At six-thirty, we have our first meditational yoga class!"

Annie had packed up the twins and their small suitcases. To Mara, she said, "I know your aunt and grandmother graciously offered to watch Salvi and Cece, but they have grown quite attached to Aisha in this short time."

Both twins fervently agreed, calling out her name in true toddler fashion, "Eesha!"

Ramone explained further, "We decided to hire Aisha to accompany us for the rest of the week. Her brother offered to pick her up in Canggu where we plan to fly out this weekend."

Then Annie said with an undeniable smirk on her face, "That will also allow us to have a separate room since Aisha can stay with the children." Ramone, with a wink at Wayan, pulled Annie close, leaving her friends with no doubt as to why they wanted a private room!

Wayan took Mara's hand and gave it a light squeeze, touched that Mara's friends were becoming his own and seemed to support their relationship. He took a deep appreciative breath. Maybe true authenticity lies in these unique moments of love and connection among friends and family.

They loaded up Kadek's car and Ramone's rental, then Mara took the lead driving them to the batik factory where Mara first discovered her ability to translate her sketches to wearable designs. It was a nostalgic moment for her, revisiting the place where her creative journey began. Looking around at the meager décor and humble building, the contrast to her fast-paced, elegant studio in Milan was astounding. There was a new manager who Mara didn't know, but she quickly told him of being a past employee and asked if she could show her friends around the factory. He then seemed to recognize her, beckoning the group to follow him to his office. On the wall, there was a picture of Mara. The man explained how proud they were of her and how her success story inspired others who worked there. Tears sprang to Mara's eyes in disbelief.

The manager offered to give the tour himself with Mara and Wayan sharing in the translation. However, before they started, he showed Aisha and the twins to an outdoor terrace where brightly colored small bags of rice were part of a game to throw into a wooden box with a hole cut out. They all laughed as Salvi and Cece "negotiated" who was going to get which color!

The work space was brimming with memories and inspiration for Mara. Sarah and Hans were also particularly moved since they had met Mara in Australia right after she worked in this very place although they'd never seen it in person. There were primitive wooden shelves lining the walls, filled with hundreds of carved blocks that had been used over the years. Wayan walked slowly by, picking up one after the other trying to visualize a young Mara seeing her art come to life on the fabric.

The manager held up his finger to wait, then went to retrieve another block. When he brought it back, Mara could hardly believe her eyes. It was the block that had been used on the dress that Allison Ford had sold in the catalog for years! With his own eyes glistening, he held it out with both hands offering it to Mara to keep. Touched beyond words, Mara hugged the stranger who now held a place in her heart.

CHAPTER 37

The visit to the batik factory had touched something in all of them. Theirs was a group that was not lacking in material comforts. They all had the resources to pursue their dreams. Perhaps that is what made the time there such an eye-opening experience. Annie was supported by her grandfather, Don Marco. Sarah received El Amir's patronage beginning when she was a young girl. What made Mara and Wayan's situation different was that their patrons were also personal relationships.

The next part of the journey would be a visit to Mara's cousin Nuri's silver studio, where gleaming metals came to life in the form of intricate jewelry. Wayan remembered watching his father for hours as he pumped the torch, softening the silver to make it pliable to his tools. Memories of his father came flooding back. Sadly, not all of them were good. He had not seen his father since he left Capri. His mother had visited him in Milan once, but his father had never bothered.

Hans was another who was fascinated to see this art form remarkably similar to his own glass-blowing, yet so different in its heartier nature. With glass, any wrong manipulation carried the threat of the piece breaking. While metal, or silver in this case, was stronger, it could be manipulated into the most delicate designs. Hans could not wait to try it.

When they arrived at what looked more like a shack than a studio, Mara's cousin, Kadek, was there to greet them. Salvi saw the outdoor swing set and excitedly pulled Aisha and his twin over to it. Kadek smiled at Annie and went to embrace her, thanking her again for the kindness she showed at her wedding and pointing at the necklace Mara wore around her neck.

After Mara made the introductions, Kadek glanced between Mara and Wayan speculating about how their relationship was going. She got her answer when Wayan took Mara's hand with an intimate nudge.

Kadek showed them inside where a wall was covered in exquisite silver jewelry pieces. "Like some of you, my husband is an artisan who is passionate about his craft. This will be a chance for you to try your hand at making a ring or bracelet."

Hans and Wayan eagerly watched Nuri pump a foot pedal that fired the torch that they would use. Sarah commented, "Hans, do you remember the glass maker in Australia when you were first learning? There was a girl working there at a table with a small torch and a cup filled with multicolor glass sticks that looked like straws. She was making the small, intricate pieces that would make a scene inside a paperweight."

Nuri explained in halting English. "You will find several bowls with small pieces like you are talking about." He showed them a bowl with different small-sized silver leaves, another with an assortment of round beads, along with a variety of other small pieces. The girls moved over to the side of the table in front of the bowls. Ramone wasn't sure where he fit in. Kadek was quickly at his side pointing to a chair at the table and brought over a gorgeous men's hammered silver ring. He loved it so she placed a bench pin with a clamp and a hammer on the table in front of him.

Annie decided to make a bracelet. Sarah stole a meaningful look at Hans and decided on a ring. Mara also planned to make a bracelet.

Nuri nodded at the selections. "Now we will pair up. Wayan, you will work on the base of Mara's bracelet while she makes her design." Mara had already drawn two lines on the paper in front of her to use as a pattern while she made her design. "Then the design will be transferred piece by piece to the base."

"Hans, you will do the same for Sarah's ring. Annie and Ramone, I will work with you both."

Mara and Sarah creatively worked on their designs and helped give ideas to Annie. The next hour and a half was filled with friendship and creativity. The air was electric with collaboration and inspiration, and the time passed quickly. Even Ramone was enjoying creating a ring that he would wear proudly. Hans was putting the final touches on Sarah's ring...buffing, rinsing, and polishing. Then, instead of handing it to Sarah, grinned at her and put it in his pocket.

Sarah pouted. "Can I at least see it?"

Nonchalantly, Hans answered, "It's not time yet. Soon perhaps." In that moment, they all knew Hans and Sarah had just made her wedding ring together.

Aisha was enjoying a tea party with the twins outside, but everyone was getting hungry, and it was time for Salvi and Cece to take a nap. Nuri closed his studio and they all left to go to Kadek's family home where her mother, Mara's aunt, and their grandmother lived with a large extended family.

Kadek and Mara, obviously close cousins, led the way into the family compound with tiny houses surrounding a lotus pond with a center shrine. The pond was filled with beautiful blossoms and colorful fish which had the twins fascinated. There was a long table set up outdoors in the courtyard, large enough to seat twenty or more. They could tell the gathering had already begun since the air was filled with the aromas of Balinese spices and the chatter of cousins sharing stories and laughter.

Kadek introduced her aunt as Bibi and grandmother, Nenek. Mara's group was greeted like old friends. They were given aromatic leis to wear around their neck with colorful local flowers, and the twins were each given a crown of flowers. Aisha was given a special matching crown and said to the children, "Ah, look at us! We are very important to have such crowns. Let's eat lunch so I can tell you one of my favorite stories!"

Both twins yelling "YAY!" had Annie and Ramone wondering how they could take Aisha home with them! Annie remembered Kadek and Nuri's wedding in the garden outside the guest house where she stayed during her journey. Then, as now, she marveled at how these people with such simple lives always seemed so happy.

The table, surrounded by lush greenery and the sounds of nature, was adorned with traditional dishes bursting with rich flavors and culinary delight, a testament to the love and kinship that bound this family together yet were so open to sharing with Mara's friends. Bibi and Nenek sat at the head of the table co-hosting this weekly gathering, encouraging all to not only savor the exquisite cuisine but also the bonds of friendship and family that made moments like these truly unforgettable.

There were other men at the table, but none with Bibi and Nenek. Wayan leaned over to Mara, "Where are their husbands?"

Mara turned to him with a soft voice and answered, "My uncle and grandfather were on the coast for business when an earthquake struck in the Indian Ocean. The seaside communities never expected a tsunami. It arrived within minutes at the incredible speed of 500mph!. There were communities that were totally wiped out. They were among the casualties."

Wayan touched Mara's arm. "I am so sorry. There was a tsunami with the earthquake that destroyed our home, but it did not hit Buleleng." Remembering the Balinese Hindu beliefs his family adhered to, Wayan reflected, "And death is not viewed as an end but as a transition. Since the soul is immortal, our bodies are only a temporary vessel."

Annie overheard their conversation and asked, "Can the soul or spirit be reborn as something else?"

Mara answered, "With a proper cremation ceremony, the soul can be released from its earthbound body and journey on to its next life. It is for that reason that we believe in an interconnectedness between all living things. My uncle and grandfather are here with us in spirit. So the answer is yes."

The table was quiet for a moment. Annie was lost in thought contemplating the enormity of this concept when Aisha came over and tapped her on the shoulder. She had two sleepy toddlers rubbing their eyes, one in each arm. Bibi, watching the scene, signaled Mara. Nodding in return, Mara spoke to Aisha in Balinese suggesting they retire to a small room in their house. She then said to Annie, "We have the perfect place for a nap!" She led the way with Annie following to ensure the twins were properly tucked in. Bibi met them in the small room, insisting she watch the children so Aisha could have some lunch and a little break. Annie quickly agreed and, with a loving stroke on the forehead of each of her children, left them in Bibi's care.

Walking back to the table with Mara, Annie mentioned, "You and Wayan seem much more relaxed with each other today."

Mara thought for a moment. "We know our lives are complicated back in Milan so we are doing something you always talk about, Annie. We are living in the moment without obsessing over the past or future for now. That will all have to be dealt with soon enough. For now, Wayan turned off his phone, and we plan to enjoy the rest of the time we have here with all of you in Bali."

Annie looked at her friend who she considered family. "I want to help any way I can. You mean the world to me and I see the happiness on your face when you are around Wayan. Just remember, Sarah and I can be quite resourceful."

Mara chuckled. "I would say *resourceful* is an understatement. Let's see how things progress at the retreat to see if we find any further clarity. Trust me, I know I can count on you both."

CHAPTER 38

The twins were still sleeping when lunch was complete and the cousins had said their goodbyes. Mara took Wayan's hand. "Let me properly introduce you to Nenek. My grandmother does not speak English and follows many of the old traditions."

To Nenek, Mara said, "This is my friend, Wayan, who works in Italy where I do. He sews beautiful costumes like the ones we use in our ceremonies. He was born here in Bali, in Buleleng."

Wayan nodded his head in a respectful gesture. "*Om Swastiastu*, Nenek. It is an honor to meet you. Mara told me you are an expert weaver and that she learned colors from you through flowers."

Nenek studied this man with her granddaughter, curious about their relationship. "Have you ever tried your hand at weaving, my son?"

Wayan shook his head. "I can handle using a machine for sewing, but I fear weaving is becoming a lost art. Would you show me? I would love to see how it is done."

Bibi and Kadek joined Nenek and Wayan, asking Mara and the others to follow. They went to a covered area on the far side of the lotus pond. Bibi began, "Mara shared that some of you are artists, so we thought you might enjoy a little project." Three of the cousins were seated with tuffs of undyed wool with buckets of water heating in front of them. There were stone bowls with a variety of natural vegetables and flowers ready to begin the natural dye process. Sarah and Hans were fascinated.

Hans asked Bibi, "May we try? It looks like you have red cabbage and beets from lunch!"

Sarah picked up what looked like a root and smelled it. "Turmeric?" She then noticed berries and dandelions in two other bowls.

Bibi nodded toward the floor in front of them to sit, and the couple got swept into the process, with the cousins instructing them, and Kadek translating.

The others followed further into the covered area. Bibi spoke again with Wayan, Annie and Ramone paying close attention. "You might wonder where Mara got her skill with silk." Nenek held up two folded pieces of fabric for them to see and feel. "Can you tell the difference?" Annie and Ramone felt each of them trying to understand what they were looking for.

Wayan ran his fingers across them, looking closely at the weave of each one. "They both appear to be silk." He took the one in Bibi's right hand and studied it. "This one is different. It is as soft as silk but it seems more breathable. There is also the slightest elasticity to it. What is it?"

"You are holding one of the rarest fabrics in the world, made in the most tedious fashion. The normal production of silk is produced from the silkworm. However, this fabric is made from the silk fibers of the lotus stem!"

In unison, Wayan, Annie, and Ramone said, "What!? How is that possible?"

Mara smiled at Nenek. "My grandmother is one of the very few skilled at taking the fragile fibers from the lotus stem and turning them into thread. Would you like to see how it is done?"

They all heartily agreed. Mara led them to the lotus pond and removed her shoes. "It starts by selecting the heartiest lotus stems. Would you care to join me? Don't be afraid of the muddy water. Just tread carefully."

Mara showed them how to select the stems, maneuvering around the roots secured in the mud. They each cut three long stems at their roots as instructed. She told them to choose stems that were fresh, green, and firm. Wayan stepped out of the pond first and helped the others with a foot wash there to rinse their feet.

Wayan picked up the pile of stems and took them to Nenek with the others close behind him. Their fascination was evident as Nenek sat in front of a spotless wooden table and rubbed a single drop of oil onto her hands. Bibi made sure there were no drafts that would threaten to blow away the delicate fibers.

Nenek held three stems together and made a surface cut around the outside. Then she broke off the small end piece revealing multiple fibers attached between the two ends. She turned the end piece around twisting the fibers into a single thread then stretching the two parts of the stem further apart to lengthen. She did this repeatedly, overlapping the single threads and loose filaments, then rolling it into a fine, single, continuous thread that would be strong enough to weave.

Mara smiled at the looks of astonishment on her friends' faces. Nenek then got up and motioned them over to the loom in the corner, surrounded by large spools of dyed threads. Bibi explained, "Most of our family weaves ikat patterns. See how the design is painted and placed behind the threads? That is how the weaver knows where to place the colored threads in the design."

It was as though a flash of understanding came over Wayan. Looking at Mara with a renewed appreciation, he said, "So those designs that you created for Antonella's costumes were sent to the weaver who reproduced them on the fabric?"

"The weavers make the samples. Once the samples are approved, along with how the pattern repeats, it can then be reproduced by machinery. What Nenek is doing is an artform dating back thousands of years, but it is dying out. No one wants to take the time for such a process. Can you imagine how many stems and how many hours it would take to produce one scarf? Ironically, most of the lotus silk production is exported to Italy!"

Ramone stifled a yawn. "I am afraid most of this is over my head. I am going to find the twins to see what they are up to." Looking at Annie, Ramone added, "*Querida*, I might not understand what all is involved in making it, but I would like you to pick out something made with this silk from a lotus stem."

Wayan stayed with Nenek to watch her weave, which gave Mara and Annie a chance to check on Sarah and Hans.

Sarah saw them and exclaimed, "Come see what we are doing!" Sarah's vibrant energy and boundless creativity were coursing through her with excitement. "My pot is filled with the red cabbage that has been simmering for a while. Watch this!" She took a primitive-looking strainer and poured the warm purple liquid into three equal bowls, putting the remnants of the cabbage aside. The liquid in each bowl was a deep purple. "Look what happens if I add a touch of baking soda!" The color of the liquid changed to a vibrant blue. "And look at this with adding the juice of a lime!" The liquid in that bowl became bright pink! "Three colors from one cabbage!" Sarah marveled at the vibrant hues produced by plants, roots, and flowers, realizing the endless possibilities for creative expression that existed in the natural world.

Hans had an equally curious and creative nature, testing the yellow liquid produced from the turmeric, by adding some blue from Sarah's new color to make green and red from the beet to make brown. "What a wonderful experience. I have always loved blending colors with paint, but I have never seen the process of creating dyes from natural ingredients. This day has been nothing short of magical, Mara! The warmth and generosity of your family with their passion for their artistic traditions has truly inspired me."

Annie stood to the side reflecting on the day, absorbing every detail, every texture, every scent, realizing this was the journey she craved, with stories woven into each moment. She felt a deep sense of gratitude for Mara and her family, for opening their hearts and sharing their rich cultural heritage with them.

It was time to move to the next part of the journey. Mara gathered her friends. She laughed when she found Ramone with the twins, each with a plate of multicolor noodles. Aisha had gotten a cup of several colors of the natural dyes and let the children dye the noodles. They were happily eating as Aisha and Ramone taught them the names of the colors.

Mara could tell Wayan was also touched by the day in how he said goodbye to Nenek and Bibi. Her heart exploded with gratitude for her family, knowing this day could not have been more special. It was a day that seamlessly intertwined creativity and culture amidst the vibrant colors and sounds of the island. And her beloved family had welcomed Wayan and her friends with open arms, treating them as family, not as guests.

After yesterday's doubts, Mara and Wayan had started fresh, and with him by her side, Mara felt alive and inspired to begin the next part of their journey.

CHAPTER 39

After two days filled with adventure and cultural experiences, the group arrived at *Mundur Kesehatan*, the retreat nestled in the heart of Bali's terraced rice paddies, curious about what to expect next. From the moment they stepped foot on the grounds, they felt a calm and rejuvenating energy envelop them, setting the tone for a transformative experience ahead. Surrounded by towering trees and colorful flowers with the fragrant scent of frangipane in the air and wind chimes softly tinkling, the retreat beckoned them toward a more introspective journey.

After receiving a welcome wellness drink served in a coconut embellished with an orchid and straw that tasted amazing, they checked in to their cozy rooms, each adorned with traditional Balinese décor and modern amenities. As they settled in, Wayan finished the last of his drink. "What was that? It is delicious!"

Mara took another sip of her drink. "It is called a Green Healer and is loaded with kale, coconut milk, apple, and cucumber, with brown sugar syrup. While we are here, the goal of the retreat is to offer us a plan that nurtures our body, mind, and spirit. After the yoga class, our instructor will give us an overview of our schedule. We only have the one full day, so I am sure everyone will want to select their options." Mara felt what was now the familiar magnetic pull that Wayan exuded whenever she was around him. His eyes beckoned her, filled with promises she was unsure how or if he would keep. For now, she put her doubts aside and went to him without hesitation. Their physical desire sprung to life as their kisses and fondling heated. It was the sound of the gong ringing through the air, signaling the yoga class, that gave them pause not wanting to let the others down.

"Later, *sayang*. I will not forget where we left this between us."

Mara loved that he used such an affectionate term. She had always liked that Ramone called Annie *querida*. *Sayang* suited her as it was the term for dearest.

The sun was beginning its descent as they gathered for the meditational yoga session led by a wise and experienced teacher. The group formed a circle on the open-air deck, with the sounds of nature providing a soothing backdrop to their practice. The gentle voice of the instructor encouraged them, as they moved through the poses, to find stillness and harmony within themselves. There were all levels of ability, and they were gently guided at their own pace to remove blockages, improve their energy pathways, and make their bodies flexible and strong. Mara's eyes sparkled with serenity, and Wayan's presence beside her created a shared sense of tranquility and unity between them.

The instructor was an older Balinese woman of quiet confidence. Her warm and welcoming attitude encouraged Mara and her friends, as newcomers to the retreat, to stay for a short orientation before dinner. Annie quickly went to check on the children who seemed to be thriving under Aisha's care. When she returned, they got started.

"My name is Kusama. Welcome to Mundur Kesehatan where we hope to give you a holistic wellness journey that both rejuvenates and inspires you. I was born into a family of healers and therapists and have been drawn to the healing arts since I was young. I am the healer who has been assigned to you during your stay here. You will find I am a good listener and will create a sacred space for any of you who seek my help on a path to heal, recharge, and find inner peace. Some of the enriching experiences we offer include: a sunrise trek up to Mt. Batur, an active volcano; the sacred water purification ritual at the Tirta Empul Temple; a couple's hot stone massage followed by a flower bath; an experience with the sound vibrations of the Tibetan singing bowls; and a powerful energy healing session with me. There will naturally be yoga classes, spa treatments, and our pool for your convenience. The children have many activities planned for them so that parents can relax your body in a space that allows you to just be, to breathe, listen, and feel. After dinner, please sign up for your preferences."

* * *

Under the twinkling lights of the night sky, Mara looked around at her friends as they shared a delicious meal made from fresh, locally sourced ingredients, served in a communal dining area overlooking a peaceful pond. She reflected over her time in Bali that would soon come to an end. *What had she learned? How would her visit affect her life and work back in Milan? Where did Wayan fit in?*

Sarah caught her attention when she asked, "Isn't this the lotus pond we saw when we arrived earlier? It was covered in blossoms but now there are none here."

The others looked over at the pond, equally puzzled. Mara nodded. "That is one of the many things that makes the lotus unique. Its roots are secured in the muddy bottom of the pond. Every night the lotus retires back into the muddy water, yet the next morning it rises back out of the water clean and pure without a trace of the mud they were cloaked in all night."

"That is incredible! I plan to be out here tomorrow morning to see this." Sarah shook her head in wonder. "So, has everyone decided what they are going to sign up for?"

Ramone was first to answer. "I plan to be up at first light to do the sunrise mountain trek. I would be happy for anyone to join me. Then, later, the couple's massage sounds good. I'm not sure about the flower bath, though."

Annie rolled her eyes hardly containing her smile. "I am in for the massage and bath if it includes my husband. However, I have been looking forward to the water purification ritual."

Hans said he would join Ramone on the trek then do whatever Sarah wanted, not sure whether the couple's massage and bath would appeal to her. Mara and Sarah agreed to join Annie for the water purification. They then all looked at Wayan in anticipation, wondering which group he would join. It was Mara who voiced their question. "Wayan, what is your plan for tomorrow?"

"It all sounds good, but I think I am going to take advantage of the energy healing session and the Tibetan singing bowls. I have experienced the effects of the sound vibrations before. It was a great experience."

Sarah thought about it. "Depending on the timing of when everything is, the Tibetan bowls would be intriguing. I'll join you, Wayan." Hans and Mara both confirmed they would join Sarah and Wayan for the Tibetan bowls.

After dinner, Kusama handed out the preference sheets. Both the trek and the water purification ritual would be in the morning. It made perfect sense for Wayan's energy healing session to also be planned for the morning. They scheduled the Tibetan bowls for right after lunch when Annie and Ramone would go to the spa. They had all enjoyed the yoga so they signed up for another session together in the late afternoon.

Annie asked Kusama, "May I have the children's activity sheet? I would like to go over it with Aisha."

Kusama handed her the schedule, then explained where to meet to start the trek and to find the transportation to the temple for the water purification. Kusama then paused to stare a little longer at Wayan. "I will meet you here when you hear the gong blast twice." To the rest of the group, she added, "Sleep well and at peace." With a final sideways glance at Wayan, she left.

Mara looked at Wayan. "I am not quite sure what you have gotten yourself into. She gave you quite a stare!"

Wayan's heart was beating a little faster. "I noticed."

* * *

Wayan made love to Mara with a bittersweet passion that night, his thoughts cloudy and confused. He wasn't sure whether the session with Kusama would help or merely unleash the demons that haunted him. Mara dozed off into a sound sleep, yet Wayan lay there awake not wanting to give in to the dreams that awaited him.

The day had been long and weariness finally overcame him, sending him into a restless sleep. Mara was standing there at the lighted entrance to what seemed like a long dark cave. He could see her reaching out her arms to him. She was calling him, encouraging him to come to her. She looked so beautiful with the light shining through her sheer nightgown leaving no question as to her physical beauty. He tried to go to her but his legs wouldn't move forward. He listened. Voices of Antonella and his father echoed in the distance, holding him captive.

In Wayan's vivid dream, he called out to Mara to help him. She represented light and freedom, standing in the doorway to a new beginning. Why couldn't he move? He tried to ignore them, but the voices continued to haunt him, holding him back from fully embracing the light and moving forward.

Mara whispered softly, "Wayan, wake up. You were calling me. Wake up. It's just a dream."

Wayan forced himself out of the dream, praying the healer could see he was at a crossroads, torn between the familiar darkness of his past and the beckoning light of his future with Mara. He desperately needed to find a way out of the darkness. His body was shaking with emotion. Mara was there, holding him, soothing away the demons. Then she repeated in barely a whisper, hoping it was true. "It's just a dream."

CHAPTER 40

The coming morning brought the next step in the spiritual journey they had embarked on as a group. They were told at the pre-dawn breakfast to focus on the pivotal moment they were at in their lives and to ask their private burning questions to the benevolent spirits. Kusama said, "If you immerse yourselves in the traditions and spirituality of the island, you will begin to unravel your innermost fears, hopes, and desires. Find the courage to embrace your truths, confront your uncertainties, and make decisions that will shape your destiny. I want each of you to summarize your individual pivotal point in your lives on this piece of paper. Hans and Ramone, think about what you wrote on your ascent. At the summit, there will be a high priestess who will take your papers and bless them. She will ask for clarity on your behalf during your descent. Write your thoughts, then join the trek."

There was something about Kusama that evoked trust, and Mara saw that her friends were taking this seriously. She personally knew this process worked and was ready to write on her paper. For now, Hans and Ramone wrote while Kusama moved to the ladies.

Hans wrote:

Although my artistic life is successful and fulfilling, I feel like I am at a crossroads in my personal life. I am deeply in love with Sarah and eager to start a life together, but she is a free-spirited painter who moves to the beat of her own drum. She has always resisted the constraints of traditional norms, including marriage. Although I want a settled life with Sarah by my side, I can't help but wonder if I am somehow holding her back from her true calling.

Ramone thought for a moment how to express his thoughts, then began to write:

I have tried to move past the murder of my father right before my eyes, the feeling of helplessness I experienced when I was held captive, and the forsaking of the profession that I loved. If I am honest, I was a good matador but I gave it up. I am devoted to Annie and the twins. Is my desire to enlarge our family in reality trying to fill a void left in my soul from these major events? What would happen to Annie's thirst for travel and adventure with more children? I love that about her. I can't help but wonder if our dreams are aligned.

Kusama nodded to Mara and her friends. "Mara, Annie, and Sarah, you will be traveling to Pura Tirta Empul to participate in the water purification ritual designed to cleanse your soul from negative spirits. You will also write your pivotal points in your lives where you need guidance. You will give them to the high priestess before entering the water. Look to them for instruction and guidance. Now you may write."

Sarah chewed on the tip of her pencil, then began:

Deep inside, I would have to admit my biggest fear is abandonment. The tragic death of my mother as a child followed by the physical abandonment of my father live in my heart no matter how hard I try to move past them. Even though Hans has been my one true love, will I ever forget that day when I knocked on his door in Hamburg after returning from Africa when Camilla answered and said she was his wife? I want to trust him but am I ready to make a lifelong commitment to him? Despite my love for him, I don't know that I am willing to take a chance and give up my artistic freedom and independence in exchange for domestic bliss.

Annie was less sure what to write. She loved Ramone and the twins with all her heart. What was she dealing with deep inside? She wrote:

Although I would never say it to Ramone, unexpectedly having twins was more than daunting. It has taken a while to get used to the constant role of nurturing mother and supportive partner. Sometimes I catch Ramone with his thoughts wandering and I worry that he gave up the bullring and the fame that he loved for me. There is a guilt that I feel yet I can't find the words to talk about it. I spent many months going to foreign countries alone, absorbing the history, wondering at the cuisine, and meeting people of different cultures. Is that time over? Wouldn't more children merely tie me down further?

Mara looked at Wayan, knowing he was dealing with his own issues. For now, she tried to focus on herself and wrote:

I thought being a success would be a testament to my skills as a fabric designer. Despite the glamour and the allure of the high-end fashion industry, sometimes I feel like all I do is chase trends and the next fashion show victory. Despite the high-profile image I achieve on the arm of the enigmatic Zayn al Farooq, the truth is he swept me off my feet with grand gestures and hints of a forever future. There is no forever future with Zayn which left an emptiness in my heart. And Wayan? Even though I feel I might have found true love, I find myself haunted by our relationship. Uncertainty about his past and what life together would look like in Milan causes me to question the authenticity of a romantic partnership with him.

Kusama looked at the slips of paper in their hands. "You are embarking on this Melukat water purification together. Do not be fooled by that. This is your own journey. Let the soothing sounds of the flowing water and the serene atmosphere of the temple envelop you in a cocoon of introspection. Follow the instructions of the high priestess through the ceremonial ritual. Delve deep into your heart to confront your fears and doubts head-on. Your goal is to find clarity and wisdom in the whispers of the ancient temple."

* * *

The group had gone their separate ways. Wayan was the only one left. He was waiting to hear what Kusama would say to him. He did not have to wait long. She slowly walked in a circle around him as if listening. "Wayan, your heart is beating faster than normal. You feel threatened. I want you to go sit by the pond and write. Tell me about your dream from last night. It is the key to finding yourself. Remember, listen for the two gong blasts, then come to me in the pavilion."

Unlike Mara, Wayan had never experienced anything like this and he was more than intimidated. *How did Kusama know of his dream?* He had never bared his soul to anyone, thinking it a sign of weakness. He walked to the pond and wandered around it trying to remember the dream enough to put it into words. For a moment, he stopped to notice the blossoms Mara had talked about. You would never know they had spent the night in the muddy water. They were perfectly clean and brilliant. Then he realized he was avoiding putting pen to paper, so he sat down to write:

In my dream, I am in a dark cave unable to move. I am kept there by the voices. Why are they there? Many would say I am a success. After years of hard work, I now live a lavish lifestyle in Milan as the exclusive costumier for the renowned opera diva, Antonella Rossi. While the opulence and prestige seemed like a dream come true on the surface, the reality was far from it. My father, a respected silversmith, had dreams of passing his skills down to me, but I had a different vision for myself. From the time of making costumes for my sisters, a passion was ignited in me to pursue a career in fashion. My father disapproved of my career choice, constantly sharing his doubts about my chances of success. A traditional man, he never believed a straight man could thrive in the fashion world and was unconvinced about both my professional capabilities as well as my sexual preference. Despite his doubts, I pursued my dreams with unwavering passion. Yet he has never visited me. But, to this day, I carry his skepticism with me that lingers like a shadow over my achievements.

When I became Antonella Rossi's costumier and we began an affair, I was convinced that my father would be proud. However, the constant demands and physical needs of Antonella haunted me every day, making me question the true meaning of the opulent lifestyle I was living. I felt drained and suffocated, trapped in a world of extravagance and excess that was hollow and unfulfilling. When I ended the affair, Antonella threatened my position as her costume designer. I did what I had to do in order to stay. The result was an existence that seemed to revolve around fulfilling the diva's physical needs which had ironically turned to the female gender and her demanding expectations that I be at her beck and call to present ourselves as a couple to the public.

Wayan heard the two gong blasts and looked down at his paper. Once the floodgates had opened on his writing, he felt like he could go on writing for a long while. However, it was time to face Kusama to see if she had answers for him. Wayan walked on dirt paths through bamboo structures and a variety of shrines overflowing with blessing baskets. He could smell burning incense. *Was it frankincense or sandalwood?* Roosters were crowing in the background. Kusama met him at the entrance. Behind her, a priest was praying in Sanskrit, waving his burning sage stick through the air.

Kusama greeted Wayan with, "It is time for you to embrace your true essence, to illuminate your path forward, and wash away your past. In order to do that, you must surrender yourself and open the door to your spirit."

Wayan's nerves were on full alert, threatening to make him turn around and abandon this method. He then thought about what he had written, but the moment he looked down at the folded piece of paper, Kusama gently took it from him and led him inside.

CHAPTER 41

The priest continued to chant and pray with the smoke of his sage stick floating in the air mingling with the smoke of the incense creating an intoxicating aroma. "Please sit. Nuriashih is a wise priest renowned for his insight and ability to communicate with the human spirit. He must first determine your energy. If it is good, we will move to the next step. If there is negative energy, he will do a cleansing before moving on. Please put your hands together in prayer and let your mind go. What we are doing here today is not the business of the mind. It is the business of your soul."

Nuriashih sat adjacent to Wayan with his legs crossed and an old notepad in his lap. There was a sketch of a man. Nuriashih began his chant again and started drawing circle after circle in a continuous motion up and down the image of the man. Kusama said, "The priest is able to tell from his circles if there is an area of your body with negative energy."

This went on for several minutes, then Nuriashih said to Kusama in Sanskrit, who in turn translated to Wayan, "He says there are three sources of negative energy that seek to cause you pain, either physically or mentally. That would be the cause for recent headaches, troubled dreams, or self-doubts." Kusama handed Wayan's paper to the priest who took it to the ledge where he again began his chant. He picked up several plumeria blossoms waving them in the air. Kusama explained, "He is giving the flowers as a blessing. Our belief is that all must be in balance in order for positive to replace the negative." Nuriashih filled a bamboo ladle with holy water and crushed the petals of the blossoms into it.

Wayan couldn't stop his mind from questioning. *Three sources?* He could figure out two, but who was the third? Nuriashih held the ladle over his head in prayer with his eyes closed, then without turning around said in perfect Indonesian, "The soul is the outer layer to the spirit that remains eternal. The soul must be reached to gain access to the negative energy that is plaguing the spirit. If you do not free your mind, I will not be able to proceed."

Kusama held out her hand for Nuriashih to pour a few drops of the blessed holy water into the palm of her hand which she, in turn, placed against Wayan's forehead. "Let your mind rest and surrender its interference." Wayan focused on the distant sounds of the roosters as his mind slowly began to drift. Nuriashih stood next to Wayan and drizzled holy water mixed with the crushed petals over his head and shoulders, washing away the negative. The hypnotic sound of the chanting became fainter and Wayan seemed to hear Kusama say, "The pain of holding on is far greater than the pain of letting go." The flow of water and flowers were no longer noticed. Wayan heard, "Give yourself permission to explore your spirituality."

"Take a deep breath...deeper." Wayan did as he was told. "Now, blow it out hard!" Kusama's hand was on his chest. Wayan could feel emotions rising under her hand. "Again, Wayan. Deep breath in. Now, blow it out hard!" This time, with his breath out, Wayan's moan of pain was guttural. Kusama's hand never left his chest making him feel safe. More water, more flowers. "One last time...get it out, Wayan." This last breath out doubled him over in a screeching sob. The emotions were almost more than he could bear, and tears were streaming from his eyes. Drained, as if from an out-of-body experience, Wayan noticed the chanting had stopped. He slowly opened his eyes to find a small dry towel in his lap and Nuriashih seated beside him again, drawing his circles.

When he gave a satisfied grin to Kusama, she nodded to Wayan explaining the negative energy had been pushed out and he was ready to receive the light. Nuriashih took an orange coconut and made three sharp slices at one end, then held it up to bless it and the healing water it contained. He came back over and now blessed Wayan sprinkling the coconut water over him. Wayan's hands were still together in prayer. Then Nuriashih cut the coconut open and brought it to Wayan to drink. A feeling of such peace and serenity overcame him. Clarity appeared within reach.

Nuriashih seemed to disappear. Kusama shifted to face Wayan and took his hands. In that moment, Wayan knew she did not need the paper to know his innermost thoughts. "The paper was for you to start the journey. Tell me about your dream, Wayan. Do you not recognize its symbolism?"

Wayan looked at Kusama with hope and a sudden clarity. "The voices of Antonella and my father are reminding me of the expectations and pressures that encourage me to stay in the familiar darkness. They do not seem as strong, but there are only two voices. The priest said there was a third source of negative energy."

Kusama took some holy water in her hands, resting them on Wayan's shoulders. "Yours is the third voice. You have been caught between the past and the present. Your dream reflects the inner turmoil you have felt. Close your eyes and look deeper into the cave. What do you see?"

Wayan squinted in the darkness trying to see the image hidden in the dark. "It looks like blossoms and water, like the lotus pond where you told me to write."

Kusama, a perceptive healer, saw beyond Wayan's external success and delved into his soul. It was time for her to reveal the profound truth, recognizing the lotus within him. "Wayan, YOU are the lotus. It is time to illuminate the path for you to accept your true essence and rise from the murky waters of your past and self-doubts." She reached her hands out to guide him forward. In that moment, Wayan knew that something profound had changed in him that morning. He stood on the threshold of transformation. Kusama continued, "Just as the lotus flower grows from the muddy waters to bloom into a symbol of purity and beauty, you too have the power to rise above your challenges and shine brightly in the world, finding the light of your full potential and your destiny."

Kusama's words resonated deep within him. He began to let go of the shadows that had chained him down, finding strength and purpose in the realization that the lotus had become a symbol of hope and rebirth, propelling Wayan toward a newfound sense of purpose and inner peace. The impact of Kusama's parting words would stay with him for a long time. "Your destiny lies within the light. Follow the light, Wayan. If you begin to feel worried or threatened, you will discover the third energy source. Let it go. You are cleansed. It has no place in you now."

Wayan asked, "How will I know what to do when I return to Milan?"

Cryptically, Kusama said, "You are no longer bound by the expectations of others. Look for your support and your destiny in the light." The outside midday sun lit up the entrance. He looked at Kusama in gratitude and hugged her. She hugged him back and nodded toward the lit-up entrance. As he stepped toward the light he saw the shadow of a woman. Mara stood at the doorway, a beacon of hope and love, illuminating the path ahead together.

Wayan was shocked to see her but now understood she would be the path for him. "You're here. How did you know where I was?"

Mara stopped to look at Wayan. His clothes were damp, and he had a few flower petals stuck in his hair. "I thought I was the one who did the ritual with the water. It was amazing. Sarah and Annie agree. When I got back, I couldn't wait to tell you about it so I asked at the front desk where you were. I thought we might go to the sound vibrations class together."

"Honestly, I have no concept of how long I was here, but Mara, it was so emotional and draining, it is hard to describe. I don't think I am mentally or physically up for another class. Do you think it would be possible to switch to the couple's massage? I would need to shower."

Kusama was cleaning the pavilion and overheard them. "I will arrange for the massage. My suggestion would be to take the flower bath at the beginning. The water is filled with fragrant blossoms." Kusama observed Mara to discern her level of enlightenment. "You have embarked on this journey for different reasons. However, the inner light in you both was fading in the lives you were living. To go back there, it will take reflection and meditation to understand that the shadows of the past do not define you. Rekindle the inner light in each other to flourish and reconnect with your authentic selves."

CHAPTER 42

The morning purification rituals had left Mara and Wayan feeling spiritually uplifted, setting the stage for further transformation. As they approached the area for the sacred flower bath and couple's holistic massage, the air was filled with an aura of tranquility that seemed to amplify the spiritual energy between them. They were greeted warmly with a cup of green tea to sip as they prepared for the experience.

The drapes closed behind them leaving the enclosed bath area illuminated only by candlelight. Mara dropped her sarong and stepped into the warm, fragrant water wearing only the prayer necklace hanging from her neck. Stirred by the sight of Mara's natural beauty and savoring the scents of aromatic herbs and flowers, Wayan cast aside his sarong and joined her.

Settling into the bath, their bodies intertwined, Wayan felt compelled to tell Mara about his cleansing and the emotions it evoked, along with the revelation of what Kusama shared. "I could hardly recognize the sounds that came out of me during the cleansing. I did as they told me and got outside my mind in order for them to reach my soul. When I let my breath out hard, I could feel the pain coming out. It was unlike anything I have experienced before. When the cleansing was complete, Kusama described me as a lotus, destined to rise from the murky depths of my past and flourish in the light of my true purpose. When I looked toward the doorway, it was filled with bright light and there you were."

Wayan's revelation about the lotus and its symbolism as a beacon of destiny left Mara speechless. Her heart swelled with a mix of emotions...surprise, joy, and a profound sense of clarity. Finding her voice, Mara said in wonder, "I have always been fascinated by the symbolism of the lotus. In my youth, a healer told me my destiny was intertwined with the lotus. Since then, I have carried a vision with me, believing the lotus was my guiding light and that I was meant to embody the purity and resilience of the lotus blossom. I think that was part of why I was struggling with my life in Milan."

In the serene embrace of the flower bath, Mara allowed herself to look deep into Wayan's eyes and see a reflection of her own soul. She felt a profound sense of recognition and understanding wash over her. "Wayan, the lotus that has eluded me for so long was not a flower to be reached for, but a soul to be embraced."

In that moment of deep connection and understanding, Wayan added, "Then I am your destiny as you are mine, *sayang*. Our meeting was no accident. Our paths have been leading us to each other all along; the threads of fate took us out of our country then brought us back to this place to seal our future together."

Mara and Wayan emerged from the bath, a feeling of peace and contentment settling over them, knowing they had been led to this moment to find in each other a missing piece of their own soul. As they received their Balinese massages side by side in silence, it was as if their hearts beat as one to the ancient pulse of the island.

* * *

Hans had found Sarah after his trek up to the peak of the volcano. She had just returned from the water purification ritual at the temple. They were both in a reflective mindset when they entered the tent bathed in candlelight and the scent of burning incense. A priest was seated on an array of ikat blankets that covered the floor. He was surrounded by an assortment of gold bowls and chimes. Kusama greeted them and re-secured the flap of the tent door. "I wanted to let you know all is well, but Wayan and Mara will not be joining you. As individuals, you allowed yourselves to open your minds during this morning's rituals. Through the positive vibrations and power of the singing bowls, you will be able to use this healing session to cleanse your energy field, promote balance, and enhance your overall well-being."

Kusama placed two small pillows next to each other. "Please lie down and hold each other's hand. Close your eyes and let yourselves get swept up in the resonant tones as they wash away negativity, and bring harmony to your mind, body, and spirit."

The first tone reverberated through the tent, lingering until the next tone seemed to layer over it, blending into a new tone, then enhanced by a melodic series of tones. This went on for several minutes, both Hans and Sarah engrossed with the sound. Kusama then said over the last fading vibration, "Your personal recognition of your inner concerns started this transformative day of rituals and has stirred something deep within you. Sarah and Hans, your souls are connected. Would you allow me to share the vision of what I see, then leave you to work it through together as a couple over time?" They both nodded, and there was another slow series of tones as if in response to their nods.

"Today you have reached a turning point and a crossroads in your relationship. You will not be able to move the relationship forward without laying bare your deepest fears and insecurities, discovering the cracks in a seemingly perfect relationship." Kusama let her words flow into the next series of beautiful tones. "Your love for each other is worth the risk of vulnerability. Hans, you were originally drawn to Sarah's free spirit and adventurous nature. I want you to reflect on your own fears and insecurities, particularly your fear of losing Sarah to that very same free spirit you were drawn to. You long to build a life with her, to create a home filled with love and art. Yet, with her hesitation to commit, you fear your desire for stability might be holding her back."

More softer tones drifted through the air while Sarah absorbed Hans's fear. Kusama continued, "Sarah, today has brought up your deep-rooted fear of abandonment and reluctance to fully commit and trust in love. You have always valued your independence and cherished the freedom to follow your artistic direction wherever it leads you. The idea of settling down and making a permanent commitment feels overwhelming and suffocating. The contradiction is the enormous love you have always had for Hans." A deep tone that almost sounded sad made Hans cringe and hold Sarah's hand tighter, knowing that he was partially to blame for that insecurity by his marriage to Camilla that took Sarah by surprise.

"Lie here and consider each other's feelings. Listen to the healing sounds. Be willing to have open and honest conversations to uncover each other's layers and fears so you can better empathize and understand the motivations behind their actions. Work together to overcome these obstacles and to support each other's dreams and ambitions while also creating a solid foundation of love and trust. I will leave you now to listen and meditate on what has been opened up to you this day."

* * *

After the water purification ritual, Annie met Ramone having lunch with the twins in the main pavilion. With enthusiasm, she said, "It was such an incredible experience. I loved it! How was the trek?"

Ramone began to answer, "The scenery was different but beautiful." Then tears glistened in his eyes.

Annie looked at Ramone with concern. "What is it, my love? What happened?"

"We were hiking in silence." Ramone winched. "It took me right back to hiking while lost in thought in Mallorca after my father's murder."

Cece must have sensed something was wrong and climbed into her father's lap. Ramone was holding her close. Annie was trying to think of what to say when Kusama found them. She gave Salvi's head a caress and asked, "Have you and your sister had a good time?"

She knew they had been on the playground and making crafts most of the morning and was thrilled when both twins answered her with, "YES!"

Kusama noticed the slump in Ramone's shoulders. "Would you and Annie like to join me after lunch? I am available before your massage."

Annie started with, "No, I think we are good. This morning was wonderful."

Ramone quietly placed his hand over Annie's, then looked at Kusama and responded, "I would like to join you."

"Ramone, would you like to come alone?"

Annie then noticed that Ramone's demeanor had changed. She took the hand that held hers and said, "I want to be there, my love, if you will allow me."

Ramone nodded. Kusama gave them both a gentle smile. "Come find me once Aisha returns for the children."

Kusama was waiting in the bamboo structure where Wayan had experienced his healing session. There was incense burning, but no priest. She indicated for Annie and Ramone to sit before her. Kusama lit the end of a pressed bundle of sage, getting up to waft the smoke through the small room to rid it of negative energy. She opened a young orange coconut, poured a little of the water in her hand and sprinkled a little on each of their heads, giving them a blessing. She then poured a little coconut water into Annie's hands and asked her to drink it. She then did the same with Ramone. Kusama looked at them with the insight of a healer. "You have had a Balinese blessing before."

Annie answered, surprised she knew that. "Yes, when we married, Mara did a Balinese blessing at our wedding." Kusama nodded.

She placed her hand on Annie's chest and closed her eyes as if listening. She moved over in front of Ramone and did the same, her hand on his chest. Kusama raised her eyes to meet Ramone's and said, "There is an area of emptiness in you that does not want to stay quiet. You are safe in this space. Tell me what is causing this void?" Ramone's breathing changed, trying to hold back a sob but couldn't. She took his hands. "Let it out." Annie was watching wide-eyed and filled with worry as to what was buried so deep in her beautiful husband.

Between gulps for air, Ramone began, "I remember telling Annie once that fighting the bull, staring him down as he charged, and being victorious was like defying death that day. It came with a feeling of being invincible." Annie moved closer so he could feel her body next to his. He took another deep breath. "When I was kidnapped and tortured, I felt helpless and desolate with no indication I would survive. They paraded me outside and beat me in front of my *querida*. Everything then happened so quickly. I saw the man on the boat with the gun grab the woman I love yet I could do nothing. And, if something could be worse, I saw my father come out of the shadows and charge me. I thought he meant to harm me and could not defend myself. Instead, he meant to save me and was shot and murdered right before my eyes. The feeling of helplessness and vulnerability mixed with the pain of never knowing my father when he was a good man was more than I could bear. I have never again had that invincible feeling like in the bullring."

Kusama asked the question that Annie had avoided a million times. "Ramone, do you miss bullfighting?"

The floodgate opened and Ramone let out with a sob, "Yes! I thought somehow more children would fill this void in me."

Kusama nodded, then sprinkled a little more of the coconut water over him. She placed her hand back on his chest as he calmed.

"You are close to your mother." Ramone nodded. "I see her but she moved away. Although she is happy, she misses you and your brother terribly. She still wants to be in your life. I also feel your father's spirit. You said he was murdered?" Ramone nodded. "That is strange. I can see him clearly. He is not far from your home. He has many regrets."

Kusama moved to sit in front of Annie. Taking her hands, she said, "You are reluctant to have more children. I see you in many lands. Where have you traveled since the twins were born?"

Annie answered as if resigned to her fate, "This is the first time I have been out of Spain. I have loved every minute here in Bali."

Kusama put her hand back on Annie's chest. "There is something else, something you loved that is missing." Annie hesitated, her own eyes beginning to overflow with tears. "You are okay. Give yourself permission to say it." Kusama sprinkled more holy water.

Annie's emotions were unleashed. "I was a good architect and historian. All of that has been left behind. Now, I am a wife and mother. With another child, I would be housebound again. It is as though the adventures of life are gone."

Ramone took Annie's hands. "*Querida*, I had no idea."

Kusama moved back to better face both of them. "If you rely on the basis of your love for each other and trust the other with your vulnerabilities, you will develop a clearer understanding of yourselves and each other. You have some important issues to work on together, but they are also opportunities to grow into a couple that nurtures you both. Take the time with the massage and flower bath to commit to each other on your journey toward understanding and acceptance. You have done the hard work by identifying the obstacles. I believe you are ready to confront them together."

CHAPTER 43

The three couples arrived at the far pavilion separately. They had been summoned to the jungle-like, remote location by Kusama who now stood before them, her presence emitting a feeling of calm and serenity, as if she were in tune with the rhythms of the universe. Her eyes held the wisdom of someone who had journeyed through many lifetimes. She greeted them individually by taking their hands in hers and nodding in reverence. She then indicated that they should sit cross-legged in a semicircle.

"You have each experienced a journey today, both as an individual and as a couple. It started with an opportunity to look inside yourself to find your innermost hopes, fears, and regrets. That was a huge start to how you would process today's events with those thoughts moved into your awareness. However, it also told you something important. You each had something relevant to write. What that means is that every individual surrounding us has inner conflicts locked within them that affect their actions in some way. None of us are immune."

Looking at each of them pensively, she added, "You each chose your ritual as what you thought best for yourselves. Although most of you shared an activity, the forced silence did not allow you to share your thoughts. You had to do that on your own. Many emotions were stirred up in the process, and the revelations that were given to you will continue to be revealed over the coming days. Much has happened in your short time here at *Mundur Kesehatan*. Both your bodies and minds are still absorbing the transformative clarity and enlightenment that has been shared with you. The day is coming to a close. My recommendation is to spend the rest of it quietly, reflecting on what you have discovered and how it impacts your partner and your friends. That is correct. Just as you nurture yourselves and your partner, so do you nurture your friends. Do not lose sight of that. There is a waterfall a short distance from here that has a peaceful lotus pond on the side. You now understand the dynamic importance of water. It is your connection between the natural world and spiritual realms and is revered as a sacred and essential element of life. Let the flow of its energy inspire you."

Kusama held her hands to her chest, her eyes generating age-old wisdom and compassion. "Before you go, I would ask to have a few moments with Mara, Annie, and Sarah." The three of them stood up without hesitation to follow her to an area of lush greenery and they sat facing her on the surrounding rocks.

She first turned to Mara. "Mara, you have found solace here in the tranquility of the retreat. I see in your eyes a mixture of longing and apprehension as you prepare to return to the burden of the pressure of your career and the chaotic demands of a fast-paced life." Kusama placed her hand on Mara's shoulder. "I want to offer you encouragement to carry the peace you found here back into the bustling world awaiting you. Let your vibrant designs reflect the rich tapestry of your soul, intricately woven with the colors and textures that remind you of your homeland. You must find a balance between your worldly pursuits and spiritual growth. Only then will you be able to align your heart and mind. And Mara, you must also nurture the lotus for it is the path to your destiny." Mara absorbed Kusama's words with a bowed head.

Next, Kusama spoke to Annie. "The longing in your eyes tells of the unspoken desire you feel to reclaim the sense of value and purpose you felt as an architect, as well as the adventure and freedom of travel you so love. I want you to open your eyes to the friends who surround you. Annie, you are the glue that holds these friendships together. They would not exist if it were not for that very sense of adventure and openness to different cultures and curiosity you had about their history and heritage. Do not worry. You will find a path to honor your dreams and desires while fulfilling your responsibility as a wife and mother." Kusama's gentle smile and encouraging words were like a balm to Annie's soul, instilling in her with a newfound sense of empowerment and possibility. "However, I give you one area of caution to take with you. While you find your way, you must navigate the complexities your husband faces with grace and an abundance of love."

Lastly, Kusama turned to Sarah with a tender gaze, knowing the deep wounds of abandonment Sarah carried with her. "Sarah, true healing begins with self-acceptance and self-love which will pave the way for an authentic and enduring relationship. It is time to confront your fears and insecurities. You must trust in the healing power of forgiveness if you are to embrace the journey of growth and connection ahead of you. Take the ring, Sarah. Try it on for size and absorb the energy that comes from commitment. You have loved Hans for many years, and he is deeply committed. Dare to accept that you are deserving of that lasting love." Sarah's eyes glistened with unshed tears.

With a knowing smile, Kusama whispered words of blessings and guidance, enfolding the three women in a cocoon of love and grace. "You share the sacred bond of sisterhood. Look deep within yourselves to see the strength and resilience you each possess. I encourage you to find the strength to stay true to yourself and discover balance in all aspects of life. Embrace love and connection with both your partners and each other. And when inevitably one of you falters, let the other two provide the strength and loving support to shore her up. I ask you to live your lives with courage and authenticity, having found in this place a fresh sense of purpose."

With tears in their eyes and hearts full of gratitude, Mara, Annie, and Sarah, returned to their waiting men with a deep reverence for the healing power of Kusama's guidance. The healer had guided each of them through a profound experience and had become both a mentor and confidante, offering wisdom and comfort as they explored the depths of their emotions. Through tears and laughter, the six of them said their individual farewells to Kusama, all expressing their gratitude for the time they had spent at the spiritual retreat. Wayan, having spent the most time with Kusama in such a personal way, waited until the last to say his goodbye. "Kusama, were you aware that in her youth, Mara was told by a healer to look for her destiny in a lotus?" Kusama simply gave a cryptic smile. "You helped us find the connection in our destinies. However, I still do not know how I am going to handle things when I get home. Antonella still presents a huge obstacle."

Kusama took Wayan's hands. "Trust the process, Wayan. You will know what to do. The answers you seek are within reach."

* * *

Left to confront their lingering emotions, Kusama's words of wisdom hung in the air. She had warned them the journey was far from over, that the revelations would continue to come long after they left Bali. Together, they decided to seek solace at the nearby waterfall, the sound of cascading water offering a soothing backdrop to their contemplations. Deep in thought and emotionally drained, they sat in silence, the weight of the day's revelations hanging in the air.

Each of them had faced their fears, confronted their demons, and emerged on the other side by the process of purification and healing. Their shared experiences had created an unspoken bond between them, knowing they would always carry a piece of this day with them, even as they prepared to part ways the next morning.

Ramone was the first to speak. "I don't know about the rest of you but today was unlike anything I have ever experienced before." Each of them nodded in agreement.

Wayan then said, "After our stay in Bali, I feel like I have known each of you for a very long time. You are like family to me now." Taking Mara's hand, he added, "It makes me reluctant to return to life in Milan. If it weren't for this beautiful woman by my side, I would seriously consider moving back here."

Mara sighed, realizing their world was wrapped in a safe cocoon here in this idyllic setting. Back in Milan, where their lives and careers waited, things were complicated and not so authentic. "The problem is that once we get caught up in the images expected of us, do we lose our true selves?"

Wayan nodded. "That is what happened to Antonella. We have to find a way for it not to happen to us."

CHAPTER 44

As they gathered in the dining room of *Mundur Kesehatan* for their last evening together at a dinner filled with sumptuous delicacies, the weight of their shared experiences had left them weary but content. They had each come on this journey with their own set of struggles and challenges and throughout the day had discovered hidden truths about themselves through the ceremonies. The presence of the twins, with their lively and boisterous behavior, brought happy smiles and laughter to the gathering, highlighting their innocence and joy at each new adventure.

Annie and Mara noticed the grin on Hans's face and saw that Sarah was wearing the ring they had made together at the silversmith. Once she saw they noticed, Sarah felt obliged to say, "Don't go jumping to conclusions. I am just doing what Kusama advised and trying it on for size."

Mara reached over and took Sarah's hand for a closer look. "It is beautiful, Sarah, and suits you perfectly."

They all agreed but it was Hans who said, "Whether Sarah chooses to wear the ring or not, I am not going anywhere. I have found the love of my life, and I plan to remind her of that every day for the rest of our lives." Sarah allowed happiness to wash over her and leaned into Hans for a sensuous kiss that expressed the love she had felt from the moment they met.

Annie looked at Wayan, pondering whether she should bring up the subject of Antonella. She eventually decided that perhaps she could ask a question that Mara might be reluctant to. "Wayan, Mara said you promised Antonella you would be back tomorrow. Do you have any idea what is waiting for you at home?"

Wayan shook his head in doubt. "Mara was originally planning to stay another day with Hans and Sarah, but she has decided to go back to Milan with me so we can confront the situation there together."

Hans interjected, "Yes, and now we have the day all alone to relax and enjoy the honeymoon!" At Sarah's look of shock, Hans laughed. "There's nothing wrong with a honeymoon before the wedding, right?" That got a round of laughter, even from Sarah. Hans then followed up on the conversation with Wayan. "I am feeling a little lost on the subject of Antonella. You design costumes for her and dress her to look more mature on stage. You were a couple once but you said that has passed. So why would she care if you have a girlfriend?"

Mara prepared herself for what had become Wayan's usual answer that it was complicated. Nothing could have surprised her more than when he began to open up to them.

Wayan glanced at the faces of each of these amazing people who started out as Mara's friends and were now his own as well. He had not felt such a bond of friendship for a long time, and he knew without asking that he could trust them. He glanced at Mara and she nodded her support, keenly aware this might shed some light on what awaited them.

"It started so innocently. I had just begun working in Milan at the opera house assisting some of the costume designers who provided costumes and fittings for the frequent opera stars and stage actors who performed there. One afternoon, I was returning from a fitting and noticed a wisp of a young girl sitting on a bench crying outside the theater. She had long dark hair and I could tell she was quite pretty, so I walked over to ask if she was alright."

Sarah asked, "Why was she crying?"

At that moment, Aisha came to the table to get the twins for bedtime. Contritely, Wayan realized he might be overstepping everyone's time with his story. To his amazement, Annie handed the twins over and, looking intently at Wayan, asked him to continue. Wayan no longer felt alone. It was as if they were all there to help him solve a puzzle.

He thought about that afternoon and how things would have been different if they had never met. "Practically sobbing, she told me she had just tried out for the female lead in *Tosca*. With the tears, I assumed she didn't get the part, but then she said the director told her that her voice had potential for the part, but that her age and stature did not fit the magnitude of her voice. I didn't understand until she pulled a recorder out of her bag and gave me earphones. All I can tell you is that I had never heard such a magnificent voice! Looking at her, I admit it was hard to imagine that larger-than-life voice coming out of such a small frame."

Ramone commented, "How unfair."

Wayan nodded in agreement. "I thought so too. Then, it occurred to me. As a costume designer with this ornate Balinese ceremonial background that I had, I understood how to transform someone into the role they were playing. Her name was Nella Rossellini. Through carefully padded costumes to give her bulk, and stage makeup perfected to age her, Antonella Rossi was born. Later that week, she reapplied as Antonella and got the part. The same director never recognized her. She was so elated by what she attributed to my miraculous transformation that she basically fell into my arms."

Annie saw the flush rise on Mara's cheeks but asked anyway. "That was when the affair began? Are you still involved in that part of your relationship? I can't imagine that if you were you would have begun something with Mara. Is Antonella jealous of you two?"

Wayan was noticeably uncomfortable but determined to finish. "That is where it gets complicated. The affair I began was with Nella Rossellini, but as Antonella Rossi's fame grew, she effortlessly slipped into her onstage persona, both on and off the stage. Initially, I shielded her from prying eyes to protect her illusion. What I discovered was her commanding voice and role as prima donna masked what was happening to the pretty young girl that I cared about. I realize now it was the weight of her own insecurities that made her dependency on me increase. By this time, I was her exclusive costume designer, well compensated financially, as well as her confidant, which blurred the lines between professional duty and personal entanglement. Our physical relationship ended poorly, mostly because my interest waned just as her needs and desires increased. Yet if I even looked at another woman, Antonella flew into a rage. I soon found myself caught in a web of manipulation and power dynamics."

Mara was listening and realized something didn't make sense. "But Wayan, Antonella invited Lucca and me to her home and allowed us to see her without the costume and makeup. Why would she do that?"

Wayan shook his head. "I can't answer that. It surprised me. It was extremely rare for her to invite strangers into her private space without the usual armor of costumes and makeup."

It was Sarah who seemed to unravel the pieces to the story. "I remember as a child, after my mother died in that horrible explosion, I retreated into a very dark space. My social worker suggested something that made no sense at the time. She thought I should take acting lessons. To be honest, the last thing I wanted was to be on display. But I will never forget an actor coming into class to read a play and watching him completely immerse himself into each of the characters. His voice and mannerisms completely changed. He spoke of what it took emotionally to step into the role of another character. Maybe that is what has happened to Antonella, or rather Nella. She even has a different name to step into. It could be that inviting Mara and Lucca to her home meant she was reaching out to be truly seen as herself. And trusting you, Wayan, it might have felt safe that they were in your industry."

It was like a lightbulb went off for Annie and she added, "And when she found out there might be something between you two, it seemed like a betrayal by you both. A word that has come up many times today is authenticity. What if there was a way to restore Antonella's authentic self? I think that might be just the answer for Antonella, and you might find it even reaches over to the situation with Zayn. Just think about it. You have a long flight tomorrow. Something will occur to you. I'm sure of it."

CHAPTER 45

Annie and Ramone had packed up early with the twins and Aisha in tow to make their way to Canggu for some beach time. Sarah and Hans were sleeping in. All the farewells were said the night before, so Mara and Wayan left the retreat with a final walk around the property. They both agreed the entire trip had been transformative for both of them individually and as a couple. Kadek was waiting for them when they got back to the lobby. She had insisted on giving them a ride to the airport for one final chance to see her favorite cousin before she left.

By the time they checked in at the airport and were seated in the waiting area, reality began to set in. Mara rubbed her temple and Wayan could sense her worry. "What is it, *sayang*?"

"I was thinking about Zayn. So much has happened that changes everything yet he is totally unaware of any of it. He thinks everything is the same and that I will attend the debutante ball with him Friday as planned. He and his father have done so much for me and my business. I hate that he is going to be blindsided by what has happened between us."

Wayan gave her an understanding look, pulling out his phone to turn it on, mentally steeling himself for the barrage of messages that were surely waiting for him. Amidst the pings of the incoming messages, the phone actually rang. Wayan looked at Mara and sighed. "I can't put it off forever. I should take this."

Mara nodded, listening, but could only hear one side of the conversation. All she heard was, "Yes, I'm at the airport...this Friday? There is no need to worry. We will figure it out...I will work around the clock if I need to. Don't worry. Mara can help me... We have a three-hour layover in Hong Kong. I will call you then...Yes, I will take care of everything. Stop worrying...Goodbye, Antonella."

Mara was more than puzzled. "What was that all about?"

Wayan shook his head with the irony. "It would appear you and Zayn are not the only ones going to the debutante ball!"

"W-What? Was this unexpected?" Mara responded in disbelief.

"Yes, Antonella heard from her agent last Friday. That is why she has been trying so hard to reach me. A well-known singer that was supposed to perform at the event has a bout with the flu and can't use her voice. Antonella has been asked to fill in on short notice. Although her agent knew she was in her time off, she wanted her to consider it because one of her regular producers has a daughter in the group making her debut. She has been panicking that I would not be there with an appropriate outfit to wear and to do her stage hair and makeup."

Mara asked, "What about the dress she wore at the gala, or even at the fundraiser? Would either of them work? They were beautiful."

They boarded the plane without pausing in their conversation about what Antonella should wear to perform Friday night. Wayan was busy thinking out loud. "None of the costumes from *Aïda* are ready yet." Thinking through her recent costumes, Wayan realized that by the end of a tour, the costumes were well worn and not suitable for an event such as this. "She really loved several of Lucca's designs. The one with the asymmetrical neckline is edgy and could work if it had a long skirt. But he is most likely finished with them, and they are sized to Nella."

That gave Mara an idea. "Wait, that's it! That outfit was a huge seller and I had to buy more fabric to accommodate all the orders. There should be enough matching fabric to make a long skirt. I'm sure Lucca would be thrilled to do it! I could call him during our layover to get started." Mara got out her notepad and sketched a replica of the contemporary top of Lucca's dress, then handed it to Wayan to add the skirt. He reached into his backpack for some tracing paper and began to doodle some ideas. "Lucca is brilliant at what he does. Why don't you choose your favorites between your ideas for the skirt and we will send them to him. Trust him to work his magic. I know he will come through for us. I will have Rochelle send the fabric over right away so he can get started! You can do this, Wayan. She will be perfect!"

Wayan took Mara's hand to his lips without taking his eyes from hers. "It feels good working together, *sayang*. It has been a week filled with new friends, adventure, history, and self-discovery. It seems as if we have been gone much longer. Do you feel as I do that this is a new beginning?"

Mara studied the man with the alluring smile and magnetic pull. She had felt drawn to him from the moment they met. This week had taken them far beyond mere chemistry. She had gotten the renewal and reconnection with her roots she sought and had deepened the bond with her friends. Mara knew in her heart that Wayan was now part of that bond. His eyes held a reflection of her own hopes and dreams for the future. Wayan's question hung in the air between them, a promise of possibilities yet to be explored. Her answer required no words. She reached her hands behind his neck and gently pulled him into a kiss that told him all he wanted to know.

* * *

Mara and Wayan landed in Hong Kong, noting the six-hour time difference was working in their favor since it was still early afternoon on Tuesday in Milan. Wayan was by Mara's side when she made the first call to Lucca. He had to come through for them to make their idea work. "Lucca, it's Mara. I am on my way back from Bali and need your help. Do you remember Wayan, Antonella's costume designer? Well, he has been with me in Bali and just found out that Antonella has a last-minute performance at this Friday's Bal de Salute for the debutantes."

Lucca interrupted, "Slow down. Wayan is with you? What? Oh, this is good. Do tell."

Mara's blush made Wayan chuckle. Rolling her eyes, Mara got back to the subject. "Later, Lucca. For now, Wayan thinks if a long skirt were added to your asymmetrical style, that could work perfectly for the event. Check your email. We have sent some ideas. Can you switch it over to a long skirt concept and have it ready by early Friday? My order for more of the fabric used in the bodice should have been delivered. If you give us the go-ahead, I will call Rochelle next and have her bring you the yardage you need."

The importance of the call was sinking in, and Lucca exclaimed, "Anything for you, Mara, but there is a problem. The bodice to that dress is completed and is fitted to Antonella with none of the padding Wayan uses for her costumes. I am afraid that with the way it is cut, I cannot alter it or let it out. *Meo Dio!* It is so silly anyway that such a lovely woman has to hide behind all that padding!"

In that moment, Mara and Wayan both recognized if they made this decision for Antonella, it could all go really wrong, or it might just be the path for Antonella to reconnect with her authentic self. Mara stared at Wayan and said in barely a whisper, "Remember what Sarah said about her ring...that she was 'trying it on for size'? Maybe this is Antonella's chance to sing in front of an audience as her true self. She is far from that inexperienced girl with the big voice that you were compelled to transform. Your makeup can subtly change from looking mature to enhancing her own beauty."

Wayan knew well enough that Antonella might react by refusing to perform. Perhaps if he had a backup plan, they should try it.

Mara saw his hesitation but was determined that this might be the answer not only for Antonella, but also for Wayan and herself as a couple. "Lucca, let's do it. You and I will be there to help persuade her. Wayan will have a 'just-in-case' back up. Go check your email; I will call Rochelle. Wayan and I will be back in Milan later tonight your time. Send us your thoughts about the new design tomorrow morning. Thank you, Lucca! If you are involved, it will be spectacular!"

She hung up and glanced at Wayan, who shook his head with a smile. "Look at you with all that authority! I have no idea how we are going to pull this off, much less what I am going to say to Antonella on the call I am about to make."

"Just tell her the truth that you are having the style she loved that Lucca designed re-formatted to a long dress that should be perfect for the occasion. Just leave out the part about omitting the padding. Let's not give her too much time to over-think the idea. We can do this, Wayan...and so can she."

CHAPTER 46

By the time they boarded the plane for the last leg of their journey back to Milan, Rochelle had already delivered the fabric to Lucca, Antonella was scheduled to arrive in Milan Thursday afternoon, and Zayn knew how Antonella would be performing and that Mara had to help with her outfit. Mara asked him to meet her at the ball, and in return she would arrange for a late dinner with Antonella. That seemed to appease Zayn, who was predictably pleased to be socializing with a celebrity. He asked Mara about her trip, and she briefly gave him the highlights but also predictably left out the details about who had joined her. Wayan noticed.

His arm around Mara, Wayan pulled her close to rest her head against him. "We will get through this, *sayang*. We are together. Think about it...you and I have navigated through my meeting your family and friends, supporting each other through spiritual awakening, and even building the foundation of our own love story. Just because certain things are expected of us doesn't mean we can't change the rules. Antonella's sudden call for this performance might be just the twist of fate we needed to set the record straight with both Antonella and Zayn that we are even better for them together as a couple. For Antonella, it could mean her launching into a future unafraid to show her inner beauty to the world. And for Zayn, our collaboration can only enhance his investment in you."

As they sat side by side on the plane, exhaustion weighed heavily on them, yet an undercurrent of anticipation buzzed between them. The prospect of returning to their fast-paced lives in Milan loomed ahead, where deadlines, demands, and unresolved issues awaited their arrival. Mara's heart ached at the thought of leaving behind the warmth and familiarity of Bali, yet she also felt a stirring of determination to face whatever lay ahead with courage and resilience.

They both knew, as the minutes ticked by, that the reality of their professional lives would soon intrude on their idyllic escape. Mara snuggled closer and said, "Whatever challenges are ahead, we will face them together." She soon dozed off leaving Wayan to focus on the stage outfit and makeup that would inspire confidence and self-acceptance in Antonella. Gone would be the days of hiding behind masks and pretending to be someone she was not. He deeply wished to not reach backward to the innocent and inexperienced Nella, but rather to reveal a more authentic version of herself, the opera star, with the empowerment to step into the spotlight with confidence and grace, accepting the true identity of the star that she was, Antonella Rossi.

The plane began its descent into Milan with its greeting of twinkling city lights, a stark contrast to the serene landscapes of Bali. Mara looked out the window, a wave of uncertainty settling over her, carrying with it the weight of their responsibilities and obligations she knew were waiting. As for Wayan, he had lost an important week of work. The demands to catch up threatened to consume his every waking moment, not to mention whether their plan would succeed for Antonella Friday night. Even if it did work, that would affect all the costumes in the works for the upcoming opera, *Aïda*. And all that didn't take into account how he would react to her constant demands that he cater to her whims.

As they retrieved their bags, despite the challenges and desperate need for rest, Wayan couldn't bear the thought of parting from Mara just yet. He turned Mara to him. "Please allow me to stay with you tonight, *sayang*. We need sleep but give me this chance to hold you close before all the chaos sets in."

Mara, touched by his words, looked at him with love in her eyes. "Wayan, I feel that in Bali we embarked on a shared journey. Only time will tell if the bond between us is unbreakable. For now, let's allow our growing love for each other to be the sanctuary in the storm of our hectic lives, a place where we can embrace our own authenticity together when things around us lose their grounding."

* * *

Total exhaustion overcame Mara and Wayan, both from the time difference and journey home. One of Wayan's last thoughts as he drifted into a sound sleep was a feeling of peace with Mara beside him in his arms offering a feeling of warmth and comfort. Kusama had told him the effects of the healing ritual would emerge over time. It was that remarkable first night back in Milan that Wayan's dreams began to shift. He had confronted the darkest corners of his subconscious where his fears lurked. Wayan, immersed in his dream, saw that he was still in the dark cave. This time he heard Kusama's voice telling him to ignore the voices and look toward the light. Mara's presence at the entrance, bathed in radiant light, offered him a beacon of hope and guidance as she reached out her hand. From her hand something was floating toward him, a thread of some sort. No, it was a stem. Kusama said, "The stem of the lotus symbolizes your lifeline, a connection to your inner strength. Reach out and grab it, Wayan."

When he grasped the end in his hand, he felt a surge of empowerment and courage coursing through him. For the first time, he felt a sense of control over his own destiny, no longer bound by the expectations and criticisms of others. He allowed himself to follow the stem toward the light. The voices that had once haunted him now seemed distant and faint, overshadowed by the warmth and serenity ahead. Kusama's last words referred to this as his passage to liberation. As he got closer, he saw the most beautiful purple lotus blossom in Mara's hands. Emerging into the light and Mara's embrace, he was overwhelmed by gratitude and renewed purpose.

In his sleep, Wayan smiled and pulled Mara tighter.

CHAPTER 47

Waking up next to Mara, Wayan didn't remember the dream, only that he felt energized and ready to face the day ahead with whatever it brought. He called Lucca and arranged to meet for breakfast.

Mara drove to her studio ready to pour her heart and soul into her work, invigorated and willing to tackle whatever needed her attention. As she stepped through the doors, she spotted the overflowing stack of mail and messages and braced herself for what she would find. Just as she was rolling up her sleeves to get down to business, Rochelle strode in looking quirky as ever with her red leather pants and matching leopard top and shoes. With a gleam in her eye, she said, "Hi boss! You've been missed. I've got news."

Curious and slightly apprehensive, Mara tentatively asked, "Good news or bad news?"

Rochelle gave Mara one of her mischievous smiles. "Well, actually it is good news and better news."

Mara raised her eyebrows in question. "Well?"

Rochelle handed her the business account ledger. A staggering amount of deposits had been made as a result of the orders from Fashion Week, but by far the largest was her share of Antonella's order. Lucca had split it with her fifty-fifty. Mara had never expected that and was about to call him to protest such generosity when Rochelle set a magazine on the table in front of her. It was a copy of the latest issue of the sleek and prestigious Milan fashion magazine. Staring at it in disbelief, Mara was speechless.

There, emblazoned on the cover was her photo and name in bold letters, hailed as the *"Up and Coming Fabric Designer to Watch."* Chills went up and down her arms that her talent and dedication had been validated by such a prestigious accolade. She then quickly realized who had just as much to do with this and picked up the phone with Rochelle leaving Mara to her privacy, but not without giving a loud "whoop" of excitement!

Mara unfastened the prayer necklace that she had worn during the trip to Bali. Studying it, she thought of seeing those first sprouts from the rice seeds she planted and the arrival of Wayan, to the water purification ritual she experienced with Annie and Sarah, to the time spent with the healer, Kusama. Wayan was right. It had been transformative for both of them. Deep in thought, she remembered the importance of living in gratitude. She would not forget her humble beginnings or the people who had helped her along the way.

First and foremost was Zayn. It was through his efforts that Mara gained access to crucial resources and networks that propelled her into the elite circles so necessary in the fashion industry. Despite their decision to remain friends rather than pursue a romantic relationship, he made the decision to continue to support her even though she knew he still had feelings for her. It was suddenly clear to her that success is not just about talent and hard work, but also about the relationships and connections developed along the way.

Mara thought of that day in Bajir's office when he told her Zayn wanted to buy him out and be her only investor. She had resisted, thinking he wanted more control over her. What she had not grasped was that it was an effort to prove himself to his father. She had merely fueled that situation by insinuating she didn't trust Zayn enough to have him as her sole backer. It was time to express her gratitude in a meaningful way. Mara placed the call to Bajir Al Farooq's private number.

"Alo, Mara? Are you back in Milan? How was your trip?" Bajir seemed in good spirits. Mara proceeded to tell him about the orders and the magazine cover. "That is most excellent, Mara! We must celebrate when I am next in Italy."

Mara agreed, then added, "Bajir, you have my heartfelt thanks for your support and believing in me. However, I am well aware of Zayn's role in persuading you to invest with him and, for that, I will be forever grateful. I also wanted to make sure you understood what a pivotal role your son played in connecting me with the right resources and influential circles that has turned out to be a successful collaboration."

"Mara, my dear, I have eyes in many places and I have knowledge of these things. My son has many talents, but he has not fared well in business until meeting you. He knew you and your talent were special from the beginning. In another day and time, perhaps you might have taken your partnership to another level."

Mara realized Bajir knew more than she could imagine, but she forged ahead wondering if somehow he knew she was going to ask this question. "Bajir, do you remember the meeting we had during Fashion Week when you said Zayn had offered to buy out your position? I hesitated, not sure I wanted our relationship to be so unbalanced. I have realized that we make really good business partners and would like to ask him if that idea would still interest him. Do I have your permission?"

"Of course you do, Mara. Why don't you ask him right now? He is right here."

Stunned, Mara had never anticipated Zayn actually being with his father when she called. She could hear them in the background exchanging the receiver. Zayn picked up. "Hello Mara. My father and I were just sitting here looking at the magazine. Congratulations! That is exciting news."

Suddenly suspicious that Zayn might have had something to do with the cover, Mara asked, "Thinking about it, it did seem to come out of nowhere and I don't recall speaking with anyone from the magazine. Did you know anything about this?"

"Well, it happened right after you left. I was speaking with Rochelle on another matter, and she mentioned the managing editor from the publication had called and that they were considering you for the cover. However, they were on a tight deadline to making their closing for this issue. I couldn't let such an opportunity slip by and told her I'd talk with them. The editor was extremely professional and said both Lucca and Sophia had been instrumental in their decision." Sheepishly, he added, "I gave them my approval on your behalf. You're okay with that, right?"

"Are you kidding? Of course I am. I was just telling Bajir how much you have done for the business. This is an accolade to you as well, Zayn. I also told him that I would be honored if you still wanted to be my exclusive investor. As a matter of fact, the books are looking quite healthy right now. Let's talk this weekend about whether it would be a good idea to use some of the funds to help buy out Bajir's position."

There was a long pause before Zayn answered. She had the feeling that he had moved out of the room to get some privacy. "So, you still intend to attend the ball with me Friday? After your call, I assumed you had a reason to go separately other than to dress the entertainment."

"No, there are some serious issues going on with Antonella right now. If all goes as planned, you might see quite a different performer since the night of the fundraiser." Mara took a deep breath. "Zayn, I can't begin to tell you how much I appreciate all you have done for me and the business, and I honestly want to stay friends. But I also want you to know I've met someone. It could be the beginning of something important. But, Zayn, I would never want to lose your friendship."

"Mara, you will not lose me as a business partner or a friend. I already knew there was someone else."

Shocked, Mara asked, "How, when?"

"The reason that I called Rochelle was regarding the Bali trip. I felt bad about you being there with the two couples by yourself, so I thought I would come surprise you. Rochelle did not want to betray you in any way, but she also did not want me to show up in Bali unannounced. She let me know the costume designer followed you right after you left. He was going to the farm where your parents were. I am certain he fit in more than I would have. Fortunately, I didn't make a buffoon of myself by dropping in unannounced. Believe it or not, Mara, I am actually rooting for you two. You are a special woman and you deserve the future you want. I would never have been able to give you what he can."

Mara sat at her desk in disbelief until she remembered something her grandmother had told her years before.

"It is said that when you choose to follow a certain path to the result you seek, if it has the blessing of the ancient spirits, the path will go smoothly. Pay heed to the signs and omens that guide your way."

Zayn's understanding and willingness to continue their friendship and their business relationship, knowing she might be with someone else, was the sign she was hoping for to confirm the path with Wayan was meant to be.

CHAPTER 48

After a rejuvenating week in Bali with Wayan, her family, and close friends, Mara felt reconnected with her roots and inspired to push the boundaries of her design skills even further. Upon returning to Milan, her business was booming, and she was grateful the magazine feature had highlighted her fabrics that captured the essence of Balinese culture with a modern twist. Despite the allure of her success, she was determined to remain grounded, thanks in part to the conversation with Zayn, who appeared eager to remain a pillar of encouragement and acceptance in their business arrangement.

Wayan, on the other hand, faced a daunting challenge as Antonella's performance at the Bal de Salut loomed on the horizon. Wayan had gone to Lucca's studio early to see how the dress was unfolding. He was feeling the weight of her expectations knowing she assumed he would deliver, never dawning on her what she was about to discover.

Lucca sensed the tension in Wayan and sought to reassure him. Retrieving the dress, he shook it out to fluff the layers of tulle netting he had used to create the effect of a ball gown. The feature was still the fitted asymmetrical bodice, but the new skirt no longer had any resemblance to the original. "Wayan, Antonella is going to look lovely tomorrow evening. I have blocked out the entire day so we can make any changes you feel are necessary before she arrives for her fitting."

His nerves were on edge and tight as a knot. He knew well the diva-like behavior that could erupt if she felt manipulated. *What had he been thinking?* Antonella's fierce dependency on him to create a show-stopping stage look for her was a double-edged sword. It had pushed him to hone his creative skills and become a master artisan. But it had also meant his work was infused with Antonella's notoriously fickle reactions that required an immense amount of skill and diplomacy.

Assessing the merits of Lucca's work, Wayan knew the design would excel in the fashion world, but it lacked the embellishments to take it from couture to performance ready. "Lucca, you have created a masterful work of art in such a short amount of time. If you will allow me to step in and help, I think we can give it the signature 'Antonella touch' to make it irresistible to her and to the audience."

Lucca assured Wayan he could count on his help but was catching some of Wayan's nerves. He asked, "Have you ever seen Antonella perform as herself?"

"Never. At least, not on the professional stage. When I met her four years ago, the directors and producers had rejected her time and again because of her slender frame and delicate features not fitting the standard opera diva mold, and especially the powerful voice that emanated from her. Her confidence was crushed. Behind the curtain of fame and success, Antonella struggled with insecurities about her appearance."

Lucca nodded. "So, through clever padding and expert makeup, you created the illusion of a regal, middle-aged diva, befitting of a larger-than-life voice. I think I understand. As time has passed, Antonella has begun to feel a disconnect between the persona she portrays on stage and her true self." With a smile and a flamboyant wave of his arm, Lucca added, "Well, I think it is about time to change all that. Let's get this showpiece to a point that she can't turn it down."

* * *

Wayan had hired a private car to pick up Antonella in Lake Como and bring her to Milan to avoid her traveling on public transportation alone. The car arrived precisely as scheduled, and Antonella sat in the back seat prepared for the long drive, giving her plenty of time to think about how she had gotten into this predicament.

Antonella allowed her mind to wander back to her childhood. She was born in a small town in the heart of Italy to a humble family with a deep love for music. From a young age, her powerful voice filled with emotion captivated all who heard her sing. Everyone said her talent was undeniable, and it was clear she was destined for greatness. As she became a young teenager, her passion for opera only intensified, driving her to pursue a career in the spotlight.

At age fourteen, Antonella tried out for a lead role in a musical to be held in Siena, not too far from her home. They did not give her the lead because of her youth but they did give her the role of the daughter, which gave her a good part to feature her voice. Her parents were so proud of her and insisted they come to opening night to see her perform. Antonella remembered the pain she felt looking from the stage toward the empty seats she had reserved for them. Later, her worst fears were confirmed that both of her parents had been killed in a car accident on the way to Siena. The grief she felt was only surpassed by the guilt. If she had not left home to go perform in that play, her parents would still be alive. There was no consoling her.

Antonella felt her eyes glisten and stiffened her resolve to remember. Many months went by while members of her family tried to decide her fate, who should take her in or should she go to foster care. All her dreams of the opera were shattered. Moved between different families, Antonella slowly began to regain her passion and found singing to take her to a place of comfort.

Antonella never told Wayan that the day he found her crying on that bench outside the theater she had just turned seventeen.

She had never had a boyfriend and Wayan was like a hero to her. She remembered the tears in his eyes when she let him hear the recording of her voice.

So much had happened since then. They had been good together, and her stage appearance worked so well, it had brought a continuous stream of work for them both. It was strange always being treated like an older woman. Antonella thought about it. Had she lost her entire youth? The fact was, after her parents died, she didn't have a memory of just being free or having fun. The only times she felt even close to what she thought was normal were around Wayan. The truth, if she were being honest, was somewhere along the way she had lost her own happiness. She had experienced a fleeting moment of it with Wayan but that didn't last. *Was that why she begrudged him having the chance at happiness?*

When Wayan made the rash decision to rush to Bali in pursuit of the young fabric designer, he just disappeared leaving her without her usual support system. Yes, she was angry. Not at Wayan, but simply at the unfairness of it all. But then, the pressure came to step in at the debutante ball for the ailing singer. Wayan was nowhere to be found. Really? A debutante ball! All those young girls looking beautiful and enjoying this special time in their lives. *What about her? Where was her chance to be young, pretty, and carefree?*

Did she even want to do this anymore? She would be old soon enough. *What if Wayan leaves her and goes to Mara? Just where does that leave her?* Antonella sighed. So many questions. So few answers.

CHAPTER 49

"Hi Wayan. I thought you might want some moral support. Would you like me to come to Lucca's studio for the fitting?" Mara's phone call came at the perfect time and Wayan let out a sigh he didn't know he was holding.

"Now that is a voice I needed to hear. Wait until you see the dress! All the fabric you sent over has been interwoven and draped to create drama from every angle. It is a vision! My hope is that Antonella will be so entranced by the dress that she won't mind losing the padding. Can you come now? Antonella should be here within the hour, and I would love you to be here for reinforcements." He hung up and Lucca patted him on the back.

"Look at the gown, Wayan! You have nothing to worry about. This could be a redefining moment for Antonella. Those standards she faced are antiquated, and she is already famous. I dress women every day in all sizes, and I consider it my job to make them feel beautiful. I want nothing less for Antonella."

Mara arrived in full anticipation to see what creation a collaboration between Wayan and Lucca had produced. When Lucca proudly held it up for Mara, it took her breath away! "It's unbelievable. Wow! With this dress, you two have set the stage for Antonella's transformation. She is going to look incredible."

Lucca's assistant announced Antonella. He had assured the opera star that her identity was safe in his studio which included the confidentiality of his assistant. Antonella's head was high, exuding an air of elegance and refinement as she stepped into Lucca's luxurious private showroom. Dressed in a simple silk blouse and tailored trousers, her presence commanded attention and respect. Her eyes, filled with a mixture of anticipation and weariness, glanced at Wayan. He knew the look of disapproval and had expected it. He stepped up. "Hello Antonella, you look lovely as usual. I realize this isn't your normal type of performance, but I think you will be pleased with our surprise."

Antonella's expression turned to boredom. "Well, let's get on with it." Noticing Mara off to the side, she added, "What is she doing here?"

Wayan was about to answer when Mara spoke up. If Antonella's wrath was going to come out, she was ready to take some of the responsibility too. "The decision about the dress was last minute, as you know. Fortunately, I had just received an order of fabric used in one of Lucca's styles you liked, so I rushed it over to Lucca so he could get started. I have just seen the finished product myself and it is stunning."

Curiosity piqued, Antonella looked back at Wayan, her arm outreached for the usual padding forms. Wayan ushered her to the dressing room exchanging a worried glance with Mara. "You won't need those this time."

"What do you mean? That is outrageous! I can't go on stage without them."

Wayan reached into the dressing room and held it up for her to see. "Antonella, you have seen the gowns these debutantes wear. In this dress, you will outshine them all."

It was the thought of the debutantes that made her pause and think about it. She was accustomed to hiding behind layers of embellishments and extravagant costumes during her performances. She felt exposed and vulnerable at the thought of unveiling her true self to the world. Antonella looked at Wayan, then at Lucca, a wave of uncertainty washing over her. "How do I know they will accept me as I am, without all the artifice we have used for years when I am on stage?"

Lucca walked up to Antonella and took her hands. "Antonella, you are a star! If anyone says anything, just casually say you have dropped a few pounds. It is done all the time, darling."

Antonella stole another look at the showpiece dress they had created for her, taken aback by its sheer beauty and audacity. The deep jewel tones of ruby and amethyst shimmered, blending seamlessly together to create a rich tapestry that seemed to dance with its own rhythm. Gold accents ran like streams of sunshine through the fabric, adding a touch of regal elegance, while subtle Balinese influences could be seen in the intricate patterns and embroidery. She reached for it and closed the curtain to the dressing room behind her, with Wayan ever ready to fasten it down the back and make any adjustments. As he helped delicately drape the dress over her slender frame, Antonella stood before the mirror, her breath catching at the sight of her reflection. The gown hugged her body in a way that felt both restrictive and liberating, revealing a raw beauty that she had long forgotten existed beneath the dazzling façade she presented to the world.

Wayan opened the curtain. Lucca and Mara watched anxiously as Antonella examined herself in the mirror. They knew that the true challenge lay not in the dress itself but in whether Antonella would embrace her authentic self on stage. Lucca whispered, "*Bellissima!*"

Mara smiled, catching Antonella's eyes in the mirror. "I think it is time to shed those layers and reveal the beautiful young woman behind the diva, don't you agree?"

While standing there facing her insecurities and doubts, Antonella felt something stir inside her. Images of her parents, the girl crying on the bench, and the debutantes, floated through her mind. She recognized that this was more than just a fitting for a dress. It was a reckoning with her own artistry and identity. With a deep breath, she made a decision that could change her future.

* * *

As the night of the Bal de Salut arrived, Wayan, Mara, and Lucca, were backstage giving Antonella their unified support. Wayan expertly applied her makeup to still be recognizable as Antonella Rossi, but with a much more youthful look. He looked satisfied with the results, but it was Lucca who said, "You will have all of Milan speculating whether you had work done, my dear!"

Antonella laughed. "But there are no scars."

Lucca chuckled. "Oh sweetheart, you would have used the finest doctors, and they don't leave scars!" That got a genuine smile back from Antonella.

Mara could feel how important this night was. The illusions were falling, first with Zayn and now with Antonella. Looking at Antonella, Mara shook her head. "You look stunning, Antonella. The world is ready to see the real you. I have something for you to keep with you tonight. On the side of your dress, I had Lucca put a small pocket." Mara unfastened the prayer necklace from around her neck and handed it to Antonella. "The lesson I came back from Bali with was to live your most authentic life. Tonight, you are making the choice to do that. I would like to give you this necklace to support you as you make this transition. I am proud to know you as the real Antonella. Just watch, others will be too."

Touched beyond words, Antonella took the necklace and found the pocket. She then gave Mara a heartfelt hug. "Thank you for this. I'm sorry if I misjudged you."

The presenter came in and announced, "You are on in five minutes."

Antonella received encouraging words from Wayan, Lucca, and Mara, then took a deep breath and steeled herself to step out onto the stage. Her heart was racing with a determined sense of purpose. As Mara said, it was time to embrace her authenticity.

The audience was spellbound by her beauty, and then she began to sing. With each note she sang that night, Antonella felt a sense of freedom that had eluded her for a long time. Her voice resonated throughout the grand hall and the sea of debutantes. She felt like one of them, making her debut on the stage as herself. And when the final curtain fell on the performance, the room went wild with its applause. In that moment, she knew she had embarked on a new chapter of her life. The producer, who was there presenting his daughter, came up on stage with an enormous bouquet of flowers and thanked her on behalf of the entire Bal de Salut. When he handed her the flowers, he stepped up to Antonella and said, "Your time off is suiting you...you look marvelous!"

Stifling an unfamiliar giggle of delight, she couldn't wait to share with Lucca that he hadn't even noticed the change. When she told him, he grinned. "There you go. He was none the wiser. Now you can just enjoy being you."

Zayn had come backstage to find Mara, but when he saw Antonella, she was far from what he remembered the night they met at the fundraiser. He had already been mesmerized by her voice. Now seeing her, he was fascinated to know more. Taking her hand, Zayn smiled at her with a twinkle in his eye. "Whatever you have been doing, keep it up! My family yacht is sailing out of Antibes this weekend. I would be most honored if you might join me."

Antonella actually blushed! She then winked at Mara, patting the side of her skirt where the prayer necklace was tucked into her pocket. Wayan and Mara looked at each other in stunned shock. When Antonella hesitated to answer, Zayn added, "I simply won't take no for an answer. You deserve to be spoiled, and I think I might be just the person to do it."

Mara and Wayan joined them. Zayn gave Mara a hug and shook Wayan's hand. He thought it would be harder to see them together as his eyes wandered back to Antonella. He asked Antonella to dance, leaving Mara and Wayan to marvel at the turn of events.

Wayan put his arm around Mara and drew her close, both enveloped in a deep sense of peace and harmony. Mara looked into Wayan's loving eyes and asked, "Do you think all of this would have unfolded if we had not gone to Bali?"

Wayan thought for a moment. "I think Kusama guided us well. We had to change ourselves before we could change our circumstances." As they danced together, surrounded by the spirit of the Lotus as the healer had foretold, Mara and Wayan understood they were meant to be together, ready to follow their own journey of love and authenticity.

THE END

Glossary

Balinese Family Names

Mara's Cousin: *Kadek*

Mara's Mother: *Ni Luh*
When Mara calls her "Mother": *Ibu*

Mara's Father: *Putu*
When Mara calls him "Father": *Bapek*

Mara's Brother: *Gede*

Mara's Grandmother: *Nenek*

Kadek's Husband: *Nuri*

Wellness Resort Healer: *Kusama*

About the Author
Nina Purtee

Nina Purtee is a worldwide traveler, philosopher, and award-winning, adventure/romance, women's fiction novelist.

Nina draws from her travels to embrace multicultural characters seemingly from different worlds, and allow them to compromise, co-exist, accept each other's traditions, and even find love. Throughout her historical *Annie's Journey Series*, Nina "shares her gift and craft of writing for young women with a strong element of inspiration or timeless message."

"Purtee's sheer brilliance of her pen adroitly explores themes of love, loss, resilience, and courage."

A "natural storyteller," Nina loves to dig into the heart of her stories with touching insights added along the way.

Her love of the sea and sailing brought Nina to the coast of Florida where she calls home when she is not traveling the globe seeking new experiences to write about.

Learn more about Nina at **www.ninapurtee.com**

PREVIOUSLY PUBLISHED BOOKS BY NINA PURTEE

Annie's Journey Series

Beyond the Sea: Annie's Journey into the Extraordinary (© 2023)
Crossing Paths: The Road to Destiny (© 2023)
Finding Sarah: A Phoenix to Behold (© 2024)
Moroccan Sunset: Dawn of a New Beginning (© 2024)